BLACKMAILER'S DELIGHT

A GEORGIAN ERA ROMP

DAVID LAWRENCE

Copyright © 2023 by David Lawrence Johnson

ISBN (ebook): 979-8-9898319-1-3

ISBN (Paperback): 978-1-17377233-9-4

ISBN (Trade): 979-8-9898319-0-6

ISBN (Large Print): 979-8-9898319-2-0

Library of Congress Control Number: 2024900010

Title production by Broadbound Publishing

Book Cover by 88dsgnr

First edition February•2024

For my mother,
and for everyone who never had that conversation

Author's Note

Central to *Blackmailer's Delight* is an episode from 1795 often referred to as 'The Revolt of the Housewives'. As a history buff, I was of course immediately intrigued when I came across a reference to this in my reading. The origins of the so-called 'revolt' are usually traced to the Enclosure (or Inclosure) Laws of the previous decades. Before enclosure, much of the land owned – either privately or collectively – was considered common land over which the commoner had the right to graze animals, cut turf for fuel, or cultivate. Parliamentary acts to enclose land, done both for sound agricultural reasons as well as for financial benefit to the landowners, greatly reduced the land previously available to the public.

This change was felt particularly by the squatter, the small farmer, and the cottager. More money was now required to purchase fuel and feed, and, more often than not, many simply chose to keep fewer cattle. This reduction in overall economic health affected their ability to either grow or purchase the basic foodstuffs.

The situation reached crisis point in 1795. With an increase in food prices in the early nineties, together with the recent uprising in France, many were feeling a pinch at a time of public empowerment. Beginning in March of this year, the unrest around this issue erupted into a series of local uprisings, from Seaford to Carlisle, during which flour, bread, butter, and meat were seized for redistribution. Most of the food was reported to have been sold at a price those who were suffering could afford, the original owners then compensated from the proceeds.

This episode is known as 'The Revolt of the Housewives' due to the large number of women involved in the seizures and redistribution. Why this was is not entirely clear, but they were unusually prominent during this remarkable episode in English history.

Prologue

*M*arch 1795

A revolution in France. Food shortages at home. And now a damned tax on wig powder.

"This world is going to hell," said Daniel Thornton to his lover, Clarence, one morning over toast and marmalade. "What is the name of that local sect I was telling you of the other morning? The one predicting the end of the world in the year 1800?"

"What?" said the younger man, who had been gazing out the first-floor window of their Westminster townhouse. "Haven't they all gone to America?"

"It was in the paper last week. I distinctly recall telling you about it."

"Oh, you know I don't listen to anything you say at the breakfast table."

"Don't you?"

"I'm slow to rise, Danny. Once I am awake, I must plan my day; I cannot attend to your little newspaper articles."

Daniel observed his companion for a moment – perhaps the longest moment of his life. This was the end, of course. Not of the world, but for them. For six weeks he had been expecting this, cynic that he was. They were both cynics – and, apart from the sex, he supposed Clarence's pessimism had been his primary attraction. They saw the world identically. They liked to laugh at things like sects predicting the end of the world in five years. Or they had. If Clarence couldn't be bothered to listen to him at the breakfast table, if they hadn't even this anymore, after the misery this man was putting him through, there really was nothing for them.

He eyed the orange juice Clarence was sipping lazily. Should he?

They weren't sleeping together anymore. And this, incredibly, before he had understood why, had actually *bonded* him to this man. Clarence had made no excuses: "It's the way of all things, isn't it? We are simply two old men grown comfortable with each other," though this was absurd as Clarence was just twenty-six. No man likes being rejected in bed, but Clarence had won him by appearing to join him in their common plight – wasn't it just the way of this miserable world?

"What?" he said, lowering his orange juice to glance over his shoulder. Daniel hadn't spoken – Clarence must have heard the memory of his words ringing in his companion's head. Narcissists only listened to hear the echo of their own words. Only observed to see their reflection in your eyes. This was the person Daniel had credited with great candour, so ready was he to believe they had evolved from mere sexual attraction to true companionship. To love. Aside from an uncle in Grantham, Clarence Hopper was the first man he had truly loved. The first in thirty-four years.

Daniel looked around their breakfasting room, which seemed just now to have been organised for different people entirely. A table far too big for them – a thick block of oak fifty years out of date, shoved too close to a window where there was nothing to look at but a street vendor singing the same old tune. What *was* Clarence looking for down there?

He must be waiting for his latest to arrive. It had been six weeks since he'd discovered Clarence's first indiscretion. Many in their set held that dalliances while in a relationship were not only to be expected, but the privilege of their class. Accordingly, Daniel had tried to accept it – tried, and failed, to have one of his own. He had failed because the pain of Clarence's unfaithfulness was so intense it had bypassed even his wish for revenge. It had gone straight to his heart.

Yet, he hadn't left him. He had lowered his eyes and purchased a ticket to this new production in which Clarence performed with his partners while Daniel observed from a darkened pit. He was soon hearing from their friends of Clarence's sleeping with not only every man he could find, but every woman, every off-duty carriage horse be it tall, dark, and handsome enough. Each fling was another poisoned nick at his heart. Another wound which could not heal before another was inflicted.

Being a particularly tall, well-built man, Daniel Thornton filled a room with his presence. When his mood darkened, even his shadow could cause concern, as happened now as he rose from the table. Clarence looked up at him, though at a noise from outside his attention returned to the street.

Daniel lifted him by the scruff of his dressing gown. Before the younger man could summon anything but incoherent outrage, the orange juice was plucked from his hand and held over his head.

"Don't, Danny!"

"Hold still."

"*Dan—*"

He let one drop, then four, then a thin, even dribble spatter onto Clarence's lovely morning locks. Not too quickly. Gradually. He maintained the weaker man easily in one hand, indifferent to his blows, cutting off his airway by tightening his lapel when the wretch became too lively. Once the glass had been emptied of every drop, Clarence was permitted to sink to the floor, blue and teary, gasping for breath, shuddering at the sodden mess that was his tangled, matted hair.

"*Bastard*!" he gasped. "You will regret this, Danny!"

"Not as much as I regret waiting to do it. Two months is the limit; I shall take not one day more of your infidelity. I loved you."

"*You don't know what love is!* That was the worst decision you've ever made, Daniel Thornton! You mark my words; you shall have *nothing* but misery the rest of your days!"

Daniel walked out of the room. The rest of his days? To hell with doomsayers and doomsdayers alike. The world was not ending. Not in the year 1800. Not today.

He packed a few things, then he and Collins, his valet, took lodgings in Mill Street. The place was somewhat modest – just three rooms, no meals provided. But they were the best he could afford, Daniel being one of those men who, unlike Clarence, remained independent only by adhering closely to a budget. Leaving his wealthier lover was a blow not just to his heart, but to his pocketbook.

By the following morning he had experienced many of the emotions one might expect to feel – displacement, shame at letting his temper get the better of him. A fresh, bracing freedom. Moments of terrible regret. And something he was finding difficult to categorise.

"You wish to be a better person, sir?" said Collins, with an arch look.

"Christ, not if you say it like that. But I do wish... to be open to the goodness in the world. Do you know what I mean? To allow that there *is* goodness. I'm not saying it very well. You see, I don't wonder that the relationship with Clarence turned out as it did, because, in a way, that was what I was looking for."

"You moved to London to discover the evil in the world?"

Daniel considered. Coming to the metropolis was not so much a decision after his aimless years at Cambridge, but rather a horror of returning to the confines of his native Aylesbury. "I was a sexually frustrated man of two and twenty when I moved. I came looking for—"

"Yes, sir. London gave you the anonymity to pursue your... interests."

"And don't call Clarence evil. I was no different from him at that age. Surely."

Ignoring this prompt to be contradicted, Collins went about his business for a time. The man had been his valet for twelve years, Daniel's entire residency in the metropolis. He understood he was at liberty to speak, and to remain silent, as he chose. Under the rolls of his Sunday buckle wig, his valet was a balding, well-put-together man of about fifty, a father figure in many ways, Daniel's own parents having passed years before. Albert Collins was also a friend – perhaps his only true friend. He had been raised to disapprove of Pathics, but as he was also a social snob, Albert accepted the sight of Daniel in bed with a man as a privilege of his class.

At last, he offered, "When you were that age, sir, you weren't claiming to be in a relationship with any of your gentlemen friends."

"*Precisely*," said Daniel, perhaps too eagerly. "Precisely that. I never was the kind, was I?"

"No, you were not. And though I shall never understand your interests entirely, I must have thought far worse of you had they included sporting freely with young ladies. As Clarence has done."

"He is terrible."

"Young ladies have their reputations to maintain. There was just the one, that I know of. One too many if you ask me. Then, of course, there was that matter of her carriage horse."

"I *never* believed that. Outrageous. Even I cannot... it is outrageous." Daniel fell silent; this did savour of protesting too much. He looked desperately at his valet.

Collins remained silent a moment, then he said, "That Clarence is sufficiently hated to have the accusation made is my point. It says something about him, in its way."

Daniel merely nodded – because it said something about him, too, for having remained with him so long. At last, he said, "I suppose I'm realising I am not the world-weary cynic I liked to believe I was. There is safety in cynicism. Something in Clarence, or in myself with the passage of years, has shown me that it is simply a wall to hide behind. Without intending to, I let that wall down. I don't know what I wish for in its place, but for all the pain of having gone without, I do not wish for that wall again."

Albert grew uncomfortable at too much talk of emotions. The man was, after all, his valet. *Personal advisor* was not in his job description, and Daniel always felt some guilt after bending his ear. They spoke instead of taking an apartment in Soho, of fetching things from the townhouse. Daniel believed he should return today to end things with Clarence on a more civil note; Collins believed the man would have already fled to his parents in Charing Cross, which was his habit whenever anything went wrong.

Then, a knock sounded at the door – a runner bringing a message sent first to the townhouse. Daniel took the note, observing from the direction it was from his uncle's estate in Grantham, Bainbridge Park. Upon opening it his brow darkened – this was a message written on *behalf* of his Uncle Erasmus.

A message to take him from thoughts of Clarence and their Westminster home.

A message to take him out of London altogether.

DAVID LAWRENCE

Grantham
Five months later

CHAPTER ONE

———— ⚜ ————

"Β y G—!" cried John Morley Esq., walking his family home from St. Wulfram's one fine Sunday. "Daniel Thornton indeed. I wished to speak to him after the service; I told you I did. But there he goes in his carriage, back to the Park with his uncle – to what? Listen to the old man wheeze? G— Almighty! I only wished a word!"

"John, your voice," said his lady, guiding her five children across Church Street into a lane of fine houses. They were coming to the Eliots' stately home, a point at which she always felt a slackening in the power of the lofty church spire to direct her cares heavenward. Margaret Morley wished to model her family after people like the Eliots; she had, in fact, fallen into step behind the couple as they departed church to admire the lady's carriage and deportment. With a little mincing step and the delicate turning up of her gown, Mrs Eliot carried herself exceptionally well onto the porch. Then, she turned to observe them as her husband rang for a footboy.

Raising a hand, Mrs Morley exclaimed upon the fine sermon and the lovely August day, to which Mrs Eliot said nothing, watching until the family were clear of their property.

"Papa, *why* must we walk on Sundays?" said Maria, the eldest of his three girls. "Walking is absurd when one has a carriage. And it's absolutely common!"

"Bah."

"Your father does not like to trouble the servants on Sunday," said her mother. "It's a fine example to some who never think on such things. The Eliots walk home, and they are an old, respected family in Grantham."

"They live just across the street! *Our* house is a mile from church! It's common!"

Luke, the younger of two boys, shot a look at his mother which said it wasn't the walking that made them common, from which Mrs Morley instantly turned in favour of her elder son. Already at twenty, Stephen was a model of elegance and decorum. She directed him to say something pacifying to his sister before returning to her husband, urging him back to that exceptionally tall, exceptionally well-built man who, upon the death of his ailing uncle, would also be made exceptionally wealthy. At four and thirty, Mr Thornton was also exceptionally overdue to be married and she had three girls of marriageable age to dispose of.

"Do leave off about Mr Thornton," said Luke.

"Hush you," said his mother. "Now John, you were speaking of Mr Thornton. What kind of life can he be leading cooped up with his uncle at Bainbridge Park?"

"Hmmm," muttered the man. "Nothing but dust and decrepitude over there; the Park's in complete disrepair. It needs a woman's touch."

"Ah, how right you are," said his lady. "Only think what that splendid old Park might be with only a woman's touch."

"Mr Thornton could do with a woman's touch as well, I reckon."

"John!" said his wife, glancing at Maria.

"A man's got needs at his age, Margaret. No use pretending he hasn't."

Mrs Morley stopped in the middle of the lane, dramatically swathed in a swirl of dust, ready to alight to the heavens if mortal man proved so immovably base. Her husband quickly returned, and with a little flourish brought her hand to his lips. "Under sanction of marriage, of course, my love." Then, a touch rakishly, he whispered, "I reckon our Mr Thornton needs his own, dear Guinie, *just like I got.*"

Going all over crimson, Margaret said, "Oh, Sir Lancelot!"

"Oh, Christ," muttered Luke, going equally crimson.

"Hush you!" said his mother. "Your father is a prince to wish Mr Thornton as happy as he is himself. Now, darling, you were saying?"

Continuing their walk, now with his wife's hand firmly in his, John Morley said, "Well, it's a D— irritation seeing a bachelor arrive each Sunday in a coach and four. Set to inherit the Park and, if my solicitor can be believed, upwards of fifteen thousand pounds, but with no thought for a bride. It is monstrous, ridiculous for a single fellow to flaunt his wealth like that. I don't say she must be one of my girls; I speak of population, as Goldsmith says. And so, to flaunt oneself like a common..." Then he hummed again, with a glance at his middle daughter, Bridget. He muttered, "Aye, that is the word," leaving his audience to decide whether *monstrous, ridiculous, flaunt* or perhaps even *aye* was this one, most meaningful word.

In twenty minutes, they were arrived at their own stately home, of newer construction at the north edge of town. The house had been purchased four years before after the family drapery and haberdashery business had become the largest in South Kesteven. What John and his brother Peter lacked in social graces, they made up for in business acumen. Among their achievements was the securing of exclusive contracts with an association of Lincolnshire sheep farmers before positioning themselves as suppliers to two competing woollen drapers in Pall Mall. Yet they *were* lacking in graces – sorely lacking, and Margaret was not much better.

"Let us try with Maria, again," she said, as they passed through the vestibule into the drawing room. "We might send her to old man Erasmus with an herbal remedy my sister swears by."

"Remedy for what? He survived that stroke in March. And there's no cure for getting old last I heard – ha-ha." At this, John turned to his family with a look which said he might be rough around the edges, but, really, could they help but get on with such wit at the ready? His youngest child, Cecilia, seeing it was her turn, let out a little laugh, though smiled with genuine pleasure when her father gave her an affectionate pat on the cheek.

"That's just it," said his wife. "Remedies are of no use to that man now; a visit from us will be understood as a wish to know them better. *Both* of them – which includes Daniel Thornton. I declare, if I were younger, and single, of course, my dear, *how* I should chase him. Only think how he would look in soldier's reds! Maria – put on your emerald gown when you see him. So sweetly trimmed. Pair it with that close bonnet run through with yellow ribbons, like rays of sunshine, you know the one."

Stephen, who was not disinclined to act the part of Sir Lancelot himself, stepped manfully forward and said, "Ma'am, Maria was a week in tears after her visit to see Mr Thornton. He left her to sit an hour in his drawing room with only our manservant for company." Turning to his sister with a significant look: "You never saw Erasmus the entire time you were there, did you?"

"Not once," said Maria, contemptuously throwing her parasol onto the sofa, "and only the back of that horrible Mr Thornton when he passed by to the library. I shall never set foot in that dreadful house again."

"You were not wearing your close bonnet with the yellow ribbons as I advised," said Mrs Morley, "you know you were not."

Maria was sufficiently her mother's daughter to let a moment pass imagining the outcome of this killing manoeuvre before banishing the thoughts in bitter reflections. "A Morley girl does not get dressed up, Mamma, even to go to Bainbridge Park, merely to be noticed by the footman. He was the only one who did, and then only to eject me from the house when he saw nobody was coming down. That is how they are at the Park – proud and disdainful. The old man was an hour deciding which of his ailments was to be his excuse for not seeing me. As for Mr Thornton, he simply forgot me."

"Bah," said her father. "Daniel Thornton is a gentleman. It was all a misunderstanding – that note he sent to apologise said just that."

"The note also said that given his uncle's delicate state of health, they were not up to receiving guests just now. He made that perfectly clear. Anyhow, you forget – I've a *beau* now."

"A *beau*? A bow is a trimming for your gown. And unless girls nowadays wish to marry the trimmings of their gowns rather than rich men, I don't understand you."

"Don't be a goose, Papa!"

"We speak English in this household."

"All high-class girls speak French; it's part of our education. And you know I also firmly believe it is one's duty to speak it whenever one can to show solidarity with those poor little starving peasants. Just as you are doing by leaving off your wig, and don't say it's because of the wig tax. You are a kind, good-hearted man. Just like Mr Shapely. He told Eliza Ringwald he is a *great* admirer of mine and *she* says he abhors my going near all other men. That makes him my *beau*, Papa, don't you see? If a Morley girl is to make a nuisance of herself at Bainbridge Park, I believe it is Bridget's turn." Bridget said nothing to this and opened the novel she had been forbidden to bring to church. "Or you might send Cecilia," continued Maria. "Cecilia was sixteen last month."

With all three sisters on offer, Luke said, "Take the lazy Susan from the dining table, drape my sisters over it, then set it spinning in the centre of the Park for Thornton's appraisal. Let him take whoever can remain without falling off or growing ill."

Running a hand through her dark hair, Bridget let out an approving laugh, but it was her brother's ungentlemanly snort of amusement which drew their mother's reproval.

"Stephen! I rely on you to be an example to Luke. He makes these jokes to get your reaction but hasn't the mind to say anything truly witty. I heard nothing funny in what he said."

"Would you like me to say it again?" said Luke. "Perhaps more slowly?"

With his Guinevere insulted, John Morley advanced on his younger son. Just as quickly Stephen hurried forward with his hand outstretched. "No! Do not hit Luke, Papa!"

Luke sighed as Stephen stepped gallantly between them. John Morley had never hit anyone in his life, least of all one of his children. The Morley men were all Don Quixote tilting at windmills – all wishing to wear shining armour. All but Luke, whose untamed tongue had started the sabre-rattling.

"Stop it you two!" cried Maria. "Mamma, make them stop! I just know they are going to act like this at the ball on Tuesday – before all the world. Before Mr Shapely!"

"All right, dear. Dry your eyes. Every family has its little conflicts behind closed doors. We shall all be on our best behaviour at the ball, you may depend upon it." Turning to her son: "And you can take a lesson, Luke, should you ever wish a fine lady to look twice at you – a woman likes to be stood up for. But for Stephen's intervention, your father would have taught you the hard way!"

Luke nodded. Then, at the rather fierce look in her eyes, he added, "Yes, ma'am."

He remained in the room looking duly penitent, waiting to hear if anything more would be said on the subject of Mr Thornton. Talk turned instead to Tuesday when Cecilia asked what she should wear to the ball. Stepping forward to make an appraisal, Maria affirmed she was very pretty but her extreme blonde fairness leant her a dreamy, rambling quality, rather too much like an airborne tuft of dandelion seeds. A good solid blue would ground her, like her darker, more strikingly featured sisters were grounded, didn't Bridget think? Having nothing in common with her elder sister besides her dark hair and eyes, Bridget looked towards Luke, as though seeing the opening to a joke about Maria's self-proclaimed *groundedness*.

Luke, however, was not inclined to joke at Bridget's prompting. He avoided her gaze. A short time later, he withdrew to change his clothes.

In another minute, he was out the back door.

CHAPTER TWO

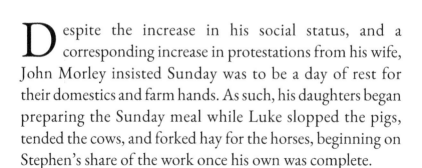

Despite the increase in his social status, and a corresponding increase in protestations from his wife, John Morley insisted Sunday was to be a day of rest for their domestics and farm hands. As such, his daughters began preparing the Sunday meal while Luke slopped the pigs, tended the cows, and forked hay for the horses, beginning on Stephen's share of the work once his own was complete.

Stephen tended to side with their mother in seeing such duties as beneath him now, and was grateful to be let off from them. Yet from Luke's perspective, his brother had the lion's share of the grunt work. The world looked to him, as the elder son, for those genteel manners, those social graces, representative of the new, finer generation of Morleys. And Stephen had those graces – had them as no one else in the family did. Growing up, Luke had often teased him for his fine ways, his speechifying and banal platitudes, and had always been closer to his sister Bridget.

Lately, however, he had begun actively to court Stephen's attentions and advice. Bridget had become involved with the son of a hard-drinking local butcher, a certain George Everett, who trailed her around town like a personal pet. Luke had watched in disbelief as his best friend and confidante, always with a sardonic quip for girls like Maria with their *beaux*, had become so entranced by Everett she was scarcely distinguishable from their sister. After nearly a week of Bridget's neglect, not trusting himself to express his hurt verbally, Luke had taken the better part of a day to put his feelings into a letter. Her response had been to organise an outing for the three of them, so certain was she that Luke would find in George the fascinating young man she was continually praising – he was everything, it seemed, that Luke was not.

For the first time in their lives, they had quarrelled. Once Luke had her alone, he had berated Everett as a moody, stoic buffoon, with nothing to say for himself but to her, who hadn't the upbringing even to engage Papa in a decent conversation. Then, he called her a fool if she believed their parents would ever let her marry the son of the town drunk. Through her tears, she had told him he was wrong about George, wrong about her – George was only a friend, and if he would only *listen* – but Luke had taken a mean pleasure in refusing not only to listen, but in refusing her company entirely so long as Everett remained in the picture.

Regrets on both sides had come. Bridget had tried to apologise for her response to his letter. But the truth was Luke didn't wish for her apology, and was too jealous to apologise himself. She had a new friend – a misunderstood, roguish fellow undeniably good-looking beneath his overgrown mop of hair. Somebody to faun over and go about with. This last week or so, Bridget had begun trying to catch Luke's eye at church or at the dinner table, exchange a look, or be noticed laughing at his jokes. And though ashamed of his unfair treatment of her, Luke was too conflicted to tell her that she had frightened him. He had said as much as he dared in that letter. She was entering into life as a young adult – the kind of life he could not join her in and for reasons he could not begin to explain.

Once he had completed the Sunday chores, Luke set his pitchfork in the ground just south of the stables. Stephen would see the pitchfork there and come to thank him for completing his share of the work. Luke then proceeded to a culvert which ran behind the property. While he waited, he hurled a few stones into the water in a rather pathetic act of defiance; he was a Morley, and in the Morley household, casting stones on a Sunday was forbidden as it was said to bring bad luck.

His parents swore by things like that. They followed all the old superstitions, certain that their success in trade had been achieved by preventing members of their house from crossing on the stairs, by never killing money spiders, and by drawing deep meaning from every coincidence. They made much of the fact that the year of Stephen's birth, 1774, had coincided with a publication second in importance for them only to the Bible. This was Lord Stanhope's *LETTERS TO HIS SON* on the Fine Art of becoming a *MAN OF THE WORLD* and a *GENTLEMAN*. Many families held it was bad luck to place anything but a book of prayers atop a Bible.

But in the Morley household, the *LETTERS TO HIS SON* often did as well. It contained lessons for both sexes in what a man should be, and was quoted from and read out over the evening fire. Luke heard in the Earl's advice merely endless ways of bowing, scraping, and toadying. Stephen, however, alone in the family, had absorbed the guidance as though he had indeed been born for such things.

The year of Luke's birth, two years after his brother, probably said as much about him. He wished independence from England if it meant a proscribed future into so-called gentility. It was said that the ultimate proof of success in business was the ability to leave it, yet one of his chief joys was working in the shop on the High Street. Assisting patrons to select textiles or moving large bolts of fabric to more eye-catching placements pulled from him a bit of creativity nothing else in his life required. Wound tight in their cubbies, which ran from floor to ceiling, the shop contained endless bolts of wool, linen, silk, and damask. Particularly choice fabrics were draped in valances across the ceiling beams – a flourish which, from his youngest days, had transformed the shop into a place of possibility, inspiring thoughts of Indian palaces, flying carpets, adventure.

At the age of ten, he had taken to spending the night in Morley's Drapery and Haberdashery. Snug under the counter in a bed of scrap fabrics, he dreamt he was a prince in other lands. Come morning, he would run about readying the place for business, unlocking the doors and lighting candles, occasionally settling with textile workers come to collect their wages. But the shop at night was what he cherished most – a magical, shrouded retreat – for even as a child he had

had a great need for solitude. In that solitude, he had begun to understand the beauty, and the power, of silence. People often felt compelled to fill silences and would say more than they had intended. As the years drew on and he discovered he had quite a lot to conceal, silence had also become a protection. And, if nothing else, it afforded him the singular amusement of provoking his mother into ordering the most silent of her children to speak still less.

The family fortunes had changed when Luke was thirteen. And though eventually Stephen began taking trips to deal with the drapers in Pall Mall, and Luke began supervising operations on the High Street, Papa's intention was to free every member of the family from work by the time Stephen was twenty-one.

Yet theirs was a fortune which changed as much as it failed to change; Luke often felt alone in understanding that the Morleys would never truly pass into the ranks of the gentry. They were a thing the gentry particularly despised. At best, they could only be second best – a lord's wife known to have previously been his mistress. For three generations, the Morleys would be labelled New Money, that class unable to distinguish fine things from established things, good dressings from good, in-the-blood breeding. And Luke, for one, did not care to be anything more.

"Don't say it," he said as his brother drew up the cuffs of his Sunday trousers and took a seat beside him.

After Stephen had settled himself gingerly down, he said, "And what is it, precisely, which I mustn't say?"

"That I didn't mean any harm but that I should have more respect for Mamma. And that one day I'll be a fine, well-mannered gentleman like you are."

"Was I going to say all that? I must be in exceptionally fine, gentlemanly form today."

"You are the only Morley who will ever be gentle-anything. I want to stay on in the shop; I want my days to have purpose. Condemn me as a common man of trade, brutish – I don't care."

"Brutish and common! Luke, you are far too hard on yourself. You've more of the boy in you, that is all. More than I ever had. You've always liked tumbling about, rolling down hills. Jokes – with a bit more sass than is good for you. Listen to me now – this is something you left out of that little speech you gave yourself in my name. Women, Luke, must always be respected. For their sake, but for your own as well, for a man is judged in this world by how he treats them."

"I *know* that. Crimenee, I was only jok—"

"It wasn't a joke to Mamma. She is serious when it comes to securing good husbands for her daughters. And she is sensitive where her intellect is concerned."

"She's sensitive whenever I say anything."

"What does Papa say when she's in a fit of melancholy?"

"Says she's got the vapours."

"Yes... but what does he say to make her feel better?"

Luke shrugged. "He calls her clever."

"*Clever. Smarter than any woman he knows and most of the men.* She never was a great beauty but being smart and clever she has always taken pride in. It's what she believes attracted Papa to her." Then, catching his brother's eye,

Stephen added, "And at the ball on Tuesday, you would do well to remember that every woman has a personal quality she values most in herself. For many it is her appearance: beauty. But sometimes a young lady, even a very pretty one, understands she has much more to offer the world than beauty. A girl like Miss Paltrow, who I daresay is not unlike Mamma in valuing her intellect. Understanding that might be just the thing to secure you the first two dances."

"I'll keep that in mind," said Luke, stretching elaborately. Then, tossing another pebble into the culvert, he said, "Come Tuesday, though, I might find tumbling down the hill behind the assembly hall more appealing than any of your Miss Paltrows."

There followed a silence – the silence every comic dreads. The joke had fallen entirely flat. Luke would be nineteen in October; far too old for such a retort. At nineteen, many young men had a steady girl. The continuing break in the conversation meant that Stephen, if not actually suspicious, was not amused and on the point of saying something more in earnest about Miss Paltrow. Luke added, "You know you cannot expect too much of me. New Money always reverts."

The quality of the silence changed. This was an expression Stephen particularly hated – not just because it was on countless tongues once the Morleys were thought to be out of hearing, but because he knew it was not, by and large, unfairly applied to them.

"I never wish to hear that kind of bloody snobbery from you again, Luke. Not even in jest."

Luke raised his brows. "Steve, you said *bloody*!"

"Bloody right I said it. Papa and Uncle Pete worked hard to make Morley's what it is. I'll be damned if we'll be looked down upon because our grandfathers hadn't everything that we have. We own land and a good estate. Papa and Uncle Pete are nearly independent men – we *are* the landed gentry."

"Alright. Jests and tomfoolery – they're hard habits to break. I know I should ask someone for the first two dances on Tuesday. If it's to be Miss Paltrow, I must do it before Tom O'Reilly asks her. But I don't know what to say."

Nothing pacified Stephen like a request to resume the role of advisor. Having been nearly two years with his own Miss Leigh, he was happy to pepper Lord Chesterfield's advice with his own, hard-won wisdom. As in most towns of three thousand souls, Grantham had a way of matching its boys and girls as they grew up. Stephen had been matched with Miss Leigh, to whom he was now happily engaged, and so it was with Luke and Miss Paltrow. Then, with a conspiratorial smile, Stephen took his brother's shoulder and confided that the young lady did rather *expect* to be asked, and her parents expected it for her. He was telling him this as one gentleman to another, and the onus would be on Luke not to make a mess of things. There now – didn't that take away most of his concerns?

Mustering a tepid smile, Luke nodded and thanked him. Internally, he chastised himself for failing to be genuinely grateful to his brother, who had spent half an hour counselling him. For his efforts, Stephen had merely shown him he would win the coming battle only to lose the war – Luke understood himself sufficiently to know why, yet insufficiently to know what he might have wished to hear in its place. He'd had a vague wish for some numbing elixir, not understanding – until his father took him aside – that what was needed was the drawing out of a rotting tooth.

That evening the cloth was laid, talk of the eligible bachelors of Grantham was the irresistible side to their mutton, and Luke remained on his best behaviour throughout the meal. Mamma dominated the table with praise of Mr Thornton. Papa, however, was unusually subdued given the energy this subject usually excited. He glanced a few times at his wife, then at Luke, but otherwise kept his eyes on his plate. Bridget appeared to sense something on his mind as well. Quite unexpectedly, she offered to take that parcel to Bainbridge Park if they thought it would do some good.

"Ah, thank you, my sweet girl. But there are other ways to skin a cat."

"I'll go first thing tomorrow; the walk will do me good."

Papa only shook his head. After the meal had concluded and Luke was departing for his bedchamber, the man took him aside.

"You are a good boy. Very intelligent. Will it surprise you to hear you are a lot like me?"

God love him, thought Luke, but observed him a bit closer to see what he could be about. That worn, slightly reddened look about the eyes likely meant his father was troubled by the thought of discord between members of his family. He understood there had been a quarrel with Bridget, a rift he'd been unable to understand or mend, and no doubt read Luke's stoicism during the meal as continued irritation with his mother. Luke felt a sharp stab of guilt. Despite the man's eccentricities, he loved his father dearly, and never doubted it was his family, even more than the business, which meant the most to him. He said, "You and Mamma wish good matches for my sisters; that is what parents must wish for."

"Precisely, Luke, precisely. Couldn't have said it so well myself."

"I know."

His father raised his brows. "Aye. Still a bit of cheek, then. You mind yourself, now."

"Yes, sir."

"I'm coming to you man to man on important business. New moons favour new ventures, and Tuesday is a new moon."

Frowning, Luke said, "Hadn't you better ask Stephen whatever it is?"

"No," said John Morley, shaking his head. "No, Stephen's a good boy."

"Papa, you just said *I* was good."

"There are many ways to be good. You are good at cards. You've a cool, analytical way and don't lose your head – you are even a bit cunning when you need to be. Stephen is not so skilled at cards, but he is good at everything else. See how you can both be good?"

Luke sighed. Then, with a nod, he listened to what his father had to say.

That night in bed, Luke thought of the man's request that he approach Mr Thornton at the ball. Grantham's most reclusive bachelor would be escorting two visiting relations, which explained this rare appearance at a social gathering.

One of these relations was a young man about Luke's age, by all accounts a very stupid fellow, who had a great taste for card-playing. So, if Luke played his cards right (really, did Luke understand the true and devastating wit in the Morley household?), he might be made to incur a small debt. A debt which the family would then forgive because the Morleys were exceptionally fine, generous-hearted people. Yet this was quite Machiavellian, as by forgiving the financial debt, Mr Thornton would feel a far greater emotional debt to the family. Accordingly, he would be receptive to more social intercourse. To an interview, which would be all they needed to get one of the girls settled well. Did Luke see?

Luke saw well enough. He wished he didn't. Wished he could be that boy again whose greatest thrill was spending the night under the shop counter, dreaming he was a prince on a magic carpet of Lincoln wool.

And yet, he *was* glad to have been asked. Glad to be pushed to speak to Mr Thornton, however it might pain him. Because he loved Mr Thornton – deeply, passionately, desperately. He loved him with an intensity which must surely kill him, because it was a love only sinners could feel, and it could never be fulfilled.

From the age of fourteen he had understood this one, profound weakness in himself. Those dreams under the shop counter had begun to evolve. One winter evening he had burrowed in deep and with a strange, new delight, begun dreaming of a shadowy bedtime companion. Of a heavy arm cast carelessly across his supine body. Of a stirring beside him as the owner of that arm awakened. Of an amused, husky laugh as Luke sought to free himself. Then another

– a knowing laugh as the man encountered something else. Luke would protest as the hand assessed the direness of his condition. Then all words would catch in his throat as the hand wrapped firmly around him and he was ordered not to make a sound.

Nearly every night for four years, this one, powerful fantasy had never lost its power to excite. On summer nights, after long days of swimming and losing himself in the forest, he'd ached for bedtime, ached to sprawl atop his bed of fabrics, stripped and exposed in the perfect privacy of the shop. Exposed to that waking, musky body beside him, to that man who understood what dirty boys like Luke wished more than anything. A man who would take him in hand, force him to cry out, then curl, sated and repentant, beside his companion whom he had formed by a special roll and tuck in a large bundle of linen. Then, Luke would beg his companion not to betray his secret, to which the man would ask, "What secret?" teasing and prodding before, mercilessly, taking hold of him. Finally, laughing like it was the grandest joke in the world, he would begin it all again.

Then in March, Daniel Thornton had arrived to care for his uncle. And in one starry-eyed moment, Luke had understood who that laugh, that meaty arm, and that roaming hand, belonged to.

And then the pain had come. The despair for his future he had not felt when he'd first understood his nature. For the life of normalcy he could never fulfil. For the dream under the shop counter, which could never be enough, now there was the face and the voice of Mr Thornton. Luke had been robbed of his fantasies above, and below, the counter of Morley's.

Tall, broad-shouldered, beautiful Mr Thornton. Kissed by the radiance of London – how the city must have adored him. You could see it in his disdain for Grantham – wishing no dinner engagements, no society, not with people like them. And who could blame him?

After first seeing him in church, Luke had wondered just how many people the man had known in his London life. Then he'd turned the question on himself. How many new faces had he encountered over the previous, say, twelve months? He had counted thirteen. A second count had confirmed the number – just thirteen. Day in, day out, dealings with the residents he'd known all his life. Visiting relations and those of his friends all met years before. Even travelling salesmen, scarcely a new face among them.

Mr Thornton must have met with titled, wealthy, international types everywhere, every day in London. Thousands of new faces in a single year.

Luke – just thirteen.

The number had been twelve before he'd added a newspaper sketch of Lord Nelson at the Battle of Genoa.

CHAPTER THREE

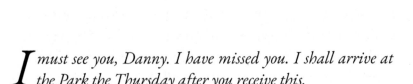

I must see you, Danny. I have missed you. I shall arrive at the Park the Thursday after you receive this.
Yours, Clarence

Daniel turned the envelope to see it had been delivered express from London.

"Sir?" He looked up to observe Collins at the sitting room door. "You made a noise."

"Did I?"

"Yes, sir. A kind of snorting, guffawing noise."

"Yes," said Daniel, smiling. "Yes, I suppose I did."

There followed a pause, after which the valet said, "It's good to see you smile again," then, with a slight bow, he departed the room.

Well, that ended Daniel's good mood. *It's good to see you smile again.* Oh, how could Collins? Had Daniel become such a sour old curmudgeon this half year with his uncle?

No. Not half a year. It had only been five months. Five months of keeping himself to himself. Five months of using Erasmus's state of health to decline every invitation to dinner or tea. Of solitary walks, carefully scheduled to avoid meeting his uncle's favourite young lady in the whole world, always prone to wandering about, Miss Williams. Daniel's lingering cynicism had served him well enough where the money-hungry and very marriageable daughter of Reverend Williams was concerned. From his uncle's first mentioning the overly helpful, insinuating Miss Williams, he had understood this was someone to avoid.

So, avoid he had – Miss Williams and everyone else in Grantham. One way of seeking the good was to avoid anything which might disappoint.

Still, five months guarding against the greed and self-interest in the world must be better than six. Surely.

At this brightening thought, light footfalls came into the room.

"Oh, there you are!" said his niece Evelina, who had arrived with her brother two days before under the care of a widowed cousin. "Upon my word, Daniel, don't you look the devil in that faun-coloured suit!" She doubled back to catch hold of her great-uncle. "Dear Erasmus, take my arm and we'll sit you in this chair. There you are. Now, look at Daniel dressed for the ball! Isn't he a lamb? How *does* he keep the ladies at bay?" She motioned to her brother who was bringing up behind. "Come Philip, stop fiddling with your cravat. Daniel has a way with cravats; he will tie it for you."

Knowing his nephew would resist if given a choice, Daniel motioned the young man briskly with two fingers. Philip advanced. He was a heavy young man without the grace or liveliness of his sister, but who nonetheless had told himself, Erasmus, and even the butler that he was very much looking forward to the ball, as his being a London man would make every girl his for the asking. It was a style of insecurity Daniel often saw and rather pitied; it always ended badly. He thought an introduction to the one young lady in Grantham he knew by name, a strong-willed, somewhat pert young woman whose father owned the best bakery in town, would take the smugness out of him – and, just possibly, make him her blissful puppy for the evening. As for Evy, he knew no young men to introduce her to. He couldn't even think where to start as, just now, a partner for himself was being rather loudly announced.

"*Miss Williams* is the name, Evy, to answer your question," called his uncle. "Daniel does not need to contend with other young ladies as it is widely known that we welcome a very sweet one here many times a week. Eldest daughter of our Reverend Williams."

Daniel gave his niece a non-committal shrug, then busied himself with Philip's cravat. He had made peace with his uncle's attempts at matchmaking. Upon arriving in Grantham, he had been grateful simply to find the man capable of stringing words into coherent thoughts. That his first words were in praise of one of his female attendants, whom he believed would make an excellent wife for his nephew, had gladdened his heart to no end. It had prevented the tears which must surely have come upon discovering a shrunken, waxen version of the man who had been the most stable and loving presence in his life – one who always welcomed him for a visit when existence with his parents became too hard, and had been a cherished correspondent throughout his adulthood. But Erasmus was now a heart-breaking reminder of the way of all things, and Daniel simply hadn't the heart to discourage him.

"Mark my words, Evy," continued the tireless man. "*Miss Williams* will get Daniel in the end!"

"Ah, in the *end*," said Evelina, returning to her uncle. "Is that where you are most vulnerable?"

Daniel went a bit red even as he understood she had intended nothing but a childish jibe. He was certain none of his family suspected his inclinations, though from no great skill on his part – they simply liked him too much to consider it. Still, such careless comments did give him a start. God help him for sounding like a curmudgeon, but this was the trouble when young people came around. So careless, so very stupid, and thoughtless – he tied Philip's cravat a bit too snugly, then, after a quick apology, retied the purple young man and sent him away.

"Well, Daniel, you *are* an old rogue," continued Evelina. "You've never mentioned the sweeter-than-sweet daughter of a holy man in your letters. I know: *a gentleman never tells.*" She sighed. "A woman must respect you for it, and so I do. One senses it immediately in you, you know – it's what makes you so attractive. That and your dashing faun-coloured jacket."

"Well, a gentleman might not tell," said Erasmus, "but an old, doddering uncle might. And I can tell you Miss Williams *is* the sweetest girl in the county; she brightens nearly every morning here at the Park with her presence. She appears just as Daniel is finishing our morning toilette and is settling me down in my sitting closet. There she is, each morning like a songbird, popping her head in my window to ask how we are. Sometimes with a basket of muffins, the most delicious muffins you ever tasted. I tell her she mustn't trouble herself, but she says it's no trouble – the Park is a favourite for her morning walk. She's a great walker, is Miss Williams. Sometimes I mistake and call her Miss Walker, I do indeed."

After stooping to kiss the man's forehead, Daniel exited the room. He wished a few minutes to himself in his bedchamber. This note from Clarence was beginning to concern him. After the surprise of receiving it, he was finding far less to be amused by. The man was coming a hundred and thirty miles to see him. Daniel's first, and only, former lover who had actually been loved. Why was he wishing to see him now? And what on earth would he say to him when he arrived?

Once inside his bedchamber, he withdrew the note from his pocket and read it through again. Then, tossing it onto the vanity, he sank into an armchair. He was slightly aware of Collins having entered the room when the man nearly tripped over his long, extended legs – still, it was a surprise to hear him speak.

"If I might crave a word, sir?" Daniel looked up, then gestured for him to continue. "I observe a note from Master Clarence on the vanity. May I assume by the care with which it has been disposed of that we shall be sending him to The George Thursday night, before returning him post-haste to London?"

Daniel straightened up slightly, then his head sank onto his hand. "Yes, of course."

"Why don't I believe you?"

Daniel took on a rather sulky expression. "I don't know. I'm trustworthy."

Collins closed the door, then approached. "Permission to speak openly, sir?"

"Speak," was the testy response.

"These last five months without Clarence have been... how shall I say it: absolute, bloody heaven for me. And for you."

"Have they?"

"Yes, they have. Do you recall what you said to me the day we left the townhouse? You said you wished to be open to the goodness in life. You said Clarence was evil and you wi—"

"I never said he was evil."

"You said he was monstrous and heartless, then affirmed he had seduced a carriage horse, and that made him evil."

"I never!"

"Then, we came to Grantham. I don't know if you've found the goodness in the world as you wished, but you have revealed it in yourself most assuredly. I've always had a good opinion of you. I don't always understand you, but I have always respected you. Yet before I observed you care for your uncle, I never understood just what a good man you are. It took patience to put up with Clarence's tantrums, his inconstancy. But it takes something altogether more to raise that poor man from bed each morning, give him his wash and help him on and off the chamber pot, without making him feel he's lost all humanity. You distract him with old stories, tell a few jokes, knowing it makes him happy to have you rather than some domestic we might easily hire from town."

Daniel was quite taken aback. "Yes, I suppose so. Thank you."

Collins raised a hand. After glancing up at the ceiling as though for strength, he came in close. Settling over Daniel's armchair, he placed either hand on the curved wings which graced its back. "You desire to have your needs met, sir. Must I be more explicit?"

"My...?" said Daniel. "I mean, I know what you mean, no need to be more explicit."

"Good. I intend to see those needs *are* met fully and completely. To the best of my abilities, which I flatter myself are not inconsiderable. I know it's been five months since you've..." He heaved a great sigh.

With Albert now inches away, his breath quickening with intensity, Daniel went bright red and squirmed away, coming to his feet in a state of such profound shock he nearly lost his footing. Frowning slightly, the valet continued, "I am offering to assist you with your daily responsibilities once Clarence arrives. He is coming to get you back: a whim, a lark, between lovers. Perhaps he simply wishes a spell in the country. Whatever it is, he'll make it appear as though he wishes to be with you again. So, you are torn considering. Only you are *not* considering this. Not really."

"I'm not?" said Daniel, his heart recovering as he understood his valet had not been on the point of going to his knees for him in some base exchange to keep Clarence away.

"No, you are not. You are merely considering how nice it would be to... to..." He faded to inaudibility.

"What was that?"

Unable to contain a slight tremor in his voice, Collins at last whispered, "To fuck a sweet arse again."

Daniel tried to laugh. He *must* laugh. This was the most bizarre conversation he had ever had! Yet, shock had left him quite beyond laughter or indeed much else.

"I beg your pardon?"

His sallow complexion having achieved a fine shade of crimson, Collins said, "My understanding is Clarence was good at that, if nothing else; I heard you say as much at the breakfast table. He'll be offering it to win you back, and I believe you should have it. Morning, noon, night, however often he is willing before you send him away. If you'll allow me, I shall care for Erasmus. I know your daily routine. As I come from the city, the servants have a disproportionate respect for me. If need be, I shall employ my power to reorganise the schedule of this house to see you are at liberty to have your amusements. On the condition, sir, *on the condition* that you send him away in a week. Two at most. Permanently."

Because a denial seemed somehow more preposterous, Daniel said, "Very well. *If* that is the case. *If* he wants me back, which I'm very far from allowing."

"You know it isn't money. Forgive me for speaking openly about this as well, sir, but Clarence has ten times what you have where money is concerned." Daniel resumed his seat. "And may I also say, I believe it was his vast wealth which allowed you to open yourself emotionally as you did. Most of your London set were living high on borrowed sums – you had plenty of experience with rascals eager to get in your breeches, simply to help themselves to your pocketbook. That was one thing you never had to worry about with Clarence, and so you understood him to genuinely care for you."

"Will you leave me?" said Daniel, rubbing his temple. "Bring me a drink first. Whiskey. Then leave me alone with my thoughts."

Albert smiled, satisfied to see his points had found their mark. After stepping before a mirror to straighten his wig, he brought the drink. Daniel met his eyes. Then, unable to look at someone who had seen him so much more clearly than he could see himself, he looked away.

About to depart, Collins said, "No, I mistake. It's been somewhat more than five months since you've... Nearer to seven, by my reckoning."

Daniel swallowed a good measure of whiskey. "Yes."

"Yesss," echoed the valet, then exited the room.

CHAPTER FOUR

Ah, whiskey. Blurring the boundaries of time. All constraints falling away so that the past, the future, seemed somehow accessible in the here and now. It was some time since Daniel had felt the need to take the edges off. And from that first, bright sip, he leant back to feel it all fall away – the very edges of time, it seemed.

Soon, he was standing before a looking glass, about to depart for a ball. A real country ball, and he didn't mind.

Soon, they were arriving at the assembly hall – he and Evy and Philip, passing from the auburn light of a summer sunset into the festive glow of candlelight and the sounds of lively chatter. They might be, all three, of an age. No doubt there were some here ready to deride this sudden change in his social habits. Five months refusing every private invitation and public event must have been interpreted to be that one, irredeemable fault: disdain. They would see him and sneer. They would say, *Well, there's life in the old boy yet.* Or he would be accused of hypocrisy, of hoping to appear the carefree man-about-a-ball to his relations when everyone in the room knew otherwise.

So be it.

Just now the lines to the past were suddenly, and quite wonderfully, blurred. As he led his young charges about the rooms, as the orchestra made final adjustments to their instruments, and guests assessed the other suits and gowns, it seemed he might simply take a step back to the good parts of life with Clarence. Daniel had no intention of having him back. But if Collins was right and his former lover was offering a bit of fun, he might just agree. For a week, or two. He would make him no promises; Clarence would be a fool to ask. And so why not?

"Oh, but that turquoise gown is lovely!" said Evelina, tugging him into the present.

Daniel was looking about to see whom she was speaking of when Philip said, "Forget her. Uncle Daniel, never in my *life* have I seen such a radiant being as that goddess she is speaking to. Who is she?"

"The friend of the one in the turquoise gown, I expect," said Daniel with a grin.

Philip was, incredibly, speaking of Eliza Ringwald, the tart, somewhat boisterous daughter of Grantham's finest baker – the only young lady in the room he had a passing acquaintance with, and to whom he had intended to introduce his nephew.

"Yes, but *who* is she?" said Philip. "*Damn* me, *tell* me she isn't engaged! I believe I shall die if she is."

With a sudden, bright joy, Daniel laughed. Could this be Philip, whom he'd taken to be that arrogant stereotype from the city? Could it be that a man, young and unsure of himself, sometimes hid behind a stereotype, believing this is what the world wished to see? Could it be he was instead exactly what he should be: a visitor filled with genuine, humble admiration for a local girl? Without artifice, arrogance. Then, his grin broadening, Daniel remembered Miss Ringwald had a brother. He had never met the brother, but he knew he was younger and certainly single. And so, Evy might well have a partner early in the night as well...

Then, he saw him – standing beside a young woman on the other side of the dance floor.

He was of medium height, lean but solidly built. Thick, rather unruly hair, just this side of chestnut. Dreadfully tied cravat. White shirt, dark green coat and waistcoat – every button of the waistcoat done up. Not a button, not a pair of buttons left open in feigned thoughtlessness. Just as the cravat was not tied in a careless, rakish fashion; the damned thing had been tortured half to death. The boy had, he would be willing to stake his life, spent half an hour attempting to tame it and simply could do no better. Lord bless him, he could do no better.

All at once, Daniel *was* his nephew – twenty-one years old, struck down, humbled. Nearly sick with sudden, violent longing as he had not felt in years.

"Who is he?"

"Who is who?" asked Evy, wincing slightly as Daniel had rather abruptly taken her arm.

Christ God, he was babbling; how would Evy know? He would give himself away. He must look away.

He did *not* look away.

Oh, the lines of that lovely torso, narrowing to a beautifully trim waist. The boy was sportive – Daniel's eyes leapt up to examine the glow of that sun-kissed face. The colour on the hands. The hands not delicate, but defined – from work, from outdoor life, from play. When the young man turned to say something to the girl beside him – Maria Morley? The one who had stopped by to see Erasmus? – he displayed, for a moment, the swell – dear God – of the tautest little bum Daniel had ever beheld.

When he leant back, Daniel observed he had commandeered the whisper to reach for a drink. Presently, he lifted the cup to his lips and took a long, deep draught. A steadying draught as one does when pursuing strength.

Then, he turned full-on to face himself, addressing Daniel in the eye. And Daniel, from the tips of his Italian cut toes to the sweep of his dashingly cut Brutus, understood that this boy, this unpretending, this good boy, was presenting himself for observation.

He must be a Morley. Not the tall, stately brother – the one you saw everywhere, parading in church and all about town.

This was *his* brother. The one who, every Sunday, when he was not turned to face the wall, was staring at the floor where his foot was tap, tap, tapping.

Luke?

Luke's eyes shone straight to him – a sweet, steady gaze, boring honey into him. Then, the gaze descended.

Understanding he was now being assessed, Daniel straightened. He stood a bit taller as those lovely, slightly dazed-from-drink eyes travelled down his body. Over the two, carefully undone buttons of his waistcoat. Down to the cut of his breeches, what was termed the city cut, whose snug fit Daniel was happily aware did him no disservice.

Yet when Luke looked up, it was not with lust, or a knowing smirk. There was something sad in his eyes. He seemed like a ravenous, wounded animal, cornered by his own desire. Presently, his cheeks were staining scarlet; they were the kind to grow ruddy from drink. Even ruddier from emotion, Daniel knew the type. A ruddiness which surged in bright splotches – across the chests of men splayed beneath him, Daniel perspiring, thrusting deeper into them, their chests arching in the throes of passion...

Good God – what would Luke Morley look like in the throes of passion?

Then, the young man stepped into a group of dour-looking chaperones and disappeared.

Daniel craned his neck to follow, even changed places with Philip, but he had lost him. At last, he stood somewhat behind his providentially rotund nephew; Christ, when had he last felt such painful arousal at such an inopportune time? He must have been about Morley's age. That throbbing urgency. Those longings – staring up as from a dry well anchored hopelessly in the earth, sights set on the distant heavens, hoping to catch rain.

Then, he recalled something else from those days – the purity of simply wishing to know. Not to conquer and move on, control, or subdue. Simply to know what it was like to be with a man. One man who would be one's all. One's everything.

"Who *are* you speaking of, Daniel?" said Evy. "I've been trying to make him out. Do you mean that one over there?"

"No, Evy. I thought I saw the brother of that angel I am to introduce Philip to. But I was mistaken. The brother I was hoping would be for you."

And Luke Morley for my bed.

He must stop, he *must* get out of here. What a time to feel, to *feel* in body and in soul, that it had been *seven months* since he'd had anyone near him. Anyone wishing his hands on him, urging him on. For months, he had kept himself from even considering such things. Only to begin at a public assembly leading his young relations about, stuffed into these miserable, city-cut breeches...

But what was this?

Was Luke approaching them? Approaching him?

"Hello, Mr Thornton," he said, stepping forward. "My name is Luke Morley."

"Pleased to make your acquaintance, Mr Morley. Somehow, we've never quite... well, I'm afraid I've never actually seen you before."

"No, sir, you haven't." Luke felt every fibre of his being trembling, but this was fine. He'd expected to tremble. A few slow, voluntary movements were concealing this. He'd expected to be unable to speak, and he *was* speaking. "I shan't make excuses for myself. I'm a bit shy around strangers. At first. Do you know..." Oh, he wouldn't say this. He really would not say this. "Once I understood you came from the metropolis, I counted all the people I had met during the previous year. Just thirteen in one whole year. Well... twelve."

Oh, of all the stupid—

Yet Mr Thornton was smiling as though he found this rather amusing. He said, "Well, I'm indebted to you for conquering your shyness and venturing over. I expect my own reputation is something worse than simply being shy. I'll wager I'm seen as downright cold and disdainful."

"No, sir, not at all. Everyone admires you for being handsome and urbane and selfless – you know, giving up your life in London to care for your uncle." There. He'd told him he thought he was handsome. Whatever else, he *had* said that.

"My goodness," said the girl beside him. "Is this the young man you wished to introduce me to, Daniel? He's perfectly charming."

"No, sweetheart. But where are my manners?" said Thornton, holding Luke's gaze for quite a long moment. A moment which seemed to contain... something. "Let me introduce you to my niece and nephew, Evelina and Philip – up from London, visiting me at the Park and forcing me to be sociable."

Luke shook first Evelina's, then Philip's, hand. "Pleased to meet you both. I know it can be difficult in a new place without introductions. If you'd like partners for the dance, I can introduce you." At this Daniel Thornton tilted his head, taking Luke's gaze in a way which nearly took his breath. The man appeared touched that he had taken the trouble, and for one red, endless moment, Luke could say nothing more.

At last, Evy, sounding somewhat affronted, asked, "Don't you dance?"

"Of course," said Luke, closing his eyes. Opening them with a smile he hoped was easy, he continued, "I'd be honoured if you would dance the fourth reel with me. I'm engaged for the first three." He looked once more to Daniel, who was observing him somewhat quizzically. "I'd be honoured if you would, Miss Evelina."

"I'd love to," she said, attempting to retrieve his eye.

"And," turning to her brother, "I reckon you know all the card games they play in the big city. Perhaps later tonight, after the dance, we might play some cards. Fancy a game of small wagers? Six penny whist, or something else you might like to show me?"

"If you can organise an introduction to that angel in the dark gown, and I can be brought down from the clouds, we'll have you back to the Park for a few hands. What do you say, Daniel?"

Mr Thornton seemed to have gone away for a moment – his eyes glazing over, his teeth grinding together. "Apologies," he said. "I thought I saw someone I knew across the room. Of course, we'd love to have you over..."

Luke heard little of what came after. *Love to have you over.* Could Mr Thornton ever suppose how he would twist this to mean something quite different later tonight, when he was alone in bed? Sometime about three – oh, the long, long hours until three! – he would pluck the words from memory. *Of course, we'd love to have you over.*

Only then, in the same, lilting bass, it would be: *Yes, Luke. I'd love to have you over.*

"So, as I say," continued Daniel, thinking frantically of a way to obstruct a situation he surely could not handle. "We'd love to have you round, but I cannot ask you to stay up so late. The dance will go to three, I'm sure, and the Park is some distance away. Out towards Londonthorpe, as I'm sure you know. We took the coach here – a terribly bumpy ride it was too, I really must have it re-sprung when next I am in town. In any event, we only planned for three passengers, not four."

Philip was regarding his uncle with wonder. "You old blockhead, what is in that drink of yours? This dance concludes at eleven, they told us when we arrived. And the coach can be made to accommodate six. Four, quite comfortably. Anyhow, you speak as though we will be taking another of my size. Look at him. He's quite slim when you come to look at him. Wouldn't you say?"

Daniel closed his eyes: "Yes."

"Slim as a boy, really."

Daniel could have strangled dear old Philip: "Yes, very slim."

"And the coach drives like a dream. Really, I don't know what's got into you tonight."

With a wilting smile, "Neither do I."

Evy added, "And you can show him your collection of foreign coins." Turning to Luke, "Daniel *has* met many people, as you imagine, but more than just Londoners. He's travelled all over Europe. Erasmus began taking him on tours when he was just nine. His coin collection is displayed in a curiosity cabinet in the front parlour. You'd adore it."

Though he knew he had lost, Daniel made one final plea. "You are certainly welcome. But you've been so kind coming over to introduce yourself, and we've all become such fast friends. I shouldn't wish to put you out of your way."

Then, smiling and saying with his schoolboy's candour, Luke delivered the *coup de grâce*. "Thank you, Mr Thornton. But I *want* to go home with you tonight."

So it was, at eleven-thirty they were departing – a party of four. In some ways it was a relief, Daniel having spent the evening feigning excuses to look away from his partners to catch sight of the young man dancing across the floor – face bright, his heightened breathing producing a post-coital glow at the end of each reel. Luke's dancing spoke of an inner point of view which was decided, direct, playful. His movements showed forethought; he had the muscle to execute lightly, but it was not until well into the second reel that Daniel understood what was so captivating about his performance. Luke danced as though he had no partner; he was before a mirror at his dancing master's, and it was like nothing Daniel had ever seen. Pity the young lady whose hand he held like a mere ribbon to twirl about. The self-possession in dance, which he did not otherwise possess, was entrancing.

Of course, now they were settling into the coach, the source of his agony was seated directly across from him. Flushed and well-spent, content to listen to the endless banter of his new, young friends, occasionally smiling shyly at his other, older one.

In each glance at himself, Daniel observed a young man opening a door to the outside world. He saw light touch places it seldom reached. Saw the hypersensitive reactions, responsive to the shading of every word, every look. Daniel had never been a particularly vain man, yet this sense that Luke had approached for him, and only him, seemed unavoidable. He was asking to be led.

And yet. If he had read the signs correctly, if this young man really was hoping to get him alone at some point in the evening, then what? What would he be opening himself to? Daniel would – hell, he already did – feel far more than he should about a potential encounter. No doubt he could, but did he wish to sport as he had done before his year with Clarence? Whatever Luke's level of experience, for a young man it was about experience. He would not intentionally seek to hurt. Yet that was small consolation when you felt the sting.

Just now, Luke seemed so much a member of that carefree, twenty-year-old set. Holding his own, if only just, against Evy's mild flirtation. Laughing at some silly observations of Philip's about a group of chaperones at the dance. Looking mildly affronted when Philip asked, "May I?" and he responded, "May you what?" and Philip proceeded to unbutton the top two buttons of Luke's waistcoat.

"*Much* better. *Damn* me, how I've wished to do that all night!"

And Daniel simmering in his seat thinking, *yes, yes, you and me both*. Then Evelina chiding Philip, and Luke – Lord bless the stubborn little angel – making a face of mild contempt before proceeding to undo all the buttons of his waistcoat.

Well, stubborn angel or no, young Mr Morley would not be having his wish about one thing tonight. Daniel was decided. The late hour declared he must sleep at the Park, but they would not make up a spare room; he would sleep with Philip. Those two would be up drinking and gambling. More than likely they would pass out together, and Daniel's bedchamber door would remain firmly locked. Should anything happen with Luke, it must be when his relations were returned to London, when they were assured of being alone together.

Of course, the likeliest outcome of this semi-righteous forbearance would be that he would miss his one chance with him. Luke would forget him, find someone else. Perhaps forget men altogether; boys that age never knew what they wanted. So be it. Daniel would not, *could* not, risk discovery. Should Philp or Evy, should Erasmus come to hear of it, it would be the end of existence as he knew it. He would be a pariah in the family. He would never forgive himself.

As the coach drew up at the Park, the partygoers tumbled out. They continued into the light of candles spilling onto the drive from a fully lit front parlour. The servants would be waiting up. There'd be a cold collation in the dining room. All would be ready for a night of gaming after a dance, nothing more, and Daniel would relinquish his guest to the blessed formality of a well-run house.

So, having firmly determined this, he took one small indulgence – just one innocent touch to last him the night; he took Luke by the arm to lead him in.

The front door opened. They were met by Collins. The butler. Evelina's maid.

And Clarence, leaning on the bannister.

CHAPTER FIVE

C oming in on the arm of Philip, Evelina turned to her uncle for an introduction. In those precious moments before he observed Clarence, Daniel was guiding Luke gently forward, savouring this one, perfectly platonic touch. Admiring his guest's defiantly unbuttoned waistcoat, his shirt wrinkled into folds where sweat from a boisterous evening had dried, and from which emanated a biscuity, boyish aroma untainted by foul perfumes. And Luke, aware of his every movement, his every look was coming over again in those brilliant red splotches.

Then, the familiar drawl. "Hello, Danny. Introduce me to your friends."

Daniel took in the scene. Allowing himself no more than a faint sigh, he gripped his companion by the shoulder. Then, he looked down at him and, with an affectionate squeeze, said, "You wish an introduction? This is Luke Morley, my dear friend."

And Luke, incredibly, looked not to Clarence, but to himself.

For a time, Daniel simply could not continue. He was so oddly touched, so taken aback by this one, instinctive reaction he could only stare at Luke – at the sparkle in his eyes, that smattering of sunlight from the happiness his introduction had made him feel. Blind to his true intention in saying it, Luke had blinded Daniel to it as well. In that moment, he wished with all his heart everything Clarence would infer about Luke would be true. Not from petty revenge; he missed being on the arm of a companion, someone who had sent light without obstruction to his optic nerve. Someone he could have all to himself after a dance – to suffocate with kisses. To draw under the covers away from the world. To love.

Clarence's eyes flashed. He had clearly been drinking but was still master enough of himself to deign no more than a glance at the tousled lad so tightly in tow. At last, Daniel said, "Evelina, Philip, this is Clarence, my nephew. Mother's side of the family. Clarence, these are relations on my father's side – my favourite relations in the whole world."

He was not surprised to see Clarence two days early. The man was an insufferable addle-pate – never one to think of inconvenience, never suppose he might be unwanted. Yet Daniel was in just that state of spirits to accept his appearance and, just as easily, to understand with astounding clarity that he did not, he would never, wish to sleep with this man again. It was the most edifying, most liberating feeling imaginable. Clarence Hopper continued to be a statuesque, exceptionally well-looking man whose attractions would translate exceptionally well into older age. And this was just it. Clarence had not changed, and Daniel had. All desire for him had quite vanished.

"Pleased to meet you all," was Clarence's reply, in which Daniel heard a touch of self-pity. Clarence was the type to prefer no invitation to arriving where everyone but himself already knew each other. "Might I have a word, Danny? Privately?"

"Certainly, please come up," said Daniel, somewhat amused to be granting an interview.

Then, his amusement subsided. There, on the floor in a corner of the front parlour, lay Clarence's portmanteau. Opened and in some disarray, clothing and some papers were scattered about – no doubt he'd been searching for a fresh tin of chewing tobacco while he waited. Daniel had the twin to this portmanteau upstairs. They'd purchased the pair in Cheapside before a trip to Brighton. A month after that trip, Clarence had gone into Devonshire to visit relations. During that agonising separation, Daniel had stashed the letters he received into his portmanteau. When there were enough, he would, of a lonely, candlelit evening, open it just enough to slip a hand inside and retrieve one. He would then take the letter into bed, slowly settling in, delaying the moment he would discover which of the many it would be – so desperate had he been for that feeling of surprise, that feeling of new engagement with Clarence Hopper.

He resolved to have a spare room made up. There was something too sad about a party of young people setting up the card table, ordering a brandy decanter when just a few feet away lay that portmanteau, pulled apart in a corner because its owner had not been offered a room in which to unpack properly. The owner who had come all this way to see him.

Understanding her chaperone, Mrs Edwards, had gone to bed, Evy said with a glance at the decanter, "We'll content ourselves with making merry for a time, shall we? Then make a rubber when you two come down?"

"Don't wait for us, Evy. Clarence has had a long journey and will want to relax."

Running a hand through his curly locks and looking rather peevish, Clarence said, "Yes, and fighting a miserable cold. There was a bad night air in Bedfordshire. Rain and a leaky roof at the coaching inn in Peterborough."

Daniel approached Luke and set a hand on his shoulder. Careful to maintain his gaze on that hand rather than letting them fix upon eyes in which he had seen almost too much, he said, "Forgive my manners, but I'm leaving you in good hands. Philip, Luke can sleep with you."

"Much obliged, Mr Thornton," said Luke, sounding very much as though he wished to say something more before his host departed.

"And that's the other thing!" said Philip, drawing chairs up to the card table and motioning the visitor over. "The first was that waistcoat buttoned up to your chin. The second is this cussed formality with my uncle. He likes you, and you make him feel like an old man! From now on it is *Daniel*, alright?"

Daniel was obliged to assure the predictably horrified guest that no offence had been taken. Then, exhaling, he began to relax, understanding he was really quite pleased to see Clarence. There could be something lovely about having one's choices taken away; just now he wished all choice annihilated where young Mr Morley was concerned. Clarence was here and he had his old life again – a life which had been the most important thing to him for more than a year. A life he must put to a proper, dignified end. Not the most pleasant chore, but better by far than finding himself wandering downstairs in an hour to observe the game. Trying to prevent his arm from slipping around Luke's waist at the first opportunity. Inventing an excuse to get him alone.

Directing Clarence upstairs, Daniel fell into step behind the stomp of black Hessian boots he had thought worn only by the military. When they reached the first-floor landing, he summoned the housekeeper to make up a spare room. Then, he directed the traveller into his study.

Collapsing into an armchair and looking quite miserable, his guest accepted a whiskey, saying, "Pleased to discover your Mr Collins is the same, clawing old puss that he always was. Told me I was to go to The George for the night – at your direction."

Closing them inside the room, Daniel set the decanter on a table between them then motioned for him to keep his voice down. "Alright, alright," said Clarence, in a subdued tone, "but you know he hates Pathics with every fibre of his being, and I really cannot understand how you can continue to employ him."

"He does not hate us. Haven't we anything else to speak of?"

"No, we haven't," said Clarence, peevishly sluicing a measure of whiskey into his mouth, then inhaling over the glass in an attempt to clear his sinuses. "Because I want to know if that man has merely grown too big for those old, worn breeches of his, or if it really was you who gave him that direction for me."

"Of *course* it was me," said Daniel, fired at last by the presumptuousness of this ridiculous man. "The George is precisely what a presuming narcissist deserves. Do you expect I've forgotten the last two months I spent with you? Two months of your going behind my back; two of the most painful months of my life—"

"Ah now, let us not tell fibs," said his guest, crossing his leg. "They was two *weeks* at most. That little trifling affair with our friend Marmaduke – *very* little and very *trifling,* I can assure you, Danny," he added, with a little snort, "came to your attention after two weeks. After which you understood full well what I had been driven to."

"Now is when we blame me for driving you to sleep with all and sundry."

"Not at all. I take full responsibility; it is how narcissists try to give meaning to their meaningless existences. Forgive me for having faults, Daniel. I'm not the picture of manly perfection that you are. And if you will agree that you remained with me for six full weeks after that discovery, *fully* aware of my doings, I will tell you a little secret. Two secrets, really."

"Why you arrived here two days early?"

"Three secrets."

Daniel poured himself a whiskey, took a good portion into his mouth, and swallowed. "I knew. Pained and still too much in love to do anything but cower as you continued to walk over me, but I knew."

"Yes, you did." Clarence scratched his nose. "Here is my first secret: I came to see you earlier than intended to escape my parents. They had learnt from my valet, whom they have taken to bribing for information about me, that I intended to come. They would have been two days haranguing me not to come. And I knew I *must* come at all costs, because of my second secret, which is that I found no meaning in my life or even gratification behaving as I did. Not a bit of it."

Supposing this was as close to an apology as he would ever get, Daniel nodded.

Then, in a lowered voice, Clarence said, "My third secret is I still love you. Never stopped. Never ceased feeling guilt for what I was doing, even after you left me, and I have *never*, Daniel Thornton, *ever* been made to feel guilt by any man. So, I ask," he sniffed, for he tended, somewhat paradoxically, to grow theatrical when moved by actual emotion, "have I come all this way merely to be sent to The George? Or do you, perhaps, have something to tell me as well?"

Though set back on his heels by what sounded like sincerity, Daniel said with decision, "Come now. It is late, we'll speak more of this in the morning."

"No," said his guest, his eyes flashing with fear. "No, there will be no *morning* if you end the conversation like this. Do you imagine I could sleep a wink this entire night after baring my soul to you? Do you imagine I will do anything but lie awake wondering what you will say? You can't possibly be that cruel."

Nodding to silence the outrage before half this speech had been made, Daniel said, "Very well. In your shoes, I would do the same. This is what I can tell you: I cherish, I love, my memories of the good times, nothing more. I care for you. I love you as a friend, and I want you to be happy. Sincerely. But I don't love you anymore, not in the way you mean. I'm sorry."

He would not have imagined Clarence could make him feel much of anything now. Yet, seeing that moment of exquisite pain, he very nearly took back what he had said. While they were together, Clarence's declarations of love had been confined to occasions when Daniel had done something impish or purchased him something extravagant. He wouldn't have thought Clarence had any real love, or regret, in him. Not for another twenty years, when, perhaps, he wasn't quite as lovely to look at.

"You don't mean it, Danny; I see you do not. You never could lie, at least not to me. You're fucking someone. That boy downstairs, I suppose."

As Clarence finished his drink and poured another, Daniel said, "It's nothing like that. You and I simply reached an end. I have a good life here with my uncle. Until now, I haven't realised how good. I read, go for walks, swim when I can. I've changed, grown into an old man. You'd be miserable with me."

"You're thirty-four; not quite an old man – rather at the height of your attractiveness. And you *are* sleeping with that little bugger, aren't you?"

"Clarence—"

"Why not say that *I* am too old now! You prefer pups of fifteen or whatever he is, not tired old libertines of twenty-seven!"

"I have known him for exactly five hours; I am not sleeping with him. If you must know, I haven't been with anyone since we parted. Does that help you understand this has nothing to do with him? This is about me."

"Promise you aren't sleeping with him. Swear on the life of your uncle you are not."

"That is grotesque. I told you I was not, and that should be enough."

"Then I cannot believe you, and you are fucking liar! You have the power to make me just a bit happier than I am, and you won't even do that much for me."

Oh, how Daniel loved him for this. He could have kissed him. This was the Clarence of old. Clarence, who made no distinction between love and sex. Clarence, who could feel some pain, and who, were he ever to grow up, did need to feel a good deal more.

"I will *not* bring my uncle into this. I tell you this on my honour, and that should be enough."

"Ah, your beloved uncle who hates Catamites just as Collins hates us. The uncle you love more than life and who would disown you if he knew what you are. You understand you cannot love someone who hates you deep down – and if you do, you are quite seriously sick in the head. And so, perhaps part of this great and undying devotion to Erasmus is in regard to a pocketbook which was never exactly overflowing. But which will be once the old dear is old dearly departed."

Daniel was too shocked to reply. Clarence, now overfired with whiskey, jumped to his feet. "And don't give me your wounded puppy expression! I don't want that any more than your word. I've had enough of your *words*, Daniel Thornton. Do you know what I did riding up here to see you? I read and reread every letter you ever sent me – that is what someone who loves does: they keep old letters, so they can reread them on miserable three-day carriage rides only to be rejected in some God-forsaken Grantham! *I will love you forever, my dearest, my sweetest, my only. You are the love of my life. I am ruined for all others. I shall die without your love – the only thing which can quench my unslakable thirst...*"

"*I was out of my head in love with you!*" cried Daniel, pained but more than a little uneasy to be having this conversation in his uncle's house. "One writes such things wholeheartedly, not literally, but wholeheartedly because, in the moment, they are the absolute truth. And were I able to choose, I would still *be* that lovesick puppy for you! I was never happier. I... oh, just let it be – I cannot make someone who hasn't a heart understand what it is to break one."

"Haven't a heart?" said Clarence. After a contemptuous look, he said somewhat dismissively, "You fool. Of course, I have one, else you could never have loved me."

Daniel finished his drink in one scorching swallow. Feeling no relief, he turned away as he attempted to collect himself. He must put a stop to this conversation; Clarence was starting to make sense. "Tell me those are not my old love letters scattered about the parlour floor."

"Of course they are. You were so fucking delayed tonight I was obliged to pull my packing apart to search out a new tin of tobacco. It's your fault."

"Stop that now. Go downstairs and put your things away. Bring everything into the room that's making for you.

We've got three drunk twenty-year-olds down there who may well find it a lark to leave off card-playing in favour of letter-reading."

Clarence shook his head. "That's all that matters to you. Keeping up appearances. Playing the dutiful nephew. How could you even think of taking me back with your uncle still around?" At this, Clarence went silent, appearing to find solace in this thought. He paced about for a time. Then, expelling a clipped little laugh, he said, "Why, I'll bet you are even talking about some young lady he's chosen for you. You are, aren't you? Leading her on, leading your uncle on – until he dies, of course, at which point you can leave off pretending."

"Leave me now, Clarence. You are drunk, I am drunk, and if you mention my uncle once more in such a disgraceful light, I won't be responsible for my actions. And for Christ's *sake*, get downstairs and collect those letters before someone gets curious and starts to look through them!"

"Oh no, no, we couldn't have that," said Clarence, draining his glass in a leisurely manner, though at the same time retreating a few steps from his well-built and quite enraged former lover. "I'll do better than that. I'll stash every precious letter into my portmanteau and leave this house entirely. Humiliated, having bared my heart after a three-day ride from hell. But with your secrets safe with me – never to be told to anyone. I shall go to The George. It was recommended to me as the most hospitable place in Grantham. I trust your coachman hasn't put the horses away?"

CHAPTER SIX

"Mr Morley? Sir? Please to get by."

Luke came awake, scrambling to his feet, understanding he had rolled out of his makeshift bed under the shop counter to sprawl across the floor. Facing him stood Mr Jenkins, the somewhat dour clerk they had opening the shop these days, a man before whom Luke had never appeared in such disrepair and who had little time for the antics of young people.

"I was out late after the rout at the assembly hall. At my father's request. I came here afterwards as I had a lark to sleep a few hours under the counter, for old times' sake – I did as a child – that's why I'm... still in last night's suit."

"Indeed..."

Giving it up as hopeless, Luke straightened his clothes and dusted himself off. He took a broom and began to sweep around the shop, pleased to find the pocket door which gave onto Uncle Pete's haberdashery was firmly closed, the man not yet arrived. When Mr Jenkins stepped into the back room, Luke collapsed in a chair, desperate to collect his thoughts. How had he wound up here? Hadn't he been meant to spend the night at the Park? What had happened?

Slowly, the previous evening returned to him. Mr Thornton's nephew storming out of the house after some quarrel with his host. Mrs Edwards, a sombre lady in widow's weeds, coming downstairs to fetch Evelina to bed. He and Philip two hours at piquet.

Philip, every bit the poor card-player he was reputed to be, had been even worse while speaking of Miss Ringwald, with whom he was even more enchanted by the end of the evening. Damn *him – Evy had a young man, an officer stationed in Yaxley, but he had nobody. They had only planned to remain a week in Grantham, what could he do to captivate his goddess? Luke must tell him everything he knew of Eliza –* damn *him, Philip knew next to nothing. Did Luke think she would agree to write to him? How did Luke remain so damned slim,* damn *him?* During which, Luke had pocketed forty-two pounds. Wishing only a short break from cards, Philip had stretched out on the sofa and fallen into oblivion. Luke had then ventured over to inspect Daniel's collection of coins – from kronor to lira, to drachma.

Any hope of seeing Daniel himself again had seemed futile; he was likely asleep or not in the best of moods after quarrelling with his nephew. Growing uncomfortable, and not knowing which was Philip's room, he had supposed it best not to stay. So, he'd slipped out the terrace door, run across the Park, and made his way toward town, happy at the thought of presenting his parents with the large gaming loss they could now forgive.

Only he had not proceeded home.

Ah, yes. He'd wished to crawl under the shop counter like a squirrel with a fresh hoard of memories: the warmth of Mr Thornton's hand when he'd taken his arm. That intensely glowing expression when he'd introduced him as his dear friend. Various words over the course of the evening, whose meaning Luke was to have repurposed for what he had promised himself would be more than one naughty fantasy before falling asleep.

But then... what? In he had crawled, only to have fallen asleep atop a bed of old linen and wool scraps? This was *mortifying*. How could he behave like this? He should be feeling proud – he had passed from silent, terrified admiration to actually engaging Mr Thornton. He had *done* it. True, he *had* drunk too much whiskey before going to the dance. Before approaching, he *had* looked Thornton over in quite an undisguised manner. Daniel had certainly noticed but hadn't been affronted. On the contrary, he had seemed quite pleased to have been approached. Welcoming.

By the time they'd reached the Park, something seemed to have begun between them – Daniel had taken his shoulder and called him his friend. *My dear friend* – and it had felt as though they were beginning a friendship. The declaration, the look in his eyes as he held him. It hadn't been so much titillating as touching. Last night, after he had returned to the shop, he'd still been trying to decode all the subtleties of what had passed, all the words, all those strangely piercing looks. Taken together, they had simply overwhelmed him.

He let out a breath. Further consideration would have to wait until he had a clearer head. It was still quite early, just after seven. He could be home in fifteen minutes if he walked quickly.

However, just before exiting the shop entrance, he paused. A crowd was advancing down the street in the direction of Ringwald's Grain, Flour and Baked Goods. It was dominated by a number of housewives Luke had known all his life – Mrs Michaels, Mrs Kensington, Mrs Musgrove among them. And though it was by no means unusual to see them so early, it was unusual to see them come together in this way. Until recently.

The women had assembled to protest the price of bread, as had been happening all over the country. Since March, a country bakery, together with dairies and butcher shops, and the routes taken for deliveries, had become flashpoints – places of collision between the haves and the have-nots, where officials, local and national, feared the echoes of revolution from across the Channel.

Protests had increasingly become uprisings in which food was forcibly seized and sold to the poor at a price they could afford, the proceeds later returned to the business owners. They would never riot here in Grantham. Yet, something in their assembling, in joining as one in a common purpose, spoke to Luke of possibility. The movement of many, none individually powerful, when assembled in one direction, could achieve things. Because of the riots, any gathering carried with it the threat of another local uprising and the issue had garnered national attention. Discussions had arisen about changes in the daily diet. Oatmeal was a common foodstuff for people up north – if its distribution to animals was limited to post horses, the surplus could be introduced as a substitute for bread in the south.

What application this had for himself, Luke hadn't an idea, still less why it should give him pause. Yet it did, and he continued to watch the protesters, entranced as the women arrived at their destination just beyond The George.

When Jenkins returned to the shop floor, Luke was still at the window, watching as the housewives spoke to a few early patrons. They wished them to delay entering the bakery so that the owners would be prompted to come out and speak to them. Seeing this, Luke supposed it best to exit the shop via the alleyway. Departure out the front would take him directly past Ringwald's and, protest or no, the women would certainly notice him. He'd rather not have his odd and untidy appearance become known all over town.

As he stepped into the alleyway, Luke observed a darkened figure just behind The George staring at something on the ground. He supposed it must be his uncle coming to open his side of Morley's. As he approached, however, Luke understood this man was taller than Uncle Pete and decidedly dishevelled. He was not staring at something on the ground but rather supporting himself over a puddle of sick. Like a crumpled memory, in the crumpled pocket of Luke's suit, was a crumpled version of the man he'd met last night at Bainbridge Park. The man looked up. Then he began stabbing the air with an index finger as though trying to place him.

"Luke... *something*. I'm a marvel with names. Luke *something*. Glass half full, you know."

"You are Clarence. Mr Thornton's nephew."

The man let out a little howl, then lurched at him. "Will you help me to my lothings? Oh, God. You see, I've taken *lothings* in this fine *establithment*... huh! I seem to have bitten my tongue which is now swelling up on me. Anyhow, I *have* been drinking in this tavern, raising a cup for old Grantham, you know, not wishing to ascend to my room. Only now I believe I *shall,* yet I am feeling... I'm feeling, Mr Lucas, rather in need of support. Will you support me?"

As Clarence was now quite alarmingly falling away from him, Luke was quickly under him, slipping an arm around his waist. Trying not to gag at the odour of vomit the man was exhaling liberally, he helped him inside. Once they were in his room, Clarence fell onto the bed fully clothed, tossing about for a time before coming to rest on his back.

Gazing intently at the ceiling, he said, "Excuse the state of my room and my person. I absconded from the city *sans mon valet,* who I discovered likes to sell my personal secrets to the highest bidder. That is why, for the first time in his life, The Honourable Clarence Hopper, son of The *Right* Honourable Lord and Lady Ludlow, is entirely without one. Ain't he a rebel? But enough of that – I wish to ask you something, Mr Lovely Luke. May I call you Luke? Or had I better be formal and call you Mr Thornton?"

"What?"

"Only a joke, my dear! On-ly-a-*joke*. But I do have something to ask. Many things, indeed. Perhaps many, *many*..."

"What do you want to know?"

"Straight to the point, then. He really is in love with you? Daniel, I mean. You can tell me. Mr Thornton loves you?"

Luke felt the blood drain from his face. "My dear, never fear – even in my stupor, I can see you are just as shy as last night. This is the country, I know. One shouldn't speak of such things; they don't exist."

"I don't understand you."

All at once, Clarence was that foul-tempered man from last night. The one who had thrown his things pell-mell into his portmanteau, then stalked about the ground floor in and out of rooms, muttering under his breath until the coach was ready to take him away. Coming up on an elbow, he took Luke by the jaw. "*What are you playing at?* Let's not call it *love*, then. I didn't imagine it was. Is. Was. I was only thinking of your delicate sensibilities. Anyhow, he *loves* me."

"Don't. I mean." Luke pulled away, his heart nearly pounding out of his chest. He whispered, "You are not his nephew?"

Clapping a hand to his forehead, Clarence melted back onto his pillow. "Ah, yes. Daniel and his lies. No, not his nephew. I am, I was, his *lover*! Are you scandalised? And I may be many things, but I am not an incestu... *not* an instigator of... what the devil am I trying to say? I am not an incestigator, is that a word?"

Luke's mouth had dried to toast. He was panting so hard he felt in danger of falling into a genuine swoon. Mr Thornton's lover. His... *male* lover.

"Darling boy, you are blushing to the tips of your ears. But you are the same, of course – a member of the cast – I observed it in the way you were observing Danny."

"A what?"

"Member of the cast. A Catamite, a Pathic."

"No! What are you saying?"

"Apologies," said Clarence. "In the city, one likes to harness terms of derision to make them one's own. I mean no offence," he snorted, "how can I? But you are?"

Fixing Clarence's eyes, Luke took a long moment to consider. Then, he said what he never thought he would, as he was affirming what he had never truly connected to himself. "Yes."

Clarence nodded. "You really are too fetching not to be, you know. But did you really just meet him tonight?"

"Yes. I approached him at the ball. I've wished to speak to him for months, only I—"

"Yes, yes. Of course, the bastard was truthful about that so I can't even hate him properly. And now I have done a terrible thing. A pretty, terrible thing; pretty, terrible Luke. I've been up all night thinking how I can make it right. I thought I would simply return today and retrieve it. But when I stepped outside just now... the sunlight... seemed to be making me rather faint. I fear my cold has worsened, and I might actually be growing ill. But you will be returning to see him."

"I will?"

"Yes. Today."

"Today?"

"Christ, *I* don't know! I tell you, I am feeling poorly, and I must get that silly letter back. Before I departed last night, I wrote a horrible little note because Daniel had just... he had just told me he didn't wish to be with me. It hurt me terribly – the thought that he would never love me again, never wish to show me affection. Living with that damned uncle has done it, I know it has... Anyhow, I must get that note back. You did say you are going? This morning?"

His heart surging, his heart singing at the thought of seeing not just Mr Thornton, but of seeing him knowing that... *knowing*. "Yes. I am."

"Then be a dear and retrieve that note from the mantle of the sitting parlour. It's with the post. A plain envelope with just his name, no direction. Don't let him see you. Just slip it into your pocket and bring it to me. I beg you."

"I will." Luke took a sharp, bracing breath, his head nearly ready to explode. "And you say he does *not* wish to be with you now. So, if I say something of my feelings for him, he might be interested? He will know what I mean?"

Clarence glared at him. "Say what you wish, I can't stop you. If he's interested, he'll respond."

"But is he... interested, do you think?"

"You were an entire evening with him. If you must ask me, I should think the answer is no."

All went silent for a time. Luke supposed the conversation to be at an end, but when Clarence spoke, he seemed to be continuing a conversation which had not ended for him, the final word of which sounded like "revenge."

"What?"

After expelling a putrefying puff of air, Clarence repeated, "Revenge. He's never had his revenge on me, that's his trouble. A man like him is slow to recover..." He looked away. "He does *so* love to feel wanted. And if he hasn't had anyone asking..." he glanced at Luke, "asking for his *affection* this half year, he may still need to get some things out of his..."

Luke had quite lost the thread of the narrative, and when he frowned, Clarence turned a kind of bitter brightness on him. "Tell him how you feel. He has a broken heart, so more than likely he will say he likes you well enough but doesn't wish to go further. *Cannot* go further, because of his grief over losing me. You must not take it to heart." Then, after taking a long, steadying breath, he continued, "And if he does respond, just... you know, give him what he wants."

Expecting Clarence to lash out again, Luke was perplexed when he merely grew more thoughtful. Perhaps it was the drink, perhaps his energies were turned to fighting an oncoming illness, but as he looked Luke over again, his gaze softened. For a moment, a cloud dimmed the glare of that sun, and he said, "Anyhow. As to your other question – you shouldn't be afraid. I *can* promise that he will understand what you mean and will not laugh at you. Not be horrified. And he will not betray you to the magistrate."

Luke's breath caught at the directness of this assurance. The words, though meant to assure, succeeded only in bringing up a fear which far outweighed mere rejection by Mr Thornton. His brow furrowing, Luke dropped his head.

"Christ," said Clarence. "Don't cry. I'm poorly, I tell you. I haven't the wherewithal to comfort even when I am well. If I'm *not* well by this afternoon you must fetch a physician for me. Then you must send an express to my parents in London, telling them to come immediately. You must do many things for me so do be strong."

Luke nodded, smiling as he pressed the heels of his palms to his eyes. Wiping his nose on his sleeve, he looked about the room. When he returned to Clarence, the man's eyes had already closed. Luke poured him a large glass of water and told him to drink it before he fell asleep.

Clarence merely nodded and drifted away.

CHAPTER SEVEN

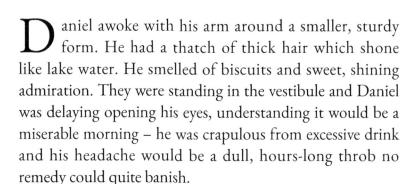

Daniel awoke with his arm around a smaller, sturdy form. He had a thatch of thick hair which shone like lake water. He smelled of biscuits and sweet, shining admiration. They were standing in the vestibule and Daniel was delaying opening his eyes, understanding it would be a miserable morning – he was crapulous from excessive drink and his headache would be a dull, hours-long throb no remedy could quite banish.

As Collins stepped about the bed, laid out his clothes and opened the bedchamber, Daniel remained with his arm around Luke, recalling his blush and the sparkle in his eyes. As Collins told him of Philip's having been sick on himself on the sofa, Daniel wondered what it would be like to love a man who could throw himself so wholeheartedly into a country dance. When Collins told him of Luke Morley's having fled the house in the middle of the night, however, he groaned and, at last, opened his eyes.

The glare in his bedchamber was glancing, the taste in his mouth a leaden weight. As he rose from bed, his valet – gleefully indifferent to the sorry state of his employer – began executing a kind of gavotte around him, scarcely able to contain his joy. Those uncommonly crisp, lively movements as he shaved him said he would not ask, he had no need to ask: it was quite enough to know that Clarence had stormed out of the house the night before and never returned. But, at last, when Daniel noted the late hour and declared he would have to postpone his bath, Collins at last grew serious.

"Go back to bed, sir. Do. Mrs Edwards offered to care for Erasmus today if you were... indisposed."

Daniel patted the man's shoulder but declined the offer, knowing his uncle would have been up half the night anxious to hear about the ball. He soon regretted this decision. Upon reaching him, he found the man more than usually ungainly rising from bed. Added to his unwieldiness, Erasmus had decided this was the day to push Miss Williams more forcibly upon him. *Yes, he was happy to hear Daniel had danced two reels with Miss Williams, but it really should have been three. Three reels would have said she was being distinguished. Really, wasn't it time Daniel showed a bit more interest? He would not be around forever, and it was high time that he settle down. He should like to know his nephew was in good hands before he passed. Let them have Miss Williams in for elevenses should she appear at the sitting closet window.*

And at the sitting closest window, at just about eleven, so she did. Daniel was half an hour rehashing the ball with her while Erasmus peered out from those watery, bloodshot eyes so very wistfully, so hopeful to see more interest from him. Miss Williams was about twenty-five, composed and engaging, and though clearly hungry to accomplish a good marriage for herself, not unjustifiably so. She valued herself, spoke without too much vulgarity of her own virtues, and would undoubtedly make the right man very happy. And so, feeling his defences quite lacking, Daniel found himself complying. He gave her a few compliments which, though half-hearted at best, sufficed to gain heightened reactions from both his harassers. How he hated himself for it.

Almost immediately after she departed, Sophia Edwards popped her head in the room and offered to bring Erasmus onto the veranda for an hour or two in the sun. Daniel might have wept with gratitude; he was now desperate to have some time to himself. The lady assured him she would be fine settling her uncle down for his nap as well, she just needed about fifteen minutes to bring a bowl of broth up to Philip. Feeling almost too grateful, Daniel readily agreed, and when she departed wondered how she had intuited his great need for relief just then.

Then again, since arriving the lady had been offering constantly to assist with their uncle. Only now did he understand she truly wished to. He was inclined to like Sophia, yet he was not entirely sure what to make of her. She was about his age, and though that dour black dress had not boded well, he had soon understood her to be an exceptionally caring woman still grieving for her husband four years after his passing. She was a firm yet caring escort to her cousins. Evy could even trick her into betraying a sense of humour.

Yet, when they found themselves alone, her manner altered. Her words seemed somehow too intent. As though she wished to express more than she said but could not because he made her uncomfortable. And what she did say was no less puzzling.

The previous evening, when he had stopped to check himself before departing for the ball, Daniel had seen her in the looking glass observing him. Fearing an awkward moment, he admitted he had been caught being overly scrupulous of his appearance. When he confessed he was a bit out of practice going to balls, she had told him he looked very nice and was assured of finding a partner.

"I thank you," he had said, smiling. "I shall take courage from that and shall press on."

"When seeking a partner, my advice is to search out the girl standing by the punchbowl."

After turning to meet her gaze with a questioning look, she had continued, "There is always one. She stands by the punchbowl because she likes to be sociable but does not like to put herself forward. She is stable, considerate, very well-read, and so more intelligent than her peers. If you take a chance and speak to her, I can all but promise you will be pleasantly engaged. If you ask her to dance, she will be grateful and will be an exceptionally pleasing companion as long as you choose to keep her with you."

Daniel had bowed and thanked her again. There was something touching in her concern. Still, he could not get beyond the suspicion that she was speaking of herself.

Once Sophia was heard ascending the stairs with Philip's broth, he asked his uncle if he found her at all reserved or strangely mannered where he, Daniel, was concerned. He half expected Erasmus would have no idea what he was referring to, but after a moment he admitted she might be a bit fearful of him. Daniel didn't know this, but before arriving with Evy and Philip, she had all but accepted his long-standing invitation to move into the house.

"Move in here to the Park?"

"I've asked her many times since her husband passed, I've told you that."

"Yes, but you hadn't mentioned she has accepted."

"Why shouldn't she? She visits me here, has done since a child, though not nearly as often as you did. She loves me and has nothing back in Northampton but the house she and her husband lived in. She hasn't the money to keep the place up as she'd like. But only after my stroke did she admit how very much she'd like to spend more time here. I told her to take the first opportunity to come up, and if she feels the same when she arrives, to simply stay on – we'll send for her things. If you sense unease around you, I'd say she fears your reaction to her moving in."

"That's rather absurd, isn't it? It's your house, not mine."

"Yes, but the house will be yours, and perhaps you won't wish her here."

Fair enough, thought Daniel, but the cynic in him sensed there must be more to it than that. If this wasn't some scheme of his uncle's to marry Daniel to her, which he would not put past him, then surely coming here to assist once the man was in declining health was a move to position herself for a larger share of the inheritance. Daniel did not begrudge this on his own behalf, though perhaps he should on Erasmus's if it was indeed a cunning manoeuvre.

In any event, Daniel himself might be seen as that scheming relation and his damned head was throbbing. He ached for a hot bath, and she was giving him the freedom to have one. It sounded so good right now, it might just be worth half his uncle's fortune.

Once he had ascended and closed himself inside his bedchamber, the bath was indeed magnificent. The headache felt scalded out of him. His mind cleared sufficiently to begin thinking more objectively of all that had happened the night before. The scene with Clarence had been ugly. He should go see him at The George, but God knew he didn't much want to. Then, of course, there was Luke. Could he even be certain he'd read his interest correctly? Last night, he had felt not an ounce of uncertainty; when they'd looked each other up and down, there had been no doubt. Yet without the drink in him, without Luke standing before him stimulating him with every reaction, he had rather lost the conviction. Might not he have interpreted Luke's behaviour according to his own experiences? According to his own wishes?

Nevertheless, by the time he observed Luke walking up the drive, he had soaked and scrubbed to his heart's content and was in decidedly improved spirits. Sighting the visitor, he fumbled to close his dressing gown as he stepped to his bedchamber window. Luke was dressed in quite a stylish powder-blue suit and knee breeches. Under one arm he held one of those oversized books of fabric samples drapers sent round to the homes of potential clients. Perhaps replacing the drapes had come up over cards last night. It was possible. So why should it be so delightful to see him like this?

He supposed Luke's having the air of making a business call prompted his being a tradesman to the front of his mind. Arriving to snag a wealthy client. There seemed something in it of role-playing which Daniel found both charming and not a little titillating. And what was this? The hillock of that untameable cowlick from the night before had today been plastered down with something – flattened as last night it had been buoyant, and not a bit less conspicuous. Daniel could scarcely keep from running to him and taking him in his arms. Smiling, he was dressed and on the first-floor landing before the butler could ascend to announce the visitor.

"To see Philip?"

"No sir, to see you. He wished to speak privately if you are available. He told me three times he would come back if this is not a good time."

"I will see him."

"He requested to be shown into the sitting parlour."

Daniel was quickly downstairs. He crossed the corridor, then stepped into the room. What he observed set him back. Standing at the mantle, book under one arm, Luke appeared to be, quite impertinently, thumbing through the post. Daniel could scarcely credit what he was seeing – Luke Morley had not at all seemed the kind. When Daniel came forward and cleared his throat, his guest started, setting a letter atop the others then turning round to face him.

"I'm sorry, Mr Thornton – Daniel – I didn't mean to be impertinent. I thought I might make room on the mantle so

I could set my book down until you came. I wanted to look out the south window and didn't wish to carry it."

Daniel believed not one word of this. Still, after the informality of last night, the command from Philip to call him *Daniel* and continually urging him to be more at ease... Luke likely hadn't had the best of educations, so perhaps... Anyhow, he did look quite marvellously fetching in his suit of soft blue cotton. Snowy white shirt and stockings, more refined than such a young man would normally go about in.

Yet this matter of the post. Fixing his eye on the place, Daniel affirmed his visitor should take in the view from the south window – it had been too dark last night to see the prospect, which was quite fine from this room. As Luke proceeded, Daniel crossed to the mantle, immediately observing the letter Luke had deposited there. No direction.

To Mr Daniel Thornton

Taking it up, he looked again at his guest, who was now gazing out the window to the green. *No direction.* Luke had *not* been going through the letters; he had left one of his own. But why the devil should he wish to leave a letter when he might simply have handed it to him? Presumably so that he would find it later. Or... had he *intended* to be seen leaving it because it contained something he did not wish to give him directly, but wished him to open all the same?

Daniel's indignance now turned to apprehension. When the maid entered to sweep round the fireplace, he said, "Mr Morley, you told the butler you wished to speak privately."

Turning from the window, he responded, "Yes, sir."

"Let us go up to my study." Then, his heart beating harder, Daniel gathered the rest of the post and led him up. Once inside the study, he turned the key in the lock. Luke remained by the desk as Daniel strode by and sat in an armchair, pleased to let his visitor stand until he understood what the hell was going on.

"You've brought a book of samples from Morley's. I take it Evy mentioned our desire to lighten the colour scheme in a couple of rooms. We've eight sets of drapes which are of that drab green so popular in the fifties."

"Have you?"

"Until Evy arrived, I had supposed my uncle to prefer old furnishings to anything newer – associating it with his younger days. I never considered he might wish a change until she suggested it."

"Yes, sir – sorry, you do prefer Daniel?"

He was a moment before nodding. "Call me Daniel."

With an attempt at airy pleasantry, Luke said, "It's quite fortunate, then, that I brought the book. You are free to keep it as long as you like. But this isn't why I wished to speak to you. More of an excuse should I lose my nerve. Some other subject to fall back on."

His throat constricting, Daniel managed, "What do you wish to speak to me about?"

"Two things."

"Very well. Just now is my time to peruse the post. Your visit was unexpected, so you won't mind if I do so while you speak."

"I don't mind while I speak of the gambling, which I will do first. I should appreciate your full attention when we come to the other matter."

Now quite sincerely frightened, Daniel tore open the letter, pulling the contents out though not quite attending to them as Luke said, "Philip and I were a couple of hours at piquet. He lost forty-two pounds to me."

Momentarily distracted from his anxiety, very nearly heartened, Daniel said, "Did he? The great blockhead. He likes to talk big when it comes to cards, but it really is just a lot of empty bravado with him. I'll fetch my pocketbook before you leave—"

"No. I don't mean to interrupt you, but Philip paid me last night. I wish to forgive the debt and give the money back. The notes are here in my pocket." He withdrew a handful of banknotes and set them on the desk. "Forty-two pounds. Count them and make sure it's all there. I told my father what happened, and he said that it is more important to be good neighbours. He insisted I return the money and think no more about it."

Daniel nodded, a frown clouding his brow. From the torn envelope, he had been obliged to catch two bits of smaller paper placed within a larger, folded sheet of stationery. He glanced up at Luke, who was watching him, before returning to what had fallen into his hands: two crudely cut scraps of stationery covered in his own handwriting. A quick perusal confirmed it was particularly ribald, explicit stuff he'd written to Clarence. Then, the note itself:

I left intact the letters with even more, shall we say, colour. It would be a shame if a certain relation came to read them. A shame if so many people came to read them. Devilish activities – quite easy to believe, however, because the citizens of small towns are always quick to understand the sins of the city. I don't mean to be cruel. Only to tell you that too much selfish thought for your inheritance might have unforeseen consequences. 'Tis better to give, than to receive, as the Bible tells us. There are some in this world very much in need, whom you don't seem to consider at all. But who, all the same, are not nearly as helpless as you seem to believe.

Returning the scraps into the letter, Daniel said, "And now, what is the second thing you wish to speak to me of? Cards on the table."

Now that Luke knew he had seen the contents of this horrifying letter, such directness seemed to set the little blackmailer back on his heels a moment. "Well," he said, "to finish the first matter, I was not quite done. I shall be honest about my father's true motive in wishing to forgive the debt. I want to be completely honest with you, always. He thought my forgiving the debt might make you more receptive to receiving visits from the family. He wishes a good marriage for one of my sisters and thought this would oblige you to us – the Morley family, I mean. I thought it all rather silly. I told him I would be happy to forgive the debt, but one must do more than that to persuade a man to marry."

Daniel raised a brow. "Did you now?"

Luke nodded, and though he smiled, he took an involuntary step back. "The second is a personal matter. But

I shall be forthright. I believe men should be forthright and direct: I understand about you and Clarence."

"Understand?"

"That he is not your nephew."

Now quite beyond fear, understanding life as he knew it was over, Daniel grew quite still, wishing only to know what his new life would look like. "He is not my nephew?"

"No need to pretend with me. You see, I've... admired you very much from the moment I first saw you. For months I was too shy even to show my face. But I'm a man now, and I did last night at the ball... with the help of a drink or two. Today, though," he laughed good-naturedly, "I haven't a drop in me. Not by choice; my stomach would revolt if I took any more just now."

Daniel said nothing.

Luke took a step forward. "I came today to tell you how much I like and admire you. Very much, indeed. And, if you're not averse, or feel you haven't the heart, I'd like to..." he took a breath, "I'd like to have some affection from you. With you. The kind you had with Clarence. I don't know what else to say. Only that I am very attracted by you."

Daniel allowed himself a moment to take this in. After running his tongue under his teeth, he said, "So long as I'm not averse."

Luke nodded. "Of course."

"Of course."

Appearing to reconsider something he had said, Luke continued, "I know I don't know the proper words for everything. I'm not as experienced as Clarence or the men you've known. I've never... you know, with anyone. Never even asked. Never felt I *could* ask; expect you know what I mean."

Luke actually seemed to be asking for sympathy. As though by drawing attention to a situation Daniel and men like them had likely all suffered, this behaviour would be somehow excusable. He had come to the Park last night, fully expecting a bit of sport, and believed he had been dismissed. Rejected. Now, he was here to take what he wanted.

Daniel wondered if he was having a stroke. After a moment he decided he must be; this was all taking on the quality of a dream. And when in a dream, he knew one should be careful not to disturb the dreamer. To wake him too suddenly, or else risk going into fits.

At last, he said, "That leaves me two things to consider, doesn't it? Which shall I address first? Marriage to a Morley girl? Or showing *affection* to a Morley boy?"

Luke said simply, "The affection. I'm only asking. I won't be offended if you turn me down."

Daniel let out a sharp, barking laugh, his jaw going slack at the audacity, the utter wickedness of this boy. This was a misjudgement of character quite beyond any he had made of Clarence. Oh, for the innocent days of Clarence. Clarence was a babe unborn to this.

"Come here, then," said Daniel, setting the hideous letter aside, careful to maintain those scraps of his own writing within. He uncrossed his legs. "Here," he repeated.

Luke's eyes had gone wide. He took one step, then another and another still, at last arriving before Daniel, who took him by the wrist and brought him somewhat roughly another step closer.

"What have you dreamed of, Luke?"

His visitor had a look which said he had expected Daniel to take it from here. He had done his part making his demands known. Luke Morley was, after all, comparatively blameless, requiring far less for his silence than his coarser and more demanding father. He wished only a bit of *affection* – the innocent in a family of blackmailers, complete with baby fat.

Receiving no response, Daniel offered, "I'm free to decide?"

Luke nodded.

"I know one thing all boys like, at least the most amusing boys. You are like them, aren't you?"

"Reckon I am. I wish to do whatever one normally does. I only want to be near you. In any way that *you* might like to be near me."

"Very considerate." Daniel reached forward and undid a button from the drop front of those blue cotton breeches. Luke watched almost comically wide-eyed as he undid the second, the final, then began on the opposing side. As the final, single button at the top centre came apart, Luke looked up at the ceiling. Through dry lips he produced a little whistle as his breeches came down his hips – a hand dropped to catch them, then he met Daniel's reproving gaze.

"Don't you trust me?"

Luke nodded. "I trust you."

Daniel could almost, *almost,* believe him. Mr Morley had missed his calling on the Grantham stage. You could almost admire the skill, the absolute separation from oneself it required to maintain such an appearance of guiltlessness while conniving in the very blackest manner.

Running his fingertips down the front of his linen small clothes, Daniel slipped a hand between his thighs. Maintaining his eyes on Luke's, he cupped him through the loosely woven fabric. Luke inhaled and began trembling. Releasing him, Daniel squeezed his decidedly unresponsive member through the slack threads.

"You're not very big, are you, Luke?"

Daniel smiled at the bright flush of embarrassment, understanding he might well be cutting his throat. That such an insult to a frightened, inexperienced young man might well sign his death warrant. In that moment, however, Daniel simply didn't care. He might later, might see it as the worst decision of his life. But in that moment, he would not deny himself the pleasure.

Yet, Luke did not become enraged. He had the guile to understand he must retain the mask of innocence, even when insulted, not for Daniel's, but for his own sake. Accordingly, he looked quite hurt. He whispered, "Please, don't tease me so. It's all... rather a lot to take in."

"I expect so – getting what you want by your chosen methods. Guilt, too, Luke, can do strange things to a man. I've known instances in which guilt has made a regular eunuch of an otherwise healthy man. Happens more often than you'd imagine. Sometimes, *quite irreversible*."

Luke said nothing to this. So, hoping to unsettle the boy even more, Daniel took the band of the linen bottoms and lowered them to his knees. Then, together with his breeches, he brought all to the floor.

For a time, Luke believed he was simply too overcome by what was happening to proceed. In all his fantasies he had never imagined uncertainty, or a bashfulness he'd never known when stripping off to have a swim. He never imagined he might be overwhelmed wondering how he measured up to the others Daniel had known. Or to Daniel himself – this worldly man before whom he was so brazenly displayed.

Closing his eyes, he recalled the warmth of Daniel's hand cupping his bollocks. That cool heat through the linen where no one had ever touched him. That warmth had been Daniel's, not his own. At last, by drawing a thread through the memory and stitching it into the present, he experienced that familiar shiver, that thickening pulse, as he stiffened before his examiner. He reached for Daniel's hand, guiding it around himself, determined to prove his manhood to every sense if he must. Daniel's expression remained unreadable.

Then, all thought of observing him vanished – he experienced that brief, pulling pain as Daniel exposed him fully. Then, slowly, he began to stroke him. Luke was now well beyond self-consciousness; this was how it felt to be held by someone else. Was this close, careful movement how Daniel pleasured himself? When he released him to cradle him once more from below, Luke understood what he meant to do. And though quite sincerely shocked by the idea, he was yet so glazed with new, pounding lust he hadn't the wherewithal to fear the encounter or consider his shame at the extraordinary intimacy of it.

Then, there was nothing to fear or to consider – he was brought into that warm, wet mouth. His knees nearly buckled as Daniel brought him underwater, speaking where no sound travelled, each flick of his tongue inspiring not his own, but Luke's voice – Luke's moans, his "Wait—" contracting around Daniel's hand where it cupped him. His "Sorry—" as he half-heartedly attempted to step away. Then, this, too, was happening. Daniel held him stationary as he spent – fully, violently, scarcely able to maintain his feet as the earth opened below him.

There passed a strange lapse in time before Luke returned to his senses. He confirmed his footing on the ground. His eyes were wet, the light prisms. He looked down as Daniel withdrew his lips, leant back in his chair, and pressed a thumb to his mouth. His heart swelling, Luke understood this was the moment to tell him he loved him. He took a breath, the words standing on his lips, waiting only for Daniel to look up, to acknowledge him in some way. Yet, something in his manner prevented him. As the silence drew on, Luke understood something had gone wrong.

Then, wonderfully, he observed unmistakable evidence of Daniel's own excitement. Grinning, he reaching for the bulge in his breeches, eager to do the same for him, eager to do anything he might wish. However, Daniel, after a quick glance up at him, slapped his hand aside with an order not to taunt him. After an impatient adjustment of his breeches, he rose to his feet and stepped to his desk.

"There," he said. "Put yourself away and go home. I've work to do."

"But—"

"Do not mention that other matter to me. I suppose your father will be requesting an interview?"

"I... Yes, I sup—"

"You suppose. And *I* suppose what you just received is enough for today. Wouldn't you say? Quite enough?"

Luke nodded, understanding none of his reaction, understanding his only course was to pull himself together and make for the door. Surely, it was Daniel's own unspent passion making him so cross. Why was he sending him away? Why didn't he ask him to do the same?

But this was not to be. By the time he had made it to the door, Daniel seemed in so foul a temper Luke dared not look at him. He twisted the key in the lock. Before departing, he said, "Thank you," then ran down the stairs.

CHAPTER EIGHT

H e would be wanted at home. His parents would wish
to know how Thornton had received the forty-two
pounds, then ask if he was open to an interview. Yet, when
Luke reached the line of Park timber and was certain of
remaining unseen, he sank to the base of a tree, drew up
his knees and looked back towards the great house. A smile
touched his lips. How incredible, all of it. He felt. He
knew. He had been accepted. Back in the study, his eyes
had passed over a sideboard, bookcases, a desk – not just
fine, but established. Well-rooted in a house which was itself
well-established, and it had meant something. He had heard
Time in the creak of the beautifully carved, richly upholstered
chair as Daniel leant towards him. Daniel Thornton had
accepted him, however briefly.

"Come here, then."

Men of a like mind required nothing more. Luke gloried
in this glimpse of how men behaved together. Daniel's taking

him as he had, though something so wicked he'd never even understood he might fantasise about it, had been the fulfilment of every wish he had ever had, ever could have or understand.

Yet things had not ended well – this was clear enough – and he was determined to understand why. On his next visit he would ask. He would be forthright as he had been today. Once he understood, and promised to be better, he would ask to touch Daniel – how he had longed to caress his dark, wavy hair, still wet from his bath. Run his fingers through it, take a handful. It had seemed too forward. Somehow impolite, though this was absurd considering what Daniel was just then doing to him. No, what they had done together.

He could only laugh at five months of longings, of fears and misunderstandings about this man. Laugh at having ever believed himself in love before. *This* was love!

And it was wonderful.

Unable to hide his delicious secret entirely, Luke returned home and admitted through a grin that the man had received the money *very well* and was now open to an interview.

"Oh, my *dear; oh*, my dear!" exclaimed his mother breathlessly, clapping her hands and pacing about. Save for Stephen, the family had been assembled in the parlour in anticipation of his return and were unable to wait for the absent member to hear the news. Upon his brother's hurrying downstairs, wiping his face of shaving cream and tossing a towel over his shoulder, Luke was pressed to tell it again.

This time he added more details from both this morning and the night before, trying his best to align them with the details he was obliged to omit. As he spoke, his chest seemed actually to swell. He felt expansive. On impulse, during this second telling, he looked occasionally at Bridget, understanding the grip of his anger at her had slackened almost to nothing. Now, there was guilt – a deep, terrible pang. He had been utterly unfair about her and George – an affair of the heart which had anything but a clear path forward. Initially, as she listened, she simply stared at the cover of *Henry* which was closed firmly on her lap. When she sensed his eyes on her, she looked up. Luke held her gaze – for one beat, then another. Then, he looked at Stephen, but not before he had seen Bridget's smile and nod of approval.

At the conclusion, his brother seized his hand and pumped it. "Excellent work, Luke! Absolutely stellar! Mother needs the carriage by one, so I must be off. We've a meeting about the fundraiser for repairing the roof of St. Wulfram's and I said I'd stop by. I'm acting secretary, you know. *By the by*," he added, speaking through his nose in that subdued tone he used when being conspiratorial, "I *intend* to manoeuvre for a seat beside Mr *Paltrow*. He's serving as treasurer and may like to hear *just how much* you enjoyed dancing with his daughter last night."

"Steve, no—"

But Stephen would brook no bashfulness. He patted Luke's shoulder, then informed the family he'd be off. Mrs Morley's continued pacing brought her rapidly to him. Taking the towel from his shoulder and giving him a peck on the cheek, she sent him on his way. Then, motioning her husband into the dining parlour, she turned to her remaining son. "Be ready in an hour, Luke; I want you with me today. Your father as well, we've some large parcels I cannot manage on my own."

Luke looked in some confusion to his father, then to Maria, whose lot it usually was to assist on Wednesdays. Wednesday was Alms Day, his mother's day to distribute food in the poor districts of town. Though Maria had been as eager as her parents to hear of the visit to Bainbridge Park, she now appeared cross and suspicious. Little prompting was required before she voiced an accusation that they were all departing to speak of Mr Thornton without her.

"*Bah and by G—!*" said their father, returning into the room. "Each week complaining of having to visit the poor and now in tears wishing to go!"

"I wish to be part of the conversation, Papa!"

Luke had evidently missed something while he'd been away – from all appearances, something rather silly. His eyes moved, as they always did on such occasions, to Bridget. She was finding her place again in *Henry*, but she looked up to acknowledge his inquiry. With an arch look, she nodded towards Cecilia, who was combing out her hair in a far corner.

Luke smiled, his heart thudding in his chest, understanding that he and Bridget had not lost what they had had. They still heard, they were still amused by the same things and his heart was warmed. He also had a pretty good idea what had passed while he'd been away, so he raised an eyebrow in the impish way Bridget liked and said, turning to

Maria, "Thornton's under consideration again, after Shapely danced two reels with Cecilia?"

"Don't speak to me of Mr Shapely!" cried Maria. "Dear Mr Thornton was never *out* of consideration, as I've been trying to make everyone understand! I was hurt by his treatment of me that day in his house *because* I am so very fond of him. A woman's heart is fathoms deep, Luke, which I don't expect *you* to understand. Anyhow," she concluded, recollecting herself and offering a flustered smile, "do have Papa put in a good word for me. And you as well, when you see him again."

Luke returned to Bridget, who was now fully engrossed in her book, or at least wishing to appear that she was. After a moment, he agreed it was best not to try for too much just yet. He had been horribly cruel to her. He followed his father into the dining parlour where the poor baskets were assembling, agreeing to help distribute them on the condition that he retain one for an errand of his own. When his parents exchanged a questioning look, he said, "Mr Thornton's nephew, who I met last night, is staying at The George. He's grown ill and can't get out, so I promised I would bring him something to eat. Then, if he wishes, I shall fetch Dr Fletcher for him."

Judging by their faces, he'd have been surprised if his parents could recall they even had another son.

"My boy!" cried his father, "what did I tell you, Margaret? He is more than capable of handling the Thornton affair. He's a late bloomer, is our Luke, but as canny in marriage negotiations as Stephen is in business. It was my idea to send him, remember? You thought it should be Stephen—"

"Tosh!" said his wife. "A mother's love is blind to all such distinctions. There never has been a day I could distinguish one from t'other." But pride was reddening her full cheeks, and Luke understood this was turning out to be the most extraordinary day of his life.

Once he had loaded the parcels into the carriage and had a moment to himself, Luke recalled with something like shame Bridget's warm reception of his news. Why had it taken success pursuing his own passion to find it in his heart to have compassion for hers? How was it he had never considered the similarities in their situations? Her wish to be with such a man as George Everett was nearly as futile as his to be with Daniel.

How strange that, just five years ago, a match with the son of a butcher, though not desirable, would not have seemed so impossible. Now, even Luke, who liked to believe he rejected this new distinction in class could not consider it as anything but absurd. When had he come to understand this? Had it been gradually? Or had it been more recent?

Had it been today?

When Daniel brought him close, he had shown him he was worth taking close. Now, he understood why Stephen tried so hard – Luke had, for the first time, experienced the reward.

The Morleys were *not* so removed from decent folks. Not so very mean, or so common. They were good people, better than many that claimed to be great. His parents, though accused by the Eliots of giving more than they could afford in the hopes of raising their social status, had quickly understood their increased prosperity obligated them to assist those less fortunate. This year particularly, with unrest throughout the country, with uprisings and riots simply for a bit of bread and butter, Reverend Williams spoke of the duty of those who had to those who had not. Since they'd come into their fortune, the Morleys *had* given. Why shouldn't they have good things? Why shouldn't Luke? Why shouldn't his sisters make good matches, the best the family could achieve for them?

His parents were somewhat delayed coming to the carriage. Then, once they had arrived, were some time more coming to the topic of Mr Thornton. They had caught the kitchen maid disrupting no less than the flow of Nature by warming milk over the kitchen fire.

"The *moment* she thought we were out of the house, she was at that fire with her pan of milk!" cried Margaret, moving aside a few baskets to make room for her feet. "But something told your father to go back inside, and so he caught the wench red-handed! She began crying that she had only wanted a mug of warm milk as she was used to drink as a child. And I gave her *such* a dressing down – marched her out to the barn. Then, she had to gall to tell me she did not *believe* warming milk over a fire would make the cows go dry, and I said I was sorry to hear it, for it reflected on her upbringing. I said it; indeed, I did. And so I set her down on the stool to rub old Betsy's udders and I told her, if Betsy is dry tomorrow and we have three days of bad luck, Lord help her!"

Her audience showed due compassion, but as they were now well on their way into town, John was obliged to intervene. He took her hand, kissed it, and in his softest tones said, "We've set all to rights, my Guinie, leastways what can be set right given the recklessness. But now we must speak about Mr Thornton, yes? We'll wish to request an interview."

This important next move was sufficient to douse the fire of vengeance and Margaret, as though suddenly remembering where she was and why Luke was accompanying them, said with a clap of her hands, "We will indeed!" She turned to her son. "Tomorrow, I think, will suit your father. About noon. That insipid Miss Williams, I understand, stops by about ten or ten-thirty nearly every morning, but afterwards the dear, compassionate caregiver can receive other callers. Once we are home, John, you must sit down and compose a letter to him."

"No!" Luke nearly shouted. "No, I shall write it. I know him better than anyone. I know what he would like to hear."

"Very well, we shall compose it together," said his father magnanimously.

"On second thought, better request an interview sometime after three," said his mother. "You should both have a haircut at noon, and Erasmus takes his nap at three."

Luke ran a hand through his hair, not wishing too much cut. But his mother was soon on to the most important part of the business.

Catching hold of her son's eye, she said, "And... Bridget, do you think?" Luke did not at first comprehend her. "You are surprised we do not recommend Maria. You may not have observed it at the ball as you were quite particularly occupied with Jenny Paltrow, but Mr Thornton danced two reels with Bridget and none with Maria. Bridget pretends to be above all this marriage talk, but we believe she is a dark horse. Though I never could understand a girl who risks being overlooked, some men are attracted by those who hold back. I knew one or two in my day to succeed quite well with the strategy."

"Hmmm," said her husband, unconvinced.

Nothing was said of Bridget's little pet, who apparently rated no mention in the discussion. When Luke introduced the name of Everett, his mother declared as a certainty that her daughter had none of *those* feelings for the young man, that she could see indifference in her eyes. Luke thought it best to say nothing beyond agreeing that Bridget would be best. A refusal would come from her, Maria would certainly accept him—

Then, with a feeling of absolute unreality, Luke understood he had been distinguishing Mr Thornton and Daniel as two distinct people. One, a commodity to be fought for and won. The other? He didn't know *what* to call it. But the thought of him *marrying*. United with someone else who must grow closer to him than anyone...

No one could grow close to Daniel but himself. After five months rejecting everyone in town, he had taken himself close in his study. *My dear friend*. Luke might have dismissed that as an offhanded pleasantry, had not the look in his eyes confirmed it. The look said he saw a friendship beginning. Not just a friendship, but something more intimate. Something Luke had never imagined he might have.

Of course, all such fears of his marrying were absurd. Bridget would never be put in a position to have to refuse him. Politeness only had obliged Daniel to accept an interview with his father. Once they met, he would politely decline the offer, and that would be that. That the scheme would fail so easily must be his comfort. Yet it did feel wrong to be deceiving his parents in this way. Wrong to raise their expectations. Wrong to put Daniel in the position of having to refuse them.

They were soon turning onto the High Street. Luke was still lost in private thoughts when the coach came to a violent halt, nearly sending all three passengers to the floor atop a banquet of bread, soup, and Cheshire cheese. He scrambled out into a volley of oaths. The coachman had jumped down from his box and was shouting at a couple in their fifties planted in the middle of the street. They were a large, bulky pair surrounded by a retinue of about ten servants. They were burdened with every appendage of fashion, from rings to hats, sun-kissed parasols to gleaming walking sticks. As Luke advanced, the gentleman's stick took aim at one of the carriage horses – or was it at the coachman as he attempted to skirt by to retrieve his fallen horsewhip?

Luke leapt forward, catching the stick in his hand. Just as quickly, he stepped back and allowed the stick to be wrenched away. The couple's retinue were now moving into a formation a history lesson had taught him was called a phalanx. Traffic now came to a dead halt on both sides of the High Street.

"In two shakes of a lamb's tail," cried the man, "I shall have the magistrate here, your most prominent citizens under investigation for unlawful practices, and lawsuits against half your businesses! Including your own, you rascally bugger! I'll have your name, sir."

"Luke Morley," he said. Then, mustering his best imitation of Stephen at his most grandiose, he continued,

"Just down the street is Morley's, the finest drapery and haberdashery in the county – investigate us any way you wish, our reputation is impeccable." He swallowed before adding, "Now, sir, I shall have your own names and business in Grantham."

Was it some gesture, some air, which gave Luke to believe that, with just a minute to consider, he could have guessed who they were?

Taking his wife's hand, the man stepped forward and announced, "Lord and Lady Ludlow, sirrah! We wish to be directed to Bainbridge Park."

Luke gaped, understanding immediately that this was not a good thing. Not for himself. Not for any in Grantham.

Lord and Lady Ludlow. These, then, were Clarence's parents.

CHAPTER NINE

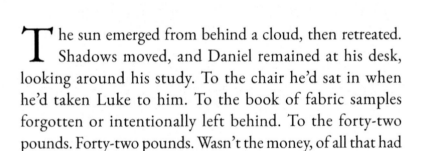

The sun emerged from behind a cloud, then retreated. Shadows moved, and Daniel remained at his desk, looking around his study. To the chair he'd sat in when he'd taken Luke to him. To the book of fabric samples forgotten or intentionally left behind. To the forty-two pounds. Forty-two pounds. Wasn't the money, of all that had just occurred, the very worst thing?

He retrieved the blackmail letter. This *was* a blackmail letter; this was his life now. Yet, he was no more able to understand that it had occurred than he could understand how he had responded to it. When faced with a threat, a blatant, degrading threat, he had simply complied. He had distanced himself; shock had returned him to that time, just moments before, he had been so ravenously hungry for that boy. He'd played a little game with himself, pretended the note had never been presented. Pretended he was the seducer, believing he might even enjoy it all the while knowing he would despise himself later. During the game, he had become aroused, which of course gave Luke to understand that what he was doing wasn't so bad. Then, as he was departing, the little beast had turned around and thanked him.

Thanked him.

Yet, somehow, that forty-two pounds was worse. Had the money actually been meant for Philip, Luke would have given it to Philip. This was meant for himself. This was what the people of Grantham thought of him. It was one thing to assume it, quite another to know it. Daniel Thornton was that scoundrel furiously guarding his sick relation for the inheritance. *Here it is,* that money said, *the thing you desire so greatly. We see it, and though we have less than you, we will make the gesture. Then, we will position ourselves for a share of the old man's money, just as you have done.*

Clarence had accused him of this. Now, the Morleys. Perhaps he *was* that person; he found he didn't quite know himself at the moment.

His was a grim smile next morning when the gardener approached at seven-thirty to say he had observed someone loitering at the edge of the woods. By stealth, he had taken him off his guard, then demanded to know what he was doing.

"By which time I had observed it was the Morley boy, as was visiting Tuesday evening. So, I said to him, 'You are the Morley boy, as was visiting Tuesday evening. I know you and your father, so now you can tell me what you want.'"

"Which was?"

"To see you, sir." The gardener handed over a note. Opening it immediately, Daniel was relieved and annoyed to find it was no more than two paragraphs of niceties and compliments before a request for an interview at three-thirty this afternoon, signed John Morley Esq.

Always pleased to appear well-informed the gardener continued, "Something about the drapes you are bespeaking from Morley's, I take it? But owing to the hour, which he admitted he'd failed to note until he arrived, he didn't like to come up so soon. So, I said that's all very well, but he might cause more trouble than he saves staring up at Mr Thornton's study window like he was – and he admitted to me it was to your window he was looking, just as I had surmised."

"Excellent, Jacob. I shall tell Erasmus of the very exceptional ally he has in his employ."

"Aye, sir, so you should," said the man, flushing. "It was all done in regard to the master, and to yourself."

"Where is Morley now?"

"Just where he was, in the forest. I told him you might not like to be disturbed, so I said I would find you and ask. Shall I send him to you?"

"No. Send him away. But first, tell me: what do you know of the family? The brothers, what are their names?"

Quick to catch the suspicion in Daniel's tone, Jacob said, like he was naming two underlings of Lucifer, "John and Peter, sir. I can tell you they are what you call *canny* in business. Came into their fortune about five years ago. Since that time, everyone says they've come to feel a bit above themselves. I can tell you, for all his riches, I shouldn't wish to be John Morley Esq. Sort of stuck between two classes, he is. His fellow tradesmen all disgusted at his airs. And the best classes, like yourself, sir, all prone to laughing at him as they ain't the airs of true Quality. Only an imitation."

"I do hate that kind of snobbery," said Daniel – for Jacob's sake because he was finding he liked this man. Jacob Elsworthy had reminded him of who he was and of a distinction in class from the Morleys that, in all his lust and fear and anger, he had somehow forgotten. He said, "Their method appears to be aggression, doesn't it? But I refuse to enter into business with them until I know more of the family. Find out what you can about them as soon as you can, Jacob. I shall be grateful, very grateful indeed. Discover their habits, their business practices. Are the rumours true?"

"What rumours are those, sir?"

"That's just it. You see, I don't know – I need you to find them out."

The gardener's eyes were sufficiently glowing at the thought of financial remuneration, he refused to question this somewhat incoherent request. "And what shall I tell the boy?"

Supposing the refusal to see Luke just now was the most he could deny them at present, Daniel said, "Tell him I agree to the request; I shall see him and his father at three-thirty this afternoon."

When the gardener departed, Daniel made a fist. These were, as yet, small acts of defiance, but it was something. It felt right to be pushing back, right to feel a kind of righteous indignation. Right to be repulsed by someone like Luke Morley.

What had Luke's visit been, from the sheepish depositing of that note on the mantle to his running off after getting what he wanted, but precisely that vulgarity the people of this town attributed to the family? How much strife there was in this world, how much unhappiness for all involved, when people sought to move from the station in life into which God had placed them. He had heard this all his life, from his parents, even in church. Yet only now was he beginning to see the truth of it. One was called a snob; one even accused oneself rather than acknowledge that the lower classes simply hadn't the breeding of their social betters. They sought to rise by buying, bullying. By charming. Yet was it charming that a man of eighteen could not comb his hair properly or tie his cravat? Was it charming this belabouring of the *sirs* and the *misters* when an education would have told him when to leave off?

Without question, blackmail was the nastiest thing anyone had ever done to him. Yet Daniel was at fault too; he should have responded differently. He should have understood it as an affront to his dignity, rather than trying to believe he was wanted again. He'd allowed his sexual inclinations to lead him most of his adult life. Indulging them had been his freedom, his defiance of any law which told him what he could and could not have.

So too had they been his burden – that hazard to his freedom he was so seldom able to resist. When he'd brought Luke close, his body had responded. He'd caught that male musk, and with it, the memory of many very pleasing escapades from his past. His nature had said, *why not beat Luke at his own game? Why not show him you love this just as much as he does?* Before the regrets had come, he had felt completely in control. It had amused him to bring Luke off so quickly. He was like an overly taut violin string, requiring nothing but a touch to loosen its peg...

At this, Daniel realised something. Albeit tentatively, he began to see a path forward. Luke was at a vulnerable period in his development as a man. Not so long ago, Daniel had been that young man; he had insight into his character. He could infer his relationship with what must be an even more revolting father. The relationship with the world he could infer by the way he sought to solve his problems. Luke was attracted to him. Attraction created a need, and if need be, Daniel would use this need for his own purposes. He didn't wish to, but should things become desperate – he would do what he had to do.

His duties were soon calling. Still, he refused to allow this train of thought far from his thoughts now he had seized upon it. Erasmus was once more in bad way rising – confused and ungainly, just as he had been the previous morning. At the time, Daniel had attributed this to his own miserable condition; today, he was not so sure. Citing his uncle's condition, he was pleased to send away Miss Williams when she appeared at the sitting closet window. When Erasmus began to chide him, Daniel cut him off with decision and was pleased to see him back down without further comment.

By eleven-thirty, his uncle was restless and eager to go onto the terrace. Daniel wheeled him onto the lawn to sit on his own for a few minutes, then retreated upstairs to his bedchamber. He needed time. Just a few minutes without distractions to consider the visit at three-thirty. He had been no more than fifteen minutes when the voice of Sophia was heard from down the corridor.

"Would you come downstairs, Daniel? It's Erasmus. Don't worry, he's alright. I happened to be passing and saw through the terrace window he had slipped down his chair and was on the point of falling over onto the lawn."

"Christ God—" said Daniel, emerging from his bedchamber and directing her downstairs.

"Everything is fine," she reaffirmed, all black, bristling motion, attempting to remain ahead of his long strides. "I reached him before he quite fell, and we had a nice sit-down on the lawn together. The footman arrived, and together we got him back into his chair."

Daniel thanked her, then hurried outside. Erasmus appeared a bit dishevelled but otherwise seemed excited at the excitement and confused by the concern. Daniel was some time apologising, reprimanding himself, thanking Sophia again, though rather wishing she would leave them alone. He didn't like to appear flustered, especially where care for his uncle was concerned. But he soon understood Erasmus wished her to remain with them. He began calling her his angel in black and thanking his stars she had been in the house. When he repeated this Daniel understood this was meant as much for himself as for Sophia. This was a prompt to let the lady know they both welcomed her here. Daniel knew immediately that he had been remiss. He had been too concerned in his own affairs, now his own misery, to do so before, and when he rose to take the man for his nap, he asked that she remain on the terrace so they could speak.

When he returned, he could think of no better opening than this: "From my heart, thank you. It *is* a blessing to have you in the house."

Sophia was too quick to mistake his meaning. Understanding that a discussion had taken place about her, she blushed. Daniel added, as lightly as he could, "You know, I've been meaning to thank you for your presence here for another reason – your advice about looking for a partner at the dance."

This sufficed to break her embarrassment and she said, "Oh my. Well, that's wonderful. Who was the lucky girl?"

At this, Daniel had to fight a grimace before naming Bridget Morley. It had not been her location in the room, but rather her easy manner, her seeming unconcern whether she danced or not, which had prompted him to approach her. Nevertheless, she had been standing at the refreshment table, and Sophia could not help but smile when he credited her with an enjoyable evening. Unfortunately, this only prolonged a topic which brought the word *Morley* so often into the air.

Sophia was particularly pleased to hear this, as she considered Margaret Morley and her daughter Bridget good friends. Last year, they had approached her upon seeing her sitting by herself at a church function. Knowing she was an infrequent visitor to the town and concerned to leave anyone sitting alone, they had introduced themselves. She assured Daniel that Erasmus had not left her alone so very long on that occasion, but there they were at her side – such good, kindly people.

Now feeling a level of anxiety to get off the subject of that family, Daniel said, "As I'm sure you've guessed, Erasmus has informed me of the likelihood of your coming to live here. I want you to know we'd all be delighted if you did. I also have fond memories of this house from my childhood. Erasmus is obviously not..." He cleared his throat. "Anyhow, this house is far too big for the two of us."

To this Sophia gave him a smile, then turned the topic back to Daniel. She wanted him to know that he was not to blame himself for this little mishap on the lawn. These things, she assured him, happened to the best of caretakers, by which she left no doubt as to whom she meant.

"I was three years caring for my husband. I married him before he was diagnosed, but I understood the weakness in his lungs and what would likely be our life together. I made my share of mistakes and used to reprimand myself terribly. But I can tell you, four years after his passing, that mistakes while attempting to do one's best are nothing one ever regrets. You protect your uncle as best you can, but you must also take care of yourself. You cannot always be present. Nobody expects you to be. So, you may rest easy."

At any time, Daniel would have been affected by such an assurance. But after the horror that had been the last twenty-four hours, he found this so poignant he seized Sophia's hand and brought it to his lips, hoping to divert the tears he felt stinging his eyes. Though setting her other hand to her breast, she appeared to take the gesture as it was meant. Then, she said it was a great pleasure, when one was able, to help someone in need. Something in her eyes made him wonder if this someone was his uncle, or indeed himself.

Once he was alone again, though supposing he had hazarded a misunderstanding, he did not regret what he had done. It was more important to feel her support fully and to show that he felt supported. Given the opportunity, he might have kissed Jacob the gardener's hand as well, for though neither could take his problems away, both had, in their way, lessened the effects.

Because of them he felt a bit more empowered. And what he lacked for in a solution, he now made up for in anger. Anger he had not felt before he'd understood this attack by the Morleys was not simply an attack on himself, his freedom, his inheritance. It was an attack on everyone who had stepped forward to assist him. An attack on the servants and visiting family. Most importantly, it was an attack on his uncle. His aim was no longer to protect his own interests. His aim was to protect Erasmus – and everyone who resided here and loved him.

***

Coming into her son's lodgings in The George, overcome by the sight of his prostrate form, Lady Ludlow cried, "Oh, my darling Clare de Lune!", overcome as well by the stench inside the room. The heavyset lady swayed on her feet as her equally well-proportioned husband opened a casement window. Once she had recovered her breath, she descended upon the patient.

"Mother?" mumbled Clarence, rousing from a fevered doze. "Are you really and truly here? What day is it?"

He was informed it was Wednesday, and this miraculously prompt appearance was owing to their having departed the city just hours after him. Clarence extended an arm to each. "I do, without question, have the best, most beautiful parents.

I have languished for hours in the very depths of despair. As soon as I arrived, I grew ill and feared I must wait a week for you. But here you are – my guardian angels."

"Rest yourself, cherub. Oh, Charles, look at him." *Him* seemed to comprise both their son's person and his lodgings, which she gestured at with distaste. Returning to the former, she sighed, "Oh, Clarey. You've seen Daniel, we know – he has rejected you."

Clarence frowned. Given his fragile state of health this seemed not the most well-judged of comments. Yet Lady Ludlow knew very well what she was about and had judged precisely. Her aim was to rouse the indignation of her husband.

"Nobody rejects our son, Edwina," he said, as though reminding her of a fact she had forgotten. He began to pace the room. "*Reject* Clarence? That man cannot have more than four thousand a year."

Edwina looked questioningly at her son, who understood it would be in his interest to pursue this course. "Rather less. Two at most, I believe."

His father rounded on him, "*Two*? And this is what you pursue after we introduce you to the daughter of Lord Easterbrook with twelve thousand per annum? Clarence, what *can* you be thinking?"

"I love Daniel—"

"Love him? *Love* him?"

"Yes, Father."

"But he was absolutely monstrous to you! Have you forgotten the orange juice?"

Averting his gaze, Clarence shook his head. Lord Ludlow let out a snorting, burbling noise, having made his point so well words were momentarily failing him. "Well, then... there you are. I want you to remember that the next time you begin to speak of *love*. To this day you go all over gooseflesh at the mere mention of a glass of orange juice. A very refreshing drink it is, full of good things..."

"What your father means," interrupted Edwina, rising to take her husband's hand, "is that this is a matter of dignity." At the look of confusion on both men's faces, she continued, "Twelve thousand per annum, I should think upwards of twenty, is your due as our son. As is that lovely daughter of Lord Easterbrook."

"Yes, Edwina – *yes*!" said her husband. "Which is why all this mucking about with men is—"

"Not unheard of in a youth born to a great family. And which, I assure you, Clarey is growing out of." After bringing her husband's hand to her bosom, she lowered her voice seductively. "You've only to think back to January to see how far he has come. Only recall those newspaper reports of his lighting up the town with Miss Easterbrook on his arm. Remember the *headlines* when he was rumoured to have kidnapped her for a weekend of debauchery! Only recall the *scandal* as that report went round the coffeehouses – how proud you were!"

"Ah, yes," said her husband, caught in some fond reflections. "Before it was learned she had disappeared only in a frantic attempt to track down her runaway lover. Where were you hiding that time, Casanova? Brighton?"

Rubbing his temples, Clarence looked pleadingly at his mother, begging her to intervene. At her steadfast refusal, however, he said somewhat grudgingly, "Tunbridge Wells. Brighton was to avoid her birthday celebration in February."

His father let out a howl of anguish. "Upon my word! Did *nothing* happen with that lovely young lady? Ever?"

"Why do you think she started that rumour about her carriage horse?"

"My point, Charles," said his lady, "is that the instinct *is* emerging in him. A mother knows. As I say, this is about his dignity. You see, *he* should have been the one to reject Thornton. Daniel's rejecting him back in March was a blow to his dignity, to his manhood, which is why he never tended his budding passion for Miss Easterbrook. As I told you when we left the city, I believe Clarence has done the right thing coming here to win him back." She gave her son a meaningful look before continuing, "He is not in pursuit of this, or of any, man, really. Once he has the man again, *he* will be free to reject him – then *accept* someone who is a far better match. Do you see?"

Charles was a minute marinating in this argument, appearing unconvinced. His subsequent nod was more from an inability to think of any other method of getting his son on the straight and narrow.

Then commenced an examination of Clarence's movements since he'd arrived in Grantham, demanded in almost military detail. All was taken in, the blackmail letter praised as a valiant effort to claim the upper hand. They saw no particular need to reclaim the note, optimistic that it might even work to their benefit if allowed to take effect. But they became concerned to learn of the youth he had asked to retrieve it. Concern became alarm when the boy's own interest in Daniel became known, then outrage to hear that their son had actually encouraged him to pursue Thornton.

"Clarence!" cried his mother.

"Do not shout at me, Mother!" shouted Clarence. "Is a man to claim his manhood subjected to hen-peckery?" Lady Ludlow experienced a moment's check. He continued, "You wouldn't understand. Father would, only he won't wish to hear about it."

"What is it, son? What will I understand?"

"Well..." said Clarence hesitantly. "All this time, our entire separation, Daniel has had no amusements. Not one. Add to this his last two months in London with, or rather without, me, while we were having our troubles, if you take my meaning. Seven months he has been lacking for affection and suffering a broken heart. Without his revenge upon me, he is still too angry to consider having me back."

"So, you encouraged some innocent to pursue him," said his mother, determined to reclaim her place in the conversation. "To sport with him and show him how much better the sport was with you."

"Mother!"

"Don't 'mother' me. We've an objective, and I haven't been a blushing virgin in thirty years." At her husband's start, she continued, "Twenty-eight. Suffice it that I understand the ways of men. With the best of intentions, you sent some fresh young thing to him, yet he may well be the ruin of all our prospects."

"But... he is a mere pup. He's quite pretty, but boys that age aren't looking for a commitment, only experiences. He will be off to his next once he's had this one."

Clarence was dismayed to see his parents exchange of look of mutual disagreement. "That may be in a metropolis," said his father, "but this is the country. The number of..." he cleared his throat, "of *men* willing to participate in such things is far more limited here. If one happens to be shopping for such a thing out here, then actually find some likeminded rascal who hasn't an aim of blackmail or turning one over to the magistrate, I should think one would hold onto him." He paused while his son lost what colour was left in his face. "I am on record as wishing you to leave off pursuing this man. But as a matter of dignity, I agree with your mother – that was a bad move. Now, what is the name of this young devil?"

Clarence recommenced rubbing his temples. "Oh, I don't remember... Duke, something. Marmaduke, I suppose. A shopkeeper's son."

"Marmaduke," said his father, inscribing the name to memory. "And just how... succulent a lad are we speaking of?"

Turning his head to the wall, Clarence groaned out a vivid description, filled with equally vivid reproaches for himself, before his father interrupted him and looked at his lady. "We know him! *Morley*. His carriage nearly ran us down on the High Street! *Luke*, not Duke – I never forget a name. He's the one who directed us here, rather than to the Park, telling us you had quarrelled with Thornton. Happy he must have been, too, to prevent anyone associated with you from contacting his new love. Luke Morley is the young devil!

A tradesman's son and nasty bit of New Money into the bargain!"

CHAPTER TEN

———— ❧ ————

O ne minute became five. Then eight. Then ten.

Father and son sat in the library of Bainbridge Park, a large, lofty room at the secluded northeast corner of the house. They stared at a plate of biscuits set beside a tea service, none of which they dared touch until their host arrived. A funnel of steam rose from the teapot and dissipated before the bookcases – floor-to-ceiling towers supporting the ornately painted heavens. At intervals, tall, slender windows showed the sweep of the front drive. Light shimmered in a nearby pond. The pale trunks of silver birch shone, like echoes of the many volumes from their former lives. The contrast was rich and somehow decadent.

Another minute passed. Then another. Still, Daniel failed to come.

"Alright Luke, just follow my lead," said his father, not for the first time, as though their host had just entered the room.

Luke glanced at the man, whose freshly cropped head of hair leant him the appearance of a baby bird just emerged from its shell. Luke had sat across from him in the back kitchen as the man's valet had hacked away, agreeing to a cut for himself only if Maria would do it. Though suspecting she was not to be the one put forward in this venture, his sister nevertheless understood the importance of this ceremony – a canny manoeuvre in initiating a new romance, symbolic of shedding the old, exposing the eyes to the new, particularly effective when performed at high noon.

"Not too much," Luke had begged her. "Just a bit off the ends."

And Maria, thank God, had done just that, giving him her best nod to a Brutus.

Now, as they waited in the library, Luke scratched his neck, hoping against hope that, if there was anything to this hair-cutting strategy, the new romance might also include himself and Daniel. Of course, John Morley must fail in his venture for Luke to feel he had succeeded in his, and so it all became rather a muddle...

The wait having become unbearable, Luke began tugging at the sleeves of his frockcoat. If he'd only been able to speak with Clarence before coming here. He had been fully prepared to confess his failure to retrieve the note. Then, after bringing him food and fetching a physician, he would have pried more advice from the grateful invalid. Instead, his coach had nearly run down the man's parents, after which he had had his services summarily dismissed as the Hopper entourage swept by. Now, even if he could be alone with Daniel today, his only idea for breaking through those unpredictable, unsettling moods of his was a continued intention to be forthright. That did, just now, seem pitifully little.

Noticing his look of distracted anxiety, John said, "Rest easy, son. Marriage is just another facet of business, which I am a master of. Business is my vocation; I do not pretend to be a fine gentleman, nor do I wish to be one. That's what you and I have in common." At his son's continued silence, he said, "Has Stephen convinced you to be otherwise?"

Luke offered his best response. "Not more than I must be."

"That's a good answer. It don't come natural to us. Twenty-one years ago, the stars aligned to make Stephen what he is. But between you and me, I don't reckon a family should have over-many of the fine sort. A family grows fine, they become soft. Business matters are turned over to attorneys and finance managers, whose real profession is smelling out weaknesses and discovering ways to line their pockets. Wives of soft men grow fat on fine things. They raise fat children, and a fortune is lost. You've negotiating skill, which is far more desirable than possessing *the graces*."

Luke stared up at the rows and rows and rows of ancient tomes.

"Your mother and I are not seeking to engage your sister just yet. If all goes well today, I shall be doing nothing more than giving my permission to court her. I would never force the hand of any of my daughters. But if I ask Bridget what she thinks, she will say what she always says: that the family speaks too much of marriage, that she could die an old maid and wouldn't care. Yet if she is asked by Thornton – a tall, dapper man with a look the ladies will always swoon for – she will likely do what she did on Tuesday and accept him. Cecilia is too young, Maria too flighty. Bridget has always been different: serious and with a maturity Thornton seemed particularly to admire. I watched them at the ball and observed he was entirely at ease with her. And I can tell you they looked very fine dancing together. Both of the fairest with the same dark hair and eyes like a black night sky approached a full, fair moon and planned it for them ages ago..." He waved his hand mystically through the air.

Luke's gaze descended the length of a window before which a desk had been organised as a rebinding station. A fan of bone folders, a punching cradle. Awl needles of all dimensions caught the light at silver angles. The rinds from two old volumes, grey-red and grey-green, had been peeled away to reveal their white spine piths.

His brow beginning to clear, Luke realised he had heard something useful in what his father had said. Daniel had responded positively to Bridget's groundedness and maturity. In romance, he was used to adults – to men, not silly boys who spent their passion in scarcely a minute. Yesterday in the study, Luke had spoken well of his feelings for him, then at the first opportunity had taken his pleasure without holding back. It was an insult, a sign to Daniel that he cared for nothing but himself. There was etiquette, no doubt, when men came together; Luke had broken it. *This* was why Daniel had become angry and sent him away. Of course it was! Now he must show him he was a man just like himself, take the first chance to apologise, and they could begin again!

"Thank you, Papa," he said, turning to him and smiling.

Grinning, his father patted his knee and said anytime, anytime at all.

When Daniel entered the room, he passed by and turned round the chair from the binder's desk. He sat before them in an attitude which should have been both candid and informal. Somehow, it was neither – it seemed stiff and oddly disjointed. Criticising his sitting posture should not have been Luke's first thought; no doubt the joy of seeing Daniel again after nearly twenty-seven hours was making him sensitive to everything in his manner. Yet, he was clearly uneasy. He bid them take refreshments without looking at either of them. Did he wish to say something to himself he could not with his father present? Looking at John, did he feel guilt for what he had done with his son? Trying not to scald himself, Luke quickly busied himself, arranging three Delftware teacups then poured out the steaming tea.

Chewing a biscuit, John said, "And how fares your uncle, Mr Thornton?"

Daniel waited until his guest had finished chewing and had swallowed to answer. Though his father failed to notice, Luke found in this delay to speak an unmistakable disdain. "He's well. I've a member of my family caring for him today. I am blessed, John, with a wonderful staff, wonderful friends, and family – all exceptionally devoted to Erasmus. And to me."

Determined to speak and to sound mature and engaging, Luke asked, "And your niece and nephew, sir?", which did come out rather too much like Sir Galahad asking if all were well on the home front.

He blushed miserably, receiving from Daniel only a very brief, non-committal nod before he said, "They are gone into town with their chaperone. You've only just missed them."

Only just gone into town? With his visitors away, might they invent a reason for him to remain after the interview?

Daniel continued, "We are here to speak of my future."

John Morley was some time finishing another biscuit, which now inspired the slightest rising of Daniel's lip. Experiencing an eternity of misery in the time it took his father to swallow, Luke was about to speak again when the man at last said, "We are, insomuch as the future can be answered for. I said in my note that I admire you as a good and generous man..."

This was said in a slightly questioning manner, as much directed to Daniel as to his son, who had written the note. Luke had been two hours composing two short paragraphs, which his father had looked over but by no means studied. Nodding meaningfully, Luke hoped Daniel would infer his contribution and begin to sense that every word had been from himself.

John Morley continued in a baritone full of gravitas, "In my opinion, coming here to care for your uncle says more about your character and your generous spirit than almost anything else could."

Daniel's face went slightly red, which might have been taken for pleasure but for the bitterness in his words. "My *generosity*. You know, before coming to Grantham I thought I had heard my fair share of euphemisms and *double entendres*, but this does about take the cake. My *generosity* has nothing to do with the situation I now find myself in. Without choice,

I am required to marry, and with very little say indeed in whom this is to be with."

This *requiring* was in reference to Erasmus, whose wish that his nephew marry before he passed was widely known. Yet as a native of these parts, this reference to his having little choice Luke must take as an insult not just to his sisters but to every girl in Grantham. It hurt him particularly. From the moment he had introduced himself, Daniel had, so immediately, so surgically cut away any fear that he might be that disdainful city man he was reputed to be. He did not wish to marry, very well – Luke understood this. But must he imply this was because no girl in what for him must be a remote and backwards part of the country had anything to offer him?

John felt the insult as keenly. He changed position in his seat and, leaning slightly forward, said, "Sir, any expectations, any limitations, I shall not address. You've made your bed and must lie in it. I am a forthright man. Do you wish to consider marriage to one of my girls or not?"

"*Consider?*"

"Consider. Nobody is forcing your hand. Take Miss Williams, take whoever has been grasping for your attention, and take the consequences. My girls do not beg for suitors."

At this, Daniel appeared to back down. "Pray, sir, let us not speak of consequences."

"What *shall* we speak of?" said John, his ire fired and, for all Luke loved Daniel with every fibre of his being, he knew justifiably so.

For the first time, Daniel turned to face Luke full on. In that brief, wonderful, confusing moment, he seemed pleading for him to intervene. Though somewhat baffled, Luke was overjoyed to find a break in that ice. This was Daniel more as he had been the night they had met and the morning they had come together. It seemed incredible that such a polished, dignified man of the world would find it so difficult to refuse. Surely this was not the first time he had had to contend with the idea of marriage.

This was Luke's moment, then. His opportunity to assist him – as a man and as an equal.

"We've come in the interest of all parties. We wish to present you with this option, believing it will benefit you as well as ourselves. We wish the happiness of our neighbours and friends just as we wish it for my sisters. But we understand there are many things to consider. You may be unable to consider marriage just now, for reasons you don't need to explain, and we will always think well of you even if you feel you must decline our proposal."

This was, without doubt, the most Luke had ever said at once, both in words and in sentiment. His father looked slightly askance at him, no doubt believing he had gone too far in his assurances. But just now, Luke had another priority. And the words appeared to have some effect. Daniel appeared surprised. He was turning every word over in his head, though Luke was dismayed at his appearing to hit obstacles then be left merely confused. What was his trouble? Here was an opening to retreat, to begin his excuses for not wishing to marry.

Instead, he turned to John and said, "I am honoured, indeed, to be considered. Your daughters are all very fine, I'm sure; the little I know of them."

"You know the fineness of one," said John testily. "I speak of Bridget, a thoughtful, beautiful young lady. Well-spoken, well-read beyond the schooling she has received, which has been very good. But aside from that, her education has been achieved by an internal fire. She's a passion for reading, for current events, and can meet anyone, man or woman, in conversation. Yet for all that, she never seeks to lord her understanding over anyone. She's a lovely, subtle way about her. She deserves the best of suitors, which I have judged, in this town of limited means and prospects, to be you, sir. Have I erred in this assumption?"

Before half this speech had been uttered, Daniel looked positively browbeaten. How could he be so ill-prepared, so confined by politeness? Luke ached to defend him, to show he was on his side. However, Daniel sought no additional support. He simply maintained his eyes on the older man as he said, "No, sir, you have not erred."

"Aye," said John, offering his own decidedly earthy style of haughtiness. "Such is the business of a parent, which I trust you will understand in time. I have judged you to be a good and reasonable man; despite your words today I continue to do so, else my son and I should have departed. You've money – I don't apologise but rather acknowledge the fact openly. Am I to seek a pauper for my daughter?"

"Certainly not."

"You are said to be made still richer by your future interests; I tell you nothing which is not commonly known."

"I expect it is common knowledge."

"But what I value most are your actions. You uprooted yourself from your life in the metropolis to come here and care for your uncle. You did this because you wish your uncle the best care. Give me the same courtesy and believe I wish the same exceptional care for my girls."

"Of course."

"We are an ambitious family near independence; you could do worse than connect yourself with us. If you wish the connection, I suggest Bridget, whom you yourself selected on Tuesday. But only if you will court her as a man should do."

"I should be very happy to speak to her, sir." John let a moment pass in which the word *speak* returned to slap Daniel's hand. Swallowing, he added, "It is time that I choose a wife. When I speak, sir, Bridget will have no doubt that I am offering my hand."

John inclined his head. Luke, however, could scarcely keep from sinking to the floor in shock and confusion. *Why* was he agreeing to this? He could so easily have declined, politely, with the slightest excuse – Miss Williams, anything! This was *absurd*, utterly absurd. So, against all that was rational—

Oh, Christ – the haircuts! What else could it be? Oh, *why* had Luke agreed to the cut?

He shot a look at his father and, for a moment, just a moment, was overpowered by the man's great, esoteric wisdom. This cooled somewhat as his rational mind began insisting that there must be another explanation, something he simply failed to understand. Yet, it was a torment to claw his way back to the rational world from where he had just descended.

Much of this must have been revealed on his face; as John proposed a day to meet with his daughter, Daniel seemed aware of Luke's state of mind. He rose and came forward to urge the tea things closer to his guests, though seemingly with no other aim than to take Luke's gaze and hold it. As John Morley *well*'ed and *perhaps, just a couple more, if you insist*'ed, Daniel returned to his chair and leant back.

He took up a large, stout awl with a polished, pear-shaped handle. Flipping it about absently, he began to praise Bridget, whom he had apparently spoken to at some length. Luke watched intently for a sign from him, yet when one did arrive, he felt unprepared. It startled and, indeed, rather excited him. As John was washing down a biscuit then deciding upon his next, Daniel ceased speaking. In one swift motion, he stabbed the awl onto the desk.

John started. Then, looking up, he let out a laugh. "That's quite a weapon you have there!"

Holding Luke's eye, Daniel pursed his lips. As he resumed speaking, he allowed a hand to drop between his thighs, where his fingers traced an inner seam. Luke's eyes were drawn as immediately as his father's had been by the biscuits, as though by an angler's line. Daniel looked at his father, whose gaze he maintained as one hand travelled up and down the leg, occasionally pinching the fabric to pull it taut, at last coming to rest on his knee. A thumb tapped the knee absently. As his knees widened, sunlight graced those extraordinarily well-shaped calves each held in the pristine shimmer of a silk stocking. Then, the pull and release, pull and release of the buttons at his knees as he fidgeted. Luke's mouth dried as the restless fingers began an ascent, reeling his gaze in, up those long, extended thighs. The hand returned to his knee, but Luke was now on a trajectory – up, up to the gathering, where the drop front of his breeches cradled so perfectly, so tantalisingly, what must be the most extraordinary, mouth-watering...

Daniel crossed his legs. Once more, the awl came down on the desk.

"Upon my word!" cried John Morley, "you are a regular menace with that thing! Are you interested in binding?"

Daniel raised an amused eyebrow, then turned such an arch look on Luke before returning to John that any response was lost to him. What was Daniel doing? He'd never seen him act like this and it was... confound it, it was bloody agitating! Everything he did was driving him mad with desire. He couldn't know how much Luke needed to be alone with him again. At last, Daniel made a comment reflecting upon their interview, which could only mean their time was drawing to an end. Struck with fear, Luke began fidgeting, pulling at this frockcoat sleeves, clearing his throat, anything to gain Daniel's attention so he might see how wretched he was to remain behind.

After a date for dinner at the Morley house was agreed to, their host said, "Now you are departing, John, I realise this interview has been unfortunately timed. Philip will be disappointed to have missed seeing your son. He wishes to thank him personally for forgiving that debt. It would be no trouble to send Luke home in my carriage. If that is a problem—"

Mr Morley had only to glance at his son to see his approval. He affirmed it was no problem, once more lulled into admiration for Thornton after the initial tenseness of the meeting.

"I should warn you," said Daniel, turning to Luke, "my lovestruck nephew has an ulterior motive. He will certainly pester you with endless questions about Miss Eliza Ringwald."

"It's no pester— no problem." Then Luke waited, breath suspended, as Daniel continued an agonisingly slow prompting of his father from the house. It was all he could do to suppress his trembling at the thought of being alone with him again after so very many hours apart.

Luke remained in the library as Daniel escorted his guest out. Minutes passed in the towering room, which felt both airy and overcrowded. At last, his host returned. When the door closed, Luke came to his feet. Daniel, however, failed to look at him as he proceeded to the desk.

He was a long moment in thought. Then, he turned around and, sighing, shook his head.

"What do we do now?" he said.

CHAPTER ELEVEN

"We?" repeated Luke breathlessly.

Furious though he was at how the interview had gone, and despising even more that bastard John Morley, Daniel was pleased to observe the state of his son. The poor wretch. There had only ever been a slim chance of remedying the matter with his father, a shameless man not to be moved by gentlemanly disdain. Of course, it must come down to Luke.

Daniel paced the floor, running hands through his hair with dramatic flair. "Yes, *we*, unless you too are abandoning me in my plight?"

"I would never abandon you. Ever."

"You know very well I have been given no choice but to marry." Luke stepped toward him. "Unless you..."

"Me?"

Daniel advanced. "Given my freedom and able to defend myself, you know I should never wish it. But I have nobody, nobody on my side. You and your father come here as a united front; you see my misery, but you do not care. You don't care at all if I am chained to someone else, I see that."

"I do care. Very much."

"But how can you help me?"

Luke frowned. "I'd do anything for you. But you must be the one to decide whether you will marry or not. I know you feel obliged to consider. Obliged even to accept."

"If this continues my attentions, my *affections*, I must begin to divert elsewhere. I am under an obligation to you as well, you'll remember. A much more pleasant obligation, of course. But I know that to court a young lady, as she ought to be courted, as your father said just now... Then to marry her. She must eventually take all my energies."

"What do you mean your obligation to me?"

Coming in so close Luke was forced to back into the binder's desk, Daniel leant over him. His hand slipping down Luke's side, a finger curled around the waistline of his breeches, then tugged playfully. "My *obligations*. Have you forgotten what we did in the study?"

"Forgotten? It's all I've thought of since! *You* are all I've thought of— I... I shall *never* forget the study!"

Daniel hummed, encircling Luke's waist with an arm. Then, he allowed his hand to descend to that ridiculously firm, beautifully rounded bottom. "A young man *should* study, shouldn't he? Should *apply* himself."

Luke nodded, breath quickening.

"But perhaps what we did upstairs is all you wish to know of the Paphian mysteries. All you wish to know of our *brotherhood*, Luke, though not a hundredth of what I could show you."

"Please."

Daniel waited for him to particularise his demand, but this seemed the extent. Luke was staring up at him, eyes wide and expectant. Yet, despite his breathing and his pleas, he could not disguise the slightest cringe, as one must cringe when demanding the unknown. That hint of fear stirred Daniel's loins; a particularly wicked kind of arousal so much more menacing than mere lust. It was that descent from the heavens, that expanding of wings as one alights upon a grounded prey – when you know a boy, desperate for initiation, for acceptance, will let you do whatever you want.

Bringing their bodies together, he said, "They do say a thing begun should continue, that is true."

"Yes, it should."

Daniel brought him closer still, smiling at the change in Luke's expression when he felt his erection pressing into his side. When he stooped to nuzzle his hair, Luke expelled a puff of air as though it was his last, dying breath. He held Daniel tightly, urging his manhood against himself, urging its demands as he wrapped his free arm around his waist.

"Very well," said Daniel. "Perhaps I will show you. But what will you do for me?"

"Anything."

Daniel hummed. "I don't believe you."

"But I will."

"You didn't do *anything* for me in the study. Not one thing."

Luke pulled back. "I wished to! Only you wouldn't let me."

"You wouldn't let yourself. You are playing a very dangerous game, Luke, very dangerous. A game in which I am to play along so you might have a clear conscience."

"A clear conscience?"

"A clear conscience. Said in clear, comprehensible English. I suspect your conscience is bothering you quite a lot these days. Perhaps you are feeling some shame, hm?"

Luke swallowed, looking, for all his heightened sensuality, as though he might cry. "I do," he whispered. "As much as I want this, I do feel shame. For my desires. Shame at what my father would think of me. When you accepted me, I began to believe there is another way of feeling about myself."

Daniel looked away, uncertain whether he was more appalled by his expression of earnestness or by his words, which were absolutely heart-breaking. He must not fall for this. Yet when his eyes returned to Luke, this young man whose words and whose countenance expressed so much of Daniel's own early years, he took him by the shoulders and said, "Do let us be open, now. Please. I want to believe the best in you. I want you to tell me this entire affair is your father's doing. Entirely his own."

"My father's?"

Daniel gave a look of helpless frustration. "Must I say it? That wretched note. You wish me to believe it was from you, but it was from your father. You learned about Clarence and me; I condemn you for that, absolutely, and for your complacence in what your father is doing. But that note to me – you never even saw it, did you?"

"Never saw it? I wrote it!"

"Listen, I know what it is like to wish for a father's approval, even at the expense of—"

"*I* handle this business with you. No one else. You saw how Papa deferred to me. You *know* I wrote the note!"

Luke appeared so momentarily crazed that Daniel had no choice but to believe him. Then, as though fearing he might be sent away before he could accomplish his end, he slipped a hand between them to cup Daniel's bollocks, extending his thumb up and down the length of what had begun to slacken. When he failed to pull away, Luke gripped it with his hand. His eyes blazed as Daniel pulsed back to life, his arousal stronger after that brief cooling. Believing he had him where he wished him, Luke began to pull at his buttons, wincing when his wrist was seized and held aside.

"I do not believe you. I do not believe you could have written that note."

"I did, you bastard!"

Daniel was nearly as shocked to hear this as Luke seemed to be for having said it. His expression instantly softening, Luke said, "I'm sorry. I didn't mean that. I would ne—"

"Bastard? And you, Luke Morley, are a little boy. An eighteen-year-old little boy who—"

"I—"

"—who will do what he is told." Luke blinked as he was pushed back a step. "You wish an education? You do earnestly wish to know what comes next?" said Daniel. "Lock the door."

Then he commenced unfastening his breeches.

Luke was a moment staring as Daniel's hands worked down the twin columns of buttons. Then, he almost ran to the door and turned the key in the lock. When he returned, he failed quite spectacularly in his attempt to divide his gaze between Daniel's face and the full, pulsing erection he had exposed after dropping his drawers and opening his shirt. Luke simply stared, waiting for instruction. Daniel gestured him forward. When he advanced, he set a hand on his shoulder. Luke understood and went to his knees.

After a moment, a cool, cautious hand took hold of him. Daniel watched him in those moments before he began – studying himself as though he were the representation of all men. Luke's own lust now gave way to simple curiosity, a curiosity which evaporated so quickly after your first time. Luke was comparing himself to Daniel. Comparing Daniel to the men he'd glimpsed furtively throughout his life when he hadn't the luxury of time for such close examination.

It was almost a surprise when Luke at last brought his tongue once, twice over him, his hand squeezing to expose him fully before taking him tentatively into his mouth. Daniel shuddered; he could not prevent himself – this was like stepping into a morning of clean air after a night of rain. He looked down again and observed Luke's partially closed eyelids. They fluttered as he worked to prevent any information but that which he had in his mouth from entering. He looked like an absolute angel...

Daniel looked up at the bookcases, reminding himself it *had* been seven months. This was something he had enjoyed countless times. Clarence had been happy enough to receive, though was more often intent upon giving as a prologue to lovemaking. And, over the years, being serviced had indeed become a mere prologue, a means to an end. When had he last understood this sense of exploration, this studied attempt at pleasuring for its own sake? Tongue wetted, endlessly curious, sensitive to any reaction which might tell him this was not to Daniel's liking. It did feel almost as new to him as it was to Luke...

Wait. No, what was he *thinking*? This little bastard was *blackmailing* him!

He gripped Luke's hair and brought him forward, forcing a mode of pleasure he was more accustomed to. Luke tried, not entirely successfully, to accommodate it. At his third inability to manage it, with one easy, determined motion, Daniel pushed him back on his haunches. Then, slipping a hand under his arm, he brought him to his feet. Luke simply stared at him, his lips trembling as though fearing a reprimand.

"How was that, Luke? What you wanted?"

"Yes, but... but I'm not done."

"You *are* done. I want you to stop."

"But," tears standing in his eyes, "wasn't I doing it right? Let me try again. I only want to make you feel good."

"Beg."

Appearing as though the air had been physically knocked from him, Luke whispered, "I beg! Please, I'll do anything, say anything. Whatever, just don't make me stop."

"Admit you did *not* write that note."

For a moment, Luke looked uncomprehendingly at the return of this topic. But he was far too desperate to protest, and simply nodded. "Alright. I did not."

"Who wrote it?"

"My father."

Luke was no great liar. With this lie he seemed trying to substitute frustrated passion for conviction. They both knew why he had said it. At last, Daniel nodded and, still holding Luke's wrist, said, "You lied to me."

The subsequent nod was so unconvincing Daniel took it as no admission at all. This had become infuriating, so he allowed a part of himself to awaken, a part dormant for perhaps ten years, when he had, after years of frustration, first understood where to go in London to discover men of a like mind. That period in which he had had no other aim for himself than to fuck as much as he could.

Luke stepped back as Daniel cleared aside items from the desk. Turning Luke around, he lay him facedown between the cradle punch and a stack of beeswax cakes. Settling over him, he drew in close. His lips just an inch from his ear, one hand slipped below to begin unbuttoning Luke's lower garment. "Can you guess what comes next?"

Scarcely above a whisper, Luke said, "Yes."

This one word, and Luke's fumbling to assist with his buttons before sliding his clothes down his hips, very nearly took Daniel's breath. He rose up, dazzled by the beauty of the taut, pale skin of Luke's buttocks. Dazzled by the obscenity of this offering of innocence so innocently. Yet, he felt no compunction in reaching for the bottle of oil he'd secreted at the far end of the binder's desk. He had known the likely outcome of his interview with John. He had always known this was his best chance of breaking the family bond to win an ally to his side.

Daniel pushed up the white cotton shirt to expose the long, delicate dell of Luke's spine. The urge to lap along that sweet valley nearly overpowered him. Instead, he uncorked the bottle, then let a line drizzle into and across the valley. Luke jumped, shivering as the sensation ran down of its own accord.

Daniel felt his pulse begin to throb in his neck. Then, as the oil ran to his extreme nether regions, Luke arched his back in what was without question the most wanton, most provocative demand to be entered he had ever seen in his life.

Luke was staring out the window, equal parts apprehension and longing, understanding Daniel was about to have him as men in Antiquity had had each other. Sheltered as he had been, there had been jokes after a lesson in Latin, his schoolfellows complaining of having to study anything so hard particularly when it had been men who liked doing *that* who had spoken it. A text taken down from a shelf and quickly returned had confirmed the rumour. The knowledge, however, though interesting, Luke had not found particularly alluring. Nothing of the kind had entered his fantasies; he had never required more than thoughts of one naughty, roaming hand reaching under his bedclothes. Perhaps, without Daniel, that hand would have sufficed for the rest of his life.

More oil ran down his back, sending sensations he could scarcely comprehend across his haunches, into his thighs, to the pads of his feet which were trembling on tiptoe. Daniel wanted this; this was something to endure, to achieve, for Daniel. He *would* endure it, forearms supporting himself across the hard, unforgiving mahogany, his body dangling off the edge of a cliff.

When the trickle of oil became hot, Luke understood the tip of Daniel's forefinger easing inside. He dropped his head, allowing it in, his heart in his throat. Soon Daniel withdrew and took him by the hips, rutting across the cleft of his buttocks, slicking himself.

Then, he came down again, slipping one arm beneath Luke's to grip a shoulder for purchase. Daniel hushed him, then began a tentative, rhythmic prodding which doubled Luke's heartbeat.

"Relax. Breathe."

Looking out to the green of Bainbridge Park, Luke's eyes watered, blurred, starred as Daniel began to make love to him. He was inside. He had him in a vice-like grip, prodding him questioningly, waiting for Luke's body to respond.

With a sudden, obscene, vanquishing, a violation Luke had never imagined he could feel, Daniel slid in completely. He moaned with pleasure. Expecting only to feel pain, Luke was so surprised by a swirling, eddying sensation of – albeit very faint – pleasure, he let out an involuntary yelp.

"Did I hurt you? Luke, did I hurt you?"

"No," he gasped, though he hardly knew. "I want you. I want you *so* much. I want you just like this," squeezing his eyes shut, determined to stay put.

Indeed, determination was now the overriding sensation. He wished the accomplishment. If there was pleasure, so be it – but he *wished* the accomplishment. His mind fell into a tailspin of thoughts – the interview, his father, the haircut.

Moving rhythmically, his breath quickening, Daniel said, "Do you like this?"

"Yes. *Yes.*"

"I'll stop," he said, his breath slackening. The affirmation had sounded less than convincing. "Shall I?"

"I want you to *fuck* me, Daniel." Luke bit his lips to keep from laughing, certain he was about to regret this, very dearly regret it. After a moment, Daniel brought him in tighter and began driving in, a thudding, brutal assault. Yet his laughter, his requesting this, *had* somehow relaxed him. Luke had broken his own will to resist. As Daniel worked, something low and glorious opened, a river of pleasure bubbling just below the pain. Daniel seemed to feel it, was sometimes overwhelmed in it, struggling to consume everything Luke was now offering.

Taking a firm hold of his hips, Daniel tilted him up and backwards. Luke cried out with a deep, undiluted joy, a sensation so strange he hadn't an idea from where in his body it had originated.

"Yes?" said Daniel, panting, a wild, wicked edge having crept into his voice. "*Yes?*"

All attempts at a response failed as Daniel tilted his hips again, once more inspiring such intense pleasure from such an intensely unknown place that Luke judged it to be somewhere in his throat.

Then, it was lost to the whirlpool, this excruciating glory as Daniel pounded him, rapidly swelling with his climax; Luke grabbed the edge of the desk as Daniel buried his face in his shoulder to muffle his cries. He drove Luke's hips ruthlessly into the mahogany as he pulsed again, and again, and again, his teeth setting gently into Luke's shoulder as the worst, and the best, was over.

His breath slackening, Daniel slipped a hand under Luke's head where it had come to rest on the desk. Lifting his head, he leant down to kiss his ear. Luke felt a tear slip down one cheek and over Daniel's fingers. Then, slowly, Daniel withdrew. He urged him to sit up, asking if he was alright.

Luke nodded, not quite looking at him as he seated himself on the edge of the desk. An understanding was dawning that Daniel had reached places no mere silence could keep at bay. He had not anticipated this feeling of exposure, this rawness inside and out. His solace must be that, of all people, Daniel was the one he wished to see and to understand.

Pushing the matted fringe from his forehead, attempting to lift his gaze, Daniel told him he had been extraordinary. More pleasure would come with experience, he promised.

Nodding, Luke looked up as Daniel said one more thing. Then everything went to hell.

CHAPTER TWELVE

A new day dawned. Before the note from Luke was opened, Lord and Lady Ludlow were enjoying a particularly pleasant morning, breakfasting richly and in their best moods since arriving.

The previous day had been devoted to feeding and raising the spirits of a son in and out of consciousness. By evening Clarence was sufficiently recovered to rise and observe himself in a looking glass – what he discovered there immediately made him ill again. A note from Daniel after he had returned to bed was, without doubt, the highlight of the day.

Holding her son's hand as he lay in bed, Edwina had read out the note which showed concern and ended with a request to see him tomorrow. She tugged the invalid's arm this way and that, assuring him his blackmail note had come to nothing and he might sleep the sleep of the blameless. But he must rest well, for Daniel wished to come before noon and Clarence did, he would admit, rather need his beauty rest.

Too pleased, and too weak, to take offence, Clarence had acquiesced. He asked her to send their response post-haste, with his endless, undying love in the postscript. To this his father had made a face, which Edwina immediately poo-poohed, assuring him all was going according to plan – just leave it to her.

"I'm concerned for my carriage," Charles had complained, as they readied for bed. "The rain nearly washed out the main road back to town. God knows what it has done to some piddling path out to Londonthorpe. We shall be here long enough without a broken machine to attend to."

Yet this morning, with his carriage safely returned, Charles was decidedly less anxious to be on his way home. Since dawn, he had received a near-constant, soothing barrage of visits from hotel management and staff seeking to assure his comfort. These were punctuated by notes sent from what seemed every tradesman in town requesting interviews and offering services. Edwina's spirits soared to find her husband so well pleased – by nine the man was breathless from all the attention and positively glutted sampling the delectables sent by food merchants.

Undoing the top button of his trousers after finishing a pastry, he said, "That was quite as good as any I've had in London. I have always observed that a few generous tips immediately upon arrival sets the tone. But the lovely people of this town do seem uncommonly ready to oblige. The chambermaid addressed me as Your Highness! Dear me – a charming place is Grantham."

"Oh, Clarey, do eat some of your sticky cake," said his mother, observing signs of anxiety in her brightened but still recovering son. Clarence had joined them at the breakfast table but without appetite. "It is only your nerves; I promise you, you do look much better today. Rest assured, Daniel's requesting an interview is just as it should be." After sipping her tea, she continued, "He's likely dismissed the note you left him as just one of many things done, on both sides, which you both regret. He cannot discount your coming all this way to see him."

Not quite able to wish his son success with Thornton, Charles said instead, "Your parents are here now, Clarey, so you may rest easy." Then, turning to his wife, "Already today we have received notes from a butcher, a baker, possibly a candlestick-maker too, I don't recall – all seeking interviews and wishing our custom. I believe it is incumbent on us to make ourselves available to the people of this town. I wonder if a *levee* might not be best practice while we are here? What do you think?"

Clarence attempted a corner of toast while his parents considered the benefits and potential challenges of admitting an audience during their morning toilette. Noticing a couple of unopened notes at his father's elbow, he asked if he hadn't better open them as one might be from Daniel. With a chuckle at the persistence of these tireless townsfolk, Charles took them up. At the first he sighed and shook his head. At the second, however, his expression darkened. He set it aside without comment.

"Who is it from?" said Clarence.

After exchanging a look with Edwina, his father said, "They are nothing, Clarey. A note from the town florist. The other..."

He rose to peer out the window. Clarence followed him, squinting through the casement to observe a form crouching on the hotel grounds, head resting on his fists.

"Send him away!" cried Clarence.

Lady Ludlow rose and hurried to the window. The sight of Luke Morley did not cause anything like alarm in her. Her eyes lit, and she placed a hand on her son's arm. "Not so fast. This *is* your rival for the hand of Daniel Thornton, is it not?"

"Yes! And I do not wish to see him! Pray, Mother – not in my fragile state!"

Yet, Clarence was no match for his mother when she had his best interests at heart; he must see his rival and learn where things stood between him and Thornton. Friends close, enemies closer.

"Do you really think that is best, Edwina?"

"I do not *need* to see him, Father! Daniel is coming to see me at eleven. His note sounded penitent, he asked if I was feeling better – almost like his old self again. That boy is here because things have gone wrong. Daniel has tossed him aside, just as I predicted, and so he wishes my advice."

"My dear Clare de Lune," said his mother, "you must never leave things to chance. What better way to secure your happiness than to accept a role, offered to you on a silver platter, as guide to the troublesome wretch?"

"But I cannot. I simply cannot bear to hear of Daniel fucking that—"

"*Clarey*!" cried his father, "Do *please* spare the feelings of your mother!"

"We are *here* for you Clarence!" cried herself, rather incoherently.

Her son crossed the room and fell onto a sofa. "But I cannot bear it—"

"I'm afraid you will *have* to bear it," said Lady Ludlow, her voice sobering. "You are being handed a gift. You must accept it if you intend to win."

Fifteen minutes later, Luke was shown up. Clarence was sitting before a teapot at a table by his window, the communicating door between his and his parents' rooms slightly ajar. Stoic, his eyes reddened, the visitor came in without a word, keeping his head down as he took a seat.

"Do you have my note?"

Luke looked up, momentarily perplexed. Then, he shook his head. "I'm sorry. I tried. Only there was no time before Daniel—"

"Do *not* speak his name. I cannot bear to hear you speak it."

Once more studying the table, Luke said, "I know you don't wish to see me. I shouldn't have come, only I have nobody else. No one at all to speak to."

Luke glanced at the open door to the interior corridor, as though anticipating his marching orders from The George. Clarence had a similar thing in mind but felt unable to give them just yet. At a rather prolonged clearing of a throat from the adjoining room, his heart sank. So, pushing a teacup at his guest, in the process bestowing as much tea onto the table as was intended for Luke, he said, "Has he got some things out of his system now?" Luke looked up, uncertain what he meant. "Have you *pursued* him, as you were intending?"

"Yes."

"Have you... you know?"

"Well..." said Luke, hesitating. "A bit. But it hasn't gone well at all. Both times he..."

"Both! No, I cannot listen to this!"

"I don't wish you to be unhappy, really I don't," said Luke, his jaw tightening.

"Doesn't matter what you wish. Daniel is coming to see me this morning, and I shall judge how he is for myself."

"He is coming here to see you?"

Clarence smiled blandly at Luke's look of apprehension. Experiencing a slight revival of his appetite, he took up his toast and chewed for a time, determined to enjoy every moment of Luke's wretchedness. His visitor was a long time thinking before he said, "If I can have just five more minutes of your time. We don't have to speak of... him. I just wanted some general advice. There is no one else I can ask. If you have it in your heart."

Clarence remained silent, receiving no direction from the other room when he might have actually wished it. "I *have* a heart," he spat. "Has Daniel been telling you otherwise?"

"No. Nothing like that. Anyhow, I want to ask you about another man."

Clarence frowned. "Another man?"

"Yes. Just some general advice, you know."

"General advice?" Clarence considered. "Well, I do have *some* experience with military men. What is his name, this general of yours?"

"His name? It's... George. George Everett."

"General George Everett. I don't know him. Are you sleeping with him?"

"I don't know what you mean by that. But he did show me affection, as you say. Twice."

"Twice with him too, you do get around." Clarence eyed him suspiciously. "Very well, what has your *General* done to upset you?"

Out it spilled, a very strange episode Luke claimed had happened the previous month. He spoke in such a disjointed, confused manner Clarence was obliged to ask for greater explanations about nearly everything to understand what had gone wrong.

"Throwing me out of his study was strange enough. But then, the day after, it was much worse. We'd only just... finished, and he looked me in the eye and said, 'You got what you wanted. Now I need your help. If you wish more of what you just had, you must put an end to your father's marriage schemes. I don't care how you do it, just do it.'"

"The scheme to marry him to one of your sisters?"

"Yes. But why won't he simply tell my father he doesn't wish it? He actually seems afraid of saying no to him. Like he can't. He keeps badgering me to confess I didn't write what he called *that wretched note*, that my father did. We were only asking for an interview, not demanding one. It's like he didn't read any of the nice things I had to say. And now, he makes it seem as though he only agreed to do what we did to get me to do his dirty work. I thought he liked me."

Whispering began in the next room, and when it began to grow excited Clarence, feeling both confused and heartened, said, "Generals, dear, often seek to manipulate those around them. Come to think of it, I believe I knew your General, and quite intimately. He had an uncle, just as you mentioned, and that man was continually pushing him to marry. No doubt your father has learned of this. If Everett feels pressure to court one of your sisters, I expect your father has approached his uncle with the same offer and the uncle is pressuring dear George. What else could explain it?"

Luke shook his head. "My father hasn't spoken to anyone else about it. I'm sure of it. Anyhow, the uncle has someone else picked for him. It makes no sense, and it makes me feel dirty. I thought he liked me for myself, not for what I could do for him."

"That is George all over! General George Everett, as I live and breathe, I most certainly know him! He was constantly doing such things. It's a weakness of his, absolutely. One of many, I'm afraid. It took a man of much experience in the world, a man like me, to curb those tendencies. I was the only one who could. When he is not with me, I expect he simply cannot control himself. What did you say after he confessed that he had only deigned to tup you in order to use you?"

Frowning, Luke said, "Nothing. I couldn't think what to say. A moment later, his valet began knocking at the door asking him to come out. We got dressed as fast as we could, and I hid in the corner until they were gone. Then, once the coast was clear, I ran out of the house."

Luke departed The George in decidedly lower spirits than when he had arrived. Clarence might have been more civil, but it hardly mattered. It mattered only that he no longer had the hope of assistance. Clarence had been his only hope.

For five months, his problem had been adoring Daniel as male perfection without a chance of attaining him. Now he had attained him, he was no longer able to see him as perfect. He *did* still adore him; he believed he adored him. Had they only been interrupted a minute or two before, had he never heard him speak of what they had done as simply *giving him what he wanted,* this all would have felt so different. It would have been glorious.

Now, he was forced to consider all the things he might have forgotten. The worst was Daniel's seeing him as a person incapable of writing that note. He'd spent two hours composing it, hoping to convey through it his own adoration and love. But, just as had happened with his letter to Bridget, Daniel had misunderstood him entirely. Indeed, he had forced him to say that he hadn't even written it. *That wretched note.* He had found it insincere. So insincere he had actually taken offence.

As he continued toward home, Luke came upon Church Street. With Church Street arrived the memory of last Sunday and the walk home from St. Wulfram's. When he looked down the street today, he recalled his parents. The way they played off one another. The little games, little trivialities. Papa's pampering and pacifying, rushing to defend his wife from every imagined offence. Mamma bolstering, guiding, encouraging her husband. Their little names for each other. It had all seemed so much stuff and nonsense.

He understood it quite differently now. They had created a world, a kind of cocoon around themselves. A way of being with each other no one else could be. That is what he wished to have with Daniel. There had been moments at the ball and in his home which seemed like openings to a private joke or a pet name. There were times Mamma and Papa seemed even to speak another language. The language was based on shared experiences both had access to – as though they shared one memory. That was not stuff and nonsense. That was almost everything.

He was crossing the road to Barrowby when he saw Bridget in the distance walking with their sisters into town. Cecilia waved to him wildly. Maria remained talking, Bridget listening though she appeared to have seen him as well. She'd never been the sort to wave wildly as Cecilia did. So why should it hurt to receive no overt acknowledgement from her now? How *had* he made such a travesty of things?

For at least a year, he had been fearing the arrival of some love interest in her life – anticipating the time she would withdraw, he had begun to withdraw himself. They'd read the myth of Cassandra in grammar school, and he understood only too well the horror of knowing the future and not being believed. When he told her she was bound to start receiving attention, and grow interested herself, she had dismissed his concerns. Then, as she usually did, she turned the conversation on him, saying maybe it was *he* who had developed some love interest and why not tell her who it was?

He had begun to fear her. Her perception. Her cutting wit. He'd never been the object of it, but it was directed almost entirely against boys, whom she was often defending herself from. One time, when she was about twelve and defending herself from a boy who had been tormenting her, she had ridiculed him, quite unjustly, for effeminacy. Then, she told him he was too weak to torment other boys, and boys would never fight *him* because everyone knew he would get unduly *excited* by the attention. Though common enough in the discourse of their childhood, that it had been said by her had remained with Luke. Lazy reprimand though it was, bestowed by a girl of twelve when she couldn't think of anything else to say, still it had remained with him.

As his sisters approached, he looked tentatively towards her. She glanced at him. Then, her gaze returned when she saw he was not himself looking away. He saw real regret in her eyes. Regret and pity, for herself and for him. Once they reached each other he found it a benefit to have their sisters present; they could be more at ease than they might have been had they been alone.

Bridget said, "We thought we'd stop by that demonstration at the mayor's house. About the price of grain. Milley Musgrove's mother and a gaggle of her friends go over every Friday and make a scene."

"It's supposed to be rare fun!" said Cecilia. "Did you see any of it?"

He shook his head.

"Luke was off doing mysterious boy things," said Maria absently, looking over his shoulder.

157

"Were you?" said Bridget, catching his eye. She was smiling, if a bit uncertainly. Luke shrugged but gave her a smile in return. A genuine smile, which warmed her visibly. She reached out and ruffled his hair.

"That's Philip Forsyth!" continued Maria, beginning to gesture. "Luke, Papa said you were to see him after you saw Mr Thornton yesterday. Did you?"

Luke turned towards Philip, who was some distance away with his sister and chaperone. Hoping to avoid being caught out in his excuse for remaining at the Park, rather than answering, he began asking about the demonstration at the mayor's house.

"Luke!" cried Maria. "I asked you about Philip. Did you speak to him yesterday?"

"I was meant to. He was late returning so I left without seeing him."

"Oh, poo. I had hoped he might have mentioned..."

"That's a secret!" said Cecilia.

The great secret, however, was immediately revealed – as to make absolutely certain Philip had not dropped some vital piece of information, Maria let him know that Eliza was mad for him and wished to know if he might declare himself before he left town.

"*Declare*?" said Luke. "They only met on Tuesday."

"He's called on her every day since," said Cecilia, with finality. "Tomorrow he's escorting his sister to Yaxley where her *beau* is stationed and where he has a friend he wishes to visit. Eliza is afraid he will never return."

Luke frowned. "He's head over ears about Eliza. He's probably headed to Ringwald's right now to declare himself."

"Do you think?" said Maria.

"Oh, *do* let's go there rather than the mayor's house!" said Cecilia. "They are a match made in heaven!"

As they proceeded, Luke fell into step beside Bridget. For the first time in months, he had a great wish to speak to her. He must know how she would handle the proposal from Daniel, yet they had scarcely any time before they met the other party. Before he could ask if they might speak alone, however, she muttered, "Revolting, isn't it, how easily things work out for some people?"

Then Philip and his party were with them.

Evelina quickly offered her arm to Luke, leaving Bridget with Mrs Edwards, and Philip to interrogate Maria about Eliza. All other conversations, and potential conversations, had been postponed.

CHAPTER THIRTEEN

When the party approached Ringwald's, they were initially aware of little more than an unusually large gathering. As this was Friday, the bakery was offering a particularly large assortment of baked goods and daily breads intended to sustain a family until Monday. Just down the street, however, Luke observed a very strange sight – a cart had intercepted a delivery wagon of flour and unprocessed grain, which was currently being transferred into the cart by three sweating, flour-laden men. Before Ringwald's itself, there appeared to be a standoff between the owners, the gathering of housewives Luke had seen here previously, and two members of the Hopper entourage he had encountered at The George.

With Mrs Ringwald in tears and her husband, a gentleman tradesman unsure what he should, or could, do, the couple stood helplessly by as six local women worked a well-choreographed operation. With two standing guard before the entrance, the other four emptied the store of its baked goods, which they were transferring into the horse-drawn cart out front. As they worked, the women told the newly arrived onlookers that they were bringing the goods to many in need who simply could not afford these prices.

"We have always set at a fair price!" cried Mrs Ringwald, "a cost commensurate with the rising cost of grain. We told you this on Wednesday!"

"Aye," said Mrs Musgrove, one of the guards at the entrance who appeared to be leading the group. "And it has been two days more of babes crying for their hungry bellies. Two days more of regular working families too prosperous to collect alms, yet unable to afford the meanest bit of bread and butter. We are done speaking to the mayor; done with talk entirely. As I say, which you can tell the magistrate and the newspapers, we will sell these at a fair price and bring you every penny we collect. But we can abide this no longer."

While she spoke, the other ladies loaded the cart, returning into the bakery to fill baskets and aprons, red-faced from exertion and perhaps some embarrassment never having crossed such a line in their lives. Nonetheless, they remained determined in their mission which appeared to have already made one stop at a butchery. Three sides of beef and a number of shanks lay at the back, well-floured.

Always delighted to witness a singular and shocking event, Maria exclaimed, "Is that you, Mrs Michaels? And you, Mrs Kensington, I declare you are about to lose that rye loaf!"

Said the latter, "If you've a heart for the needy, Miss Morley, as you claim to have when you make your rounds on Wednesday, you might help me with this bundle. Though I suppose it'll make a better story should I drop everything in the dirt, you tiresome gossip."

At this, one of the manservants from the Hopper entourage, known as Blythe, looking even more delighted with the scene, with a stealthy leap forward saved the renegade loaf from an early demise. Then, to the astonishment of nearly all, he began tearing off great hunks and popping them into his mouth.

"Ah, still warm! I'm a workin' man myself, could do with earnin' a bit more. Tell ya what – I'll keep this little beauty as a sample and give you ha'penny for that apron-full yonder!"

Going livid, Mrs Musgrove began advancing upon the hooligan while the cart driver reached for his horsewhip. Luke, however, was suddenly overtaken by some wild, unaccountable admiration for these women who, covered in flour, had no qualms sacrificing their good names for the sake of their mission. He came forward, snatched the loaf in question and shoved Blythe back a few steps.

All eyes turned to Luke – manservants, shop owners, renegade housewives. All looked, in this instant, to him for direction in this new, decidedly surreal world of rule-breaking. Yet upon looking about, the direction was anything but clear. Meeting the reddened eyes of Mrs Ringwald, Luke hadn't a clue who was the rightful owner of the rye loaf. His head and his heart said that she was. They also said she was not.

The point became moot when Blythe made to snatch back the loaf, and the subsequent exchange scattered it in fifty pieces across the road. When Blythe made to grab another from Mrs Michaels's overflowing apron, Luke was quickly upon him. He had soon brought him to the ground where he commenced to tussle with his surprisingly wiry opponent.

At this point the two Ringwald girls, Elinor and Eliza, ran out of the shop, calling for their parents to intervene. Soon they began shrieking as the second manservant, named Jennings, began aiming his boot at Luke. The cart driver overtook Mrs Musgrove, raised his whip in the air and was only waiting for a clear target to begin employing it on Jennings.

"Eliza, *dear*!" cried Philip, stumbling toward his lover. She stepped towards him but was unable to surmount the chaotic scene which was separating them by no less than twenty feet.

"Philip, my *darling*!" cried Eliza, attempting to keep clear of the airborne whip. Jennings then let off aiming his boot at Luke and, in his haste to avoid the whip, shoved Bridget aside with such force she was only saved from dashing her head against a cartwheel by the black angel herself, who, in an incredible feat of stealth, leapt to catch her, lifting her away from the shouting men and the whip dancing in the air.

But the tale most celebrated from this early incident in a day of chaos which would come to be known as the Great Grantham Food Riot, was that of star-crossed lovers Eliza and Philip, battling to reach one another. In a valiant attempt to rescue Luke, Eliza directed her boot at Blythe, the force of the blow sending her tumbling backwards into the dirt. Then, when all appeared lost, when Luke was laying on his side in the dirt attempting to catch his breath and Blythe was about to descend upon Eliza, Philip came forward, delivered a right hook which sent the manservant spinning to the ground, before sweeping Eliza into his arms and away from harm.

After a moment attempting to rise, Luke fell back to the ground to avoid four broomsticks swinging wildly from the back of the cart. The women exchanged a few words then agreed they were content with the take from Ringwald's. A moment was needed to secure the foodstuffs, which now included baked goods, flour, grain and cuts of meat. As four took up defensive positions at the corners of the cart, Mrs Musgrove shouted at the driver to resume his box and for everyone else to stand clear. Next stop: the patisserie over on Main Street!

Luke lay in the dust beside the unconscious Blythe. His lips bloodied, his ribs sore, he worked to catch his breath alive to the utter strangeness of his life, of the town, of England in this singular year of 1795.

A large crowd was gathering about. Seemingly everyone Luke had ever known in Grantham, from his primary school teacher to the gardener who had sent him away from Bainbridge Park. To Mr and Mrs Ringwald.

To the town constable.

"Alright you two," he said, kneeling down. He prodded Blythe who began gradually to come around. "Time to cool off. Some time in lockup will do you both some good. Get to your feet."

***

Clarence was deciding on the suit to welcome Daniel in when he began hearing exclamations of alarm from a room on the top floor. He hurried toward it, meeting his mother who was scurrying down the passage, and together they entered the front sitting room. Lord Ludlow stood at the window with a look of horror on his face.

"Charles? What is it?"

"The overthrow of all that is good and decent!" he shouted, then redirected his attention to what was unfolding on the High Street. *"You there! Did you see what happened? I just sent two of my employees down to fetch foodstuffs and they have not returned... orange and green livery... Good Lord, were they injured? You don't know? Damn you to hell, then find somebody who does and send them to me!"*

Once Clarence joined him at the window, Charles turned to him. "The low are rising!" he said, spinning from the scene as though repulsed. He stepped to his wife and seized her hands. "We have arrived in Versailles, Edwina – *Versailles*! Our footmen were just assaulted outside the bakery, where a troupe of local harpies had just descended to rob the place. I observed them as they passed just now with their cartful of booty – covered head to foot in flour, a pack of barbarians brandishing broomsticks! Blythe and Jennings may well have been killed! Hacked down in the streets of this lawless town for simply wishing to do a bit of shopping, and now we shall nothing for afternoon tea!"

At this, a great ruckus was heard from in the corridor. After a moment, none other than Jennings, assisted by two footmen, stumbled past on the way to the servants' chambers. He was covered in dust, his eyes rolling toward the heavens. Edwina ran after him.

Clarence took his father's hands. "Surely this won't prevent Daniel from arriving?"

"Who can say? He may be robbed. He may be set upon by that pack of lunatics before he can reach us."

"But we must warn him!"

"No. We cannot risk any more lives. We will lock ourselves down until law and order can be restored. God *help* us, if it ever can be."

A short time later, Edwina came hurrying back with the wonderful news that Jennings had only been knocked around a bit and had suffered no serious injury. What had become of Blythe, she had not discovered – Jennings had had to contend with the cart driver's whip, and the last he had seen, Luke Morley was beating the life from him.

"Luke?" said Clarence. "You cannot be serious."

"The blackguard! The bane of our existence!" shouted Charles. "Edwina, go downstairs and have the manager secure the premises. Tell him we wish this entire top floor to ourselves. Whatever the cost. Tell him we are admitting only Daniel Thornton. No one else shall be permitted on this floor without our express permission. Thornton alone shall be welcome here today – perhaps the only remaining gentleman in this town of raging hellions!"

As the lady hurried from the room, Clarence approached his father. "*Will* you welcome him? I had feared... I know Mother wishes to meet him, but I thought you might make your excuses."

"I shall meet him. I begin to understand your mother's point of view."

"You do?"

"The balance..." said Lord Ludlow, grinding his teeth, "has been *disturbed*. A tradesman's son seeks to attain a gentleman

– admittedly a gentleman of just two thousand a year, but a gentleman, nonetheless. It upsets the order. Such ambition infects the lower tradesmen. Then it infects the labourers and their brawny wives as I just observed – an uprising of the peasant stock! Soon – revolution!"

"Do sit, Father," said Clarence, bringing him onto a settee. "I shall go to the window and see what I can learn of Blythe. Then I will watch for Daniel and warn him of any lingering miscreants as he steps from his carriage."

"Palaces invaded!" continued his father. "The guillotine!"

"Do not shout!" shouted Clarence. "I must collect my thoughts for Daniel. You do wish me to have my sweetheart again, don't you?"

"Yes, I do, son," said Charles, still trembling. "You shall have your man. If it's the last thing I do, I shall see you get him. Gentlemen must stick together, however they might choose to... well, *stick*. If my son wants Daniel Thornton, Daniel Thornton he shall have. We shall not leave Grantham until he has *secured* Daniel Thornton!"

"Oh, Father!"

"Oh, *yes*! You love your father, don't you? You have a father who understands. You love what he can do for you!"

"Yes," cried Clarence, "oh, yes!"

Having inspired himself, Charles leapt up. He returned to the window to once more shout down at the crowd, promising a rich reward for anyone who could tell him what had become of his manservant. A particularly large bonus would be given for information on the scoundrel Luke Morley, of Morley's Drapery and Haberdashery, who had assaulted said manservant.

After five minutes, a voice returned the call. He asked to be shown up.

"And who is that?"

"My name is Mr Jacob Elsworthy Esq. Head gardener at Bainbridge Park and at your particular service as regards information on the Morleys."

"Daniel's gardener?" said Clarence. "Let him in."

Charles held forth a steadying hand, wishing first to assess the risk of a potential breach in the palace walls. He called down: "We are on particularly close terms with Mr Daniel Thornton of Bainbridge Park. We will wish to ask you a few things about him to verify your claim."

"Ask me anything you like. I've known the man the entire five months he's been in the house and can verify anything you like. So long as it don't infringe upon his privacy, which I would betray for no man and no sum of money once I am taken into his confidence."

CHAPTER FOURTEEN

Daniel had meant to keep this all from Collins. Not forever, but for as long as he could. Somehow, without confessing to the absolute chaos that had become his life, without receiving Albert's shake of the head and look of dismay, it was not entirely real. He was to depart in an hour for The George; after a miserable evening and morning considering Luke's visit, any change of scene – even to see Clarence Hopper – would be a relief. Perhaps when they met, they could prove they were capable of at least one successful exchange before the man left town. Perhaps then, after this one small accomplishment as a rational adult, he could face his valet and speak of the rest.

That it came out when it did was not so much a decision as an inability to keep himself in anything like a civilised attitude. By the time Albert entered the bedchamber, he had allowed himself to fall into a pose of almost comic despair – hands in his hair, twisted about on a diminutive loveseat which was far too small for him. The valet glanced at him. Then, as was his habit, he went about his business for a time, examining a suit for tomorrow, then taking out a needle and thread to darn a stocking. When he approached to ask his employer what he thought of the suit, Daniel had already collapsed internally under the man's stealthy scrutiny. He said simply, "I am in hell."

"I see," said Collins. "I was close – I had supposed you to be posing for a scene from Dante's Inferno. I have been looking about for a painter with his easel, but perhaps I had best fetch a bucket of water."

"Please don't jest with me."

"Why not?"

"Because I am feeling exceptionally disturbed and deranged."

Coming closer, the valet said, "I can see you have been disturbed since yesterday and have been waiting for you to confide in me. I would have hoped that by now you see me as a friend who cares about you and might at last leave off this nonsense about maintaining airs around the help."

"Old habits, I am sorry, Albert. It seems scarcely anything I ask of you is in your job description. I ask for too damn much already. But you know I *have* asked you to drop the *sirs* when we are alone, but to no avail."

"With a better example from my employer, I believe I should make a better go of it. Now, aside from that longstanding saga, what in God's name is the matter with you? I am worried sick and was about to send for the physician."

After some hesitation, Daniel let his head sink into his hands. "Oh, Albert. How can I tell you? Just come out and say it, I know – I am hopelessly, out of my head in love."

Such was Daniel's misery, his unease at having exposed his inner turmoil, he failed to observe the valet sink into an armchair, lean back, and clutch his upper arm. After a time, sounding deeply annoyed that Daniel was failing to respond or even appear to take notice, Collins said, "It's my heart, sir, as you are fearing. It's all coming to an end now. No time even to call the physician."

"Let them bury us together, then," said Daniel. "I feel, I really do feel I might die of this," which was so vapid, so inexcusable a response when Albert Collins, his truest friend and confidant for the past twelve years, might well be experiencing heart failure, that the man leapt to his feet with a look of horrified outrage.

"You promised me, Daniel! Yes, I *have* called you Daniel and in that disrespectful tone, for I shall not call you sir, not just now. You *swore* you could never love Clarence again and would not have him back! I have been assisting you! Sophia has been assisting, even without knowing why she is assisting! All from the goodness of our hearts!"

Rousing himself, Daniel stood and came forward. He pushed Collins back into the armchair. Then, kneeling at his feet, he put his head in his lap.

"Plead for forgiveness all you like," said the valet. "We had an agreement! *On your honour*, Daniel."

"Albert—"

"And in the *library*! Oh yes, I knew by the state of you what you had been doing – Clarence off in a corner collecting himself. Upon my word, you might have gone to The Angel. Only you decided after the Morleys had departed that you would, in your infinite wisdom, sneak him into the *library*! Did you take down Dryden for a poetry reading afterwards? Or was it those gentle fires which kindled that initial flame?"

"That was not Clarence with me in the library." The fuming valet went suddenly still, his expressive hands frozen where he had left them mid-rant. "Indeed, I have not seen him since he stormed out of here Tuesday night. I am not in love with Clarence, though you may find what I have to tell you is far worse."

To Albert's confused silence, during which hope, blessed hope, prompted the man to reach for his employer's hand, Daniel whispered, "God forgive me, I am in love with Luke Morley."

A moment passed. When Daniel leant back on his haunches to address him face to face, Collins seized his head in both hands and, in a manner which quite surpassed unbridled passion, smashed his lips across his forehead. "*Not* Clarence! Not *Clarence*! Oh sir, *forgive* me! Forgive my using your Christian name! Forgive my having ever doubted you! *Not* Clarence?"

But Daniel was obliged to withdraw some of this joy as he began upon a long, often incoherent, and confused explanation. He spoke first of being the victim of blackmail then informed him of the true purpose of John Morley's visit to the house. After a moment of speechless horror, Albert produced, "*Blackmail*!" after his shock at last knocked the word loose from him. "Good God. They are blackmailing you?"

A sigh sufficed for an answer. Then, Daniel confessed to how he had received the note and the first encounter in the study. "Oh, my good Lord. Did you really? With the wretch who is blackmailing you?"

"Because he is *not* blackmailing me!" said Daniel, now shouting what had been a certainty in his heart from the moment he received that damned note. He came to his feet. "I cannot explain it. I know I must sound mad, and I do sometimes fear I am losing my mind. And yet, despite everything, despite every evidence to the contrary, despite Luke's own words, I simply do not believe he is capable of that. I wonder, I really do wonder, if he even knew what that note contained." After studying Collins, he shook his head. "I do wish I had someone to speak to about this."

"And what am I? What is this we are doing?"

"I don't mean that. I appreciate you immensely. I mean... I don't know, a priest in a confessional, perhaps."

Holding up a hand, Collins took a moment to steady himself. Then, rising to his feet, he took Daniel by the shoulders. "Sir, after the horrible shock you just gave me, you have just made me happier than you can possibly imagine. Make use of me as you wish, even as your confessor, I *entreat*."

Daniel simply patted his shoulder.

"Do not dismiss me, sir. I am in earnest. I have served you well and will continue to serve you well. Have I not held up my end of our bargain? Have you not, because of my manoeuvrings, fucked a sweet arse again, whomever it belonged to?"

"Lord help me..."

"Haven't you?"

"Yes. Dear, sweet Albert, yes, I have, and I thank you. It is not your fault that I now feel the blackest scoundrel who ever lived. I am utterly ashamed of myself. I have not yet summoned the courage to face Luke again, but my confession, along with my apology, must be to him, not you."

"He did ask you for it. Begged you."

"Because I cold-heartedly, calculatingly drove him to desperation. I believed, as his victim, I was justified in victimising him as well. I excused myself from all responsibility and then toyed with him until he couldn't see straight. And it *was* a wicked pleasure, of the sort I have not felt in years. Taking the innocence of a sensitive young man – I knew just how much it would affect him. I expected he would be left a trembling puddle completely at my disposal. But is emotional blackmail any better than the kind I have been subjected to?"

"You feel guilt because you have convinced yourself with no evidence, indeed with all evidence to the contrary, that Luke is somehow innocent."

"I know. I can only say that there was a moment, just before you knocked on the door. Just after I had made my demand, striking when the iron was hot as I had planned, when he looked up at me. I shall never forget his expression. This deeper understanding of himself and of me, which was at the same time so lost, so utterly exposed that I knew, in my heart, that he was blameless. Logic, evidence, even his own words played no part. I also knew that he would never do what I asked. He was too horrified by the light in which I had cast everything we had just done. He saw a blackguard and a coward standing before him. I hated what he saw just as much as he did.

"In all this mess, we've known scarcely anything of the other but in a carnal sense. Yet somehow, by knowing him in that way, I *do* know him."

What could Collins say to such esoteric nonsense? Daniel must sound as though he had lost his senses. He could see the concern, the pity, enter his valet's eyes before he could quite disguise them. However, he said, "Very well. You say Luke is innocent. Besides this blackmail business, I have no reason to think ill of him. Someone wrote that note to you. I think you should consider that it was Clarence."

"Clarence? Look, I know you do not like him, but really—"

"Who else?"

"John Morley, of course. You forget, I *saw* Luke leave that note on the mantle. He had plenty of opportunity to take a few love letters the night before – I had supposed he'd simply seen an opportunity, but it is just as likely his wretched father told him to look for anything which might be useful. A young man with something to conceal is particularly desperate to please his father, no matter his own ethics or misgivings. I was myself never put in such a position, but God knows I'd have been more than capable had I thought it would get my father's approval."

"Let me see the letter," said Collins. When it was produced, he was a long time looking it over. "I find a resemblance."

"There is no resemblance. I know Clarence's handwriting."

"Clarence was drunk, *very drunk* is what you told me. Drunk and angry. This is scrawled out in a kind of half-printing, half-cursive. Not like his letter-writing hand, to be sure, but—"

Daniel took the note. "But what could he mean by writing such a thing?"

"That if you refused to have him back, he would tell Erasmus about you."

"But that is preposterous."

"Clarence *is* preposterous."

Daniel looked again at the note. "Do you really think it's possible?"

Albert looked truly pained at being unable to damn Clarence outright. "I can't explain everything. I can't explain why you saw Luke leave the note. Is it possible he was just being curious? He took it up to look it over, then replaced it when you entered the room?"

"That just isn't plausible. I won't even say it is unlike him, even though that is precisely what I thought when I saw him do it. I'll say rather that it is absurd for anyone to run to a pile of letters having only just been shown into the room. I saw him arrive and was down there almost immediately. Would you have me believe the moment the butler left him, he began immediately hunting through the post?"

"It's possible, isn't it?"

Daniel expelled a breath. "Yes, I suppose it is *possible*. But yesterday, when we were alone, before I let things go too far, I had a suspicion something was not right with his story. I told him I did not believe he had written the note, and I asked him to admit it. He insisted he had."

"Then forget pursuing that course and confront Clarence."

"Do you..." he hesitated. He would kill Albert if he was raising his hopes for no good reason. Yet, he could not prevent hope stirring in his heart. "Do you really think I should? Ask him if he—?"

"No. I think you should tell him you forgive him. Brook no opening for denials. If he is guilty, you've a much better chance of cornering him into a confession if you've already forgiven him. Many things were said and done in the heat of passion, etcetera. You both said things you regret, etcetera."

"And this isn't because you despise the man? You really think this is a possibility?"

"Yes. At the very least something worth exploring."

Daniel crossed to an armchair to retrieve his frockcoat. He slipped it on. "Very well. I'm leaving in half an hour to see him. We shall see what he says. And, failing that..."

Collins gave him a questioning look.

"Should that fail, I shall, horribly embarrassed and with my tail between my legs, find Luke and attempt to have a heart-to-heart with him – this young man I've joked with, caroused with, argued with, fucked with, and tried to emotionally blackmail. Everything, it seems, except speak to properly."

A quiet "Hello, Danny" was Clarence's decidedly demure welcome as Daniel arrived in his top-floor sitting parlour. His host was standing in the centre of the room, hands held before him like a well-behaved child, keeping all things out of reach. When the door closed Daniel came forward, kissed his cheek, and tried to ignore Clarence's hands instinctively releasing to wrap around him.

"I'm sorry for everything that I said," said Clarence, lowering his hands.

"Let's not dwell too much on what was said. I would like to speak to you about that night, but first tell me how you are."

"Well, quite well."

"Your mother wrote that you were still recovering."

"She's overly solicitous. Always has been. I am my own man, but she did come all this way and likes to feel useful. My father as well. You've never met them. Would you like to? They'd like to meet you."

This kind of rushed, overbearing earnestness set Daniel on his guard. Clarence was so obviously uncomfortable, and meeting those two was about the last thing he wished. But before he could respond, as though on cue, the pair entered the room.

After a year during which they'd never once asked to meet, their wishing to meet him now was indeed a surprise. They themselves were not. The Lady had that kind of stale effervescence women of her class often had, like champagne left out overnight. His Lordship was decidedly silent, undisguisedly assessing everything he did and said, yet with an air of wishing to find things to like. From everything he knew of them, Clarence likely had had no choice in their appearance in Grantham or in this room. Yet, it was remarkable that they were going so far in acknowledging their son's former relationship, of seeking to support him in what he was trying to do. He was only sorry that they should show their support when the object of his wishes would not be having him back. Indeed, within two minutes he was obliged to cut off Edwina, who had begun to speak of the little upsets she and her dear Charles had had during their married life. Of how they were always stronger after a reunion all the time speaking of her son's relationship in the present tense.

"Excuse me, ma'am, but I cannot mistake your intention. I am here because I value your son as a friend, nothing more. It is very important that I clear up a private matter with him."

The stale effervescence went a bit staler as the lady's expression froze. Then, tossing back her head, Edwina, refusing to take the hint, agreed only to relinquish the reigns to him. Daniel went silent as he considered what alterations to the conversation might need to be made with this unwanted audience. Smiling as the visitor collected his thoughts, Edwina was happy to fill the silence with assurances that a strong friendship *was* the basis of all strong relationships.

Daniel turned to Clarence. "I don't mean to embarrass you, but I need to clear the air about something that happened on Tuesday." When Clarence merely nodded, he continued. "I would like to know your intentions when you left me that note."

A flicker of recognition passed over Clarence's face; Daniel's heart surged, a reaction Clarence appeared to observe, though he said only, "A note? From me?"

"Yes. It was left in a plain envelope with no direction. I see from your face you know about this."

"Your little visitor this morning, Clarey," sighed his mother, looking significantly at him, before returning her two-dimensional smile to Daniel.

Determined not to be thrown by the lady's interference, Daniel continued, "It was a threatening note, Clarence. Whatever was said that night, I do not deserve to be threatened. Included with the note were scraps of old letters I had written you. There was a very ugly implication about what might be done with the letters themselves if I did not consider those *very much in need but who were not nearly as helpless as I supposed.*"

"Do you know where my letters are?" said Clarence. "They mean everything to me. I was so drunk I didn't realise until I awoke from my stupor on Wednesday that I could locate but few."

"Clarey nearly broke his *heart* when he discovered this, Daniel. And it nearly broke *mine* to see it!"

Half in disbelief, half in fear, Daniel said, "But Clarence, *you* wrote that note, surely, and still have those letters. I promise I am not angry with you, not in the slightest. If you will just admit what you did."

"Oh, dear," said Edwina, directing her gaze to her husband, "this is what that boy meant."

"Pray," said Daniel, nearly losing his cool. "Edwina, Charles, do not keep secrets from me. This has caused more pain, more confusion, over the last few days than you can possibly imagine. If you are answering for your son in order to protect him, I beg you will not. It will make no difference in my feelings for him. They are the feelings of a friend, nothing more. But I do hope to retain his friendship." Daniel returned to their son. "You wrote that note after we quarrelled because you were angry with me."

Quite a long moment passed, then Clarence said, "Luke Morley wrote it."

Scarcely able to believe his very worst fear on the lips of the last person who should be able to make the accusation, Daniel said, "What makes you say that?"

"He told me. This morning."

"He *and* his father wrote it," interjected Edwina. "After Luke stole Clarey's letters and made the whole scheme possible."

Attempting not to show just how much this upset him, Daniel said, "Why on earth would Luke come to see you?"

"Because he wished my advice about you," said Clarence. "Ask the porter. He did indeed come here to see me this morning. When he arrived, I accused him of stealing my letters. He admitted it. That is how he found out about you and me, and so knew he could approach you as a lover." Daniel had never quite considered this. "He said if I helped him, he might be able to retrieve the letters, which I assume are with his father, though he would not say for certain. He was angry with you because he said you had seduced him in an attempt to stop his father's marriage scheme. Then, he tried to tell me that his father had gone to Erasmus about your marrying, and Erasmus was pressuring you. But it does make more sense that Mr Morley simply instructed his son what to write and had him deliver that note."

Humiliated to hear that Luke had actually accused him of seduction, scarcely able to maintain coherence, Daniel said, "But... but Clarence, that is preposterous. That *cannot* be."

Lady Ludlow said, "It's easy enough to figure out I should think. Is it pressure from your uncle, or is it that note, which is making you feel obliged to court one of Morley's sisters?"

Daniel exhaled. "The note, but—"

"Luke either wrote the note, or he was complicit in the writing of it."

"But..." Daniel was unable to keep his gaze from dropping to the floor. "Did Luke really visit you here? Did he actually tell you about all that?"

"Just an hour and a half ago." This was Charles Hopper. "How else would we know it?"

CHAPTER FIFTEEN

L uke and the manservant Blythe were shown into cells in the municipal jail, as far from one another as a jail containing three cells would allow. The flustered constable made clear this stay would be an inconvenience of just a few hours, so long as both showed signs of having cooled down. He had far bigger troubles with reports of continuing food riots and would likely have to eject them simply to make room. Nevertheless, Blythe was demanding the Hoppers be sent for, demanding the restoration of his rights, demanding at the very least something to eat.

"Half the town is demanding something to eat," said one of the on-duty guards. "Your appetite started your trouble today, so you can just pipe down."

Luke's cell contained two men. As they had already commandeered the two cots, he took a seat on the cold stone floor. His eyes were some moments adjusting to the gloom as he listened to Blythe's complaints and the guards speaking amongst themselves, trying to decide who had been most accurate predicting the arrival of the food riots to Grantham.

Luke hunkered down. With the catcalls and shouting from outside the jailhouse walls, with the agitation which stirred his jailers and sent footfalls up and down the streets, he experienced a growing sense of calm. His inner turmoil felt to have been made external – set at a distance where he could step back and observe it. If he chose, he believed he might throw it to the ground, tussle with it, then step away. It was no longer in him entirely, not in the same way. He could not rewrite the rules of the world, but in himself he felt he was rewriting them. Yet what the new rules should say, he had scarcely an idea.

Clarence had confirmed many of his fears about Daniel. The new rules surely should not say none of that mattered, and he simply must have Daniel again. The longing he had felt after their encounter in the study was now an overpowering, shameless thirst. He was living in a world in which churchgoing housewives robbed Ringwald's. A world in which haircuts performed at high noon made impossible courtships possible. Wasn't he permitted to pursue Daniel despite his wishing to use him? Couldn't he pretend to speak to his father about stopping the scheme? When Bridget refused him, Luke might easily take the credit. That would leave Maria, or Cecilia, and he might not stop those schemes, but did he care? In the interim, he could have him again. Intimately. Heart-poundingly. Every feeling he was capable of, every pleasure, every fear, rolled into one, experienced at once. How could he not seek that out again?

None of this made him very easy. He looked around the cell, to a bucket with a lid in the back corner. To Old Man McKinley sitting on the edge of his cot, picking his teeth, grinning at him. Old Man McKinley was one of Grantham's established miscreants, in and out of these cells for as long as Luke could remember. The man seemed positively ticked by the commotion today, quite pleased to welcome newcomers into his world.

On the second cot, a young man sat cross-legged. He was slumped over, his long, shaggy fringe casting his face in shadow. He looked like... wait, wasn't that Everett? Luke had hardly noticed him when he'd been shown in. Why should it please him to encounter him just now? Why should he suddenly seem a kindred spirit?

Feeling uncommonly emboldened by their new, uncommon surroundings, Luke said, "Everett."

Looking up, George tilted his head at him. After squinting through the gloom of the cell, he frowned and began studying his hands again. Was he daft? They were here together for who knew how long. This was an opportunity to ingratiate himself with a member of Bridget's family and he would continue to behave like this?

"Still nothing to say for yourself, have you?" said Luke, pleased to voice not just his own long-standing disdain, but that of all in the family.

"You can fuckin' talk."

Old Man McKinley perked up at this, sensing the setup for some entertainment. Luke's first instinct was to retreat into dignified silence, refusing to give either the satisfaction of a response. Yet just now, in this cell, refusing to exercise the one freedom he had no longer felt as satisfying. In George's rebuke, he heard Bridget's own reproaches of him. Of course, they had been talking about him – how he had changed and hadn't anything to say of any meaning anymore. Until this moment, he had never understood just how alike they were, he and George.

Trying not to consider this too much, Luke said, "Bridget's changed, hasn't she? Ever since she's begun going about with you."

Though not entirely coherent, George appeared to understand this attempt to explain his longstanding dislike. He tucked the sweep of his long fringe behind an ear and looked up. "Nothing to do with me; Bridget's her own girl."

Luke was distracted from responding by the sight of George's face. He'd always been known to be a scrapper; until now, Luke had understood him to be a fairly decent one. At the moment, however, fresh wounds had been opened, presumably during the fight which got him thrown in here today, on the greenish hues of an older one. A swelling about his right eye seemed to tilt his vision towards the older damage on his cheek and crusted lip. George noticed Luke noticing this. "Suppose she's just got a soft spot for charity cases."

Unsure what to say to this, Luke said nothing. He sure as hell did not need to start feeling sorry for George Everett. George Everett had caused a rift between himself and Bridget. He was the stock villain in the piece, no good – everyone in town said so.

Still, without mention of comparable damage he had inflicted upon his assailant, or even the name of the rank bastard, Luke could not mistake what had happened.

Everyone in town also knew that things were not good at home.

"How'd you end up in here?"

"You mean instead of the butcher? He pressed the charges before I could, didn't he? His way of seeing I follow in the grand family tradition." Luke studied him, uncertain what he wished to hear, certain only that Bridget's befriending him was not at all out of her character. If he had only met his eye months ago, had only spoken with such frankness, Luke must have felt compassion for him as well. George flipped his hair back and said with a hint of pride, "This morning I got between him and those housewives when they came to collect a few haunches for the poor. When he went after Mrs Kensington, I gave him a right shove. Knocked him clean down into the dirt. Been waiting to do that since he did this to me last week."

He held Luke's gaze, sensing from his expression that he was softening towards him. For a moment Luke considered telling him his sister saw him as more than just a charity case. But did he know that? Bridget was passionate when her compassion was engaged. If she did love him, it was entirely possible she would fight their parents to marry beneath her social dues. But it would be cruel to give hope. Luke found a few words to tell him he was sorry to hear about the situation at home but said nothing more.

He looked to Old Man McKinley, who dismissed them with a wave and returned to picking his teeth. Luke drew up his knees, then set his head on them to end further attention from either of his cellmates. What was this ache in his heart at having denied George any encouragement with his sister? It felt like denying himself the hope of ever having a love of his own. One's class, one's station in life could be just as limiting as sexual persuasion.

Perhaps more so. Luke *could* marry Jenny Paltrow, daughter of an independent family one generation removed from trade. Indeed, he probably would if his coldness at the dance hadn't driven her away. He knew she liked him. Knew, too, that she would have responded to the slightest show of interest. He hadn't been a complete buffoon; he *had* said the proper things. But his mind, his heart, had been entirely occupied with Daniel. He'd danced for Daniel, hoping against hope that he would notice him as he wished to be noticed. God help him, Daniel had noticed. God help him, he had responded. He was his lover now and would be for as long as Luke could keep the marriage talk at bay. Perhaps, even if they both married, they could still see each other sometimes. They would be friends who were more than friends when they could be.

Time passed. At each opening of the jailhouse entrance, Luke expected to see Mrs Musgrove and her troupe of flour-covered miscreants. The cells were instead filled entirely with men who had been caught up in the riots. The seizures of food sounded to have gone to plan, continuing at the town patisserie, a dairy, and finally at a nearby granary on the road to Barrowby. Conversations were had by the jailers about the need to empty one cell to make room for the women. Yet as time drew on, reports of fresh riots ceased and, by all accounts, the housewives had achieved their ambitions for the day. Rumours began that they might not be arrested at all. A nearby militia had been contacted, but only to assist in the distribution of what had been seized, and to see that the merchants were compensated from what could be collected.

Luke heard in the talk, by both the jailers and the jailed, respect for these women. They had stepped from the confines of their prescribed role in society seemingly into the realm of rank barbarism. Yet none but the most mean-spirited appeared to view it as anything but a move of great humanity. What inner conviction had it taken to hazard one's good name in a town in which everyone knew you? What courage for, though perhaps avoiding jail today, the women were far from cleared. The men in Luke's cell spoke of one Sarah Rogers of Fordingbridge who, at a recent quarter session, had received a three-month prison sentence for redistributing butter. Yet that they were even speaking of a woman whom none of them would otherwise have known, and in tones of irritation at her sentence, was a judgment surely more meaningful, more enduring, than any the law could bestow.

Family members of those incarcerated were soon arriving. Luke began looking for his father or brother, certain someone would soon be coming for him. Among the arriving visitors, he observed the manservant called Jennings. Just behind him came the gardener from Bainbridge Park, Jacob Elsworthy, the man who had found him loitering in the woods. For a moment, the men appeared to be together. However, as they advanced, the connection seemed illusory. Jennings spoke to one of the attendants and continued to the cell which contained Blythe. Elsworthy, however, remained on his own, looking the men over until his eye met Luke's. He advanced. Appearing as though he did not wish to be noticed, he motioned him to his feet.

Luke scrambled up, for a moment certain Daniel had received word of his incarceration and had arranged for his release. When he stepped to the bars, however, the man merely slipped him a note.

"Message from the Main House," was all he said, then turned and departed. Despite himself, Luke was a moment looking for Daniel. Then, he returned to his place on the floor and opened the note.

Mr Morley,
After nearly six months, Thornton fails to understand that in The House there can be no secrets. He has been long understood. You will understand what is meant by this. Your friendship with him has been understood. *You have been* seen. *Thornton is a dirty Pathic; you are his unclean Ganymede. The House desires an end to this intercourse. When Thornton seeks you out, you will tell him you wish an end of your relations.* Encourage *the man's* other interests. *Allow things to progress as they* ought. *Pay not one more visit to The House. One more visit, any carnal intercourse at all with Thornton, and we will learn of it. We shall have no choice but to inform Erasmus. And your father.*
You are fairly warned.

For some reason he would never afterwards understand, Luke's eyes leapt to Everett, to whom he had said nothing more as the cell filled with men. His head continued to be cast down, his fringe curtaining his face. As Luke's eyes were drawn back to the note, his stomach seized into a fist. Tears of shame, of fear, blurred his vision, as though wishing to prevent his ability to see what he did not wish to see again.

Your friendship with him has been understood. *You have been* seen.

This must be Daniel's valet. He had interrupted them in the library. Or perhaps the butler, who'd shown him into the sitting parlour. Or, by 'The House', did the writer mean a member of the family? Evy? Philip? Mrs Edwards? Did it matter? Whoever it was, whatever interest they had in the Thorntons, they would make the same trouble for him.

When Thornton seeks you out, you will tell him you wish an end to your relations. Encourage *the man's* other interests. *Allow things to progress as they* ought.
Pay not one more visit to The House.

This, then, was the true cost of those encounters at the Park – encounters which must now last a lifetime. Was this note not the inevitable end of delusions? Was this not the reprimand of real life? One might steal from those who had and redistribute to the poor – this was the horror on the face of Mr Ringwald as his store was robbed. The tears of Mrs Ringwald. The prison sentence of Sarah Rogers.

Yet he was being given a chance. All must, all would, go back to as it had been. Nobody else would discover the truth about him. Whoever had written this had no reason to betray him to the world if he refrained from a future with Daniel. He would encourage his other interests. Daniel would probably marry; it was what his uncle wished and as it should be. His encouragement of his other interests, his silence about his own, *was* a fair exchange. Luke had had his experiences – surely more than many would ever have. If he could simply be content. If he could simply forget Daniel Thornton, he would be safe.

Such were his thoughts, repeated over and over again as a mantra, as he tore the note into long, thin strips. The mantra calmed him, the ritual of it calmed him. He took the strips and pulled them to pieces crosswise.

He hardly noticed when Stephen arrived, dusting himself off from his valiant gallop across a town brimming with lawlessness. He was scarcely interested as his deep, outraged cadences demanded to see the head jailer. He was indifferent to the time Stephen was detained in the adjoining room, declaring his brother's arrest an outrage. It was all Luke could do to look up when Stephen at last strode forward to find him in his cell.

"Be easy, brother!" he cried. "I am here now. And you may depend upon it, this outrage against our family *will* swiftly be put an end to! I shall use *all* my power, *all* my resources as one of the brightest new lights of this town to remedy this horror! Rest *utterly* assured, *dearest* Luke, all your worries are *over*!" Then Stephen ceased speaking to steady himself.

In that moment, overpowered with a sense of wonder, he understood he had delivered a speech which must go down in the annals of Morley family history to be retold for generations to come.

CHAPTER SIXTEEN

After leaving the Hoppers, Daniel sat in his coach outside The George, having asked the coachman to give him a moment before they proceeded. In his lap he held a dahlia of deep purple. His eyes were set steadily upon it as the citizens of the town ran hither and yon about them. Reports of the location of the highwaymen housewives ricocheted off the streets and buildings. This was Grantham's moment to shine, to become the focus of the country during this heady year of 1795, when laws were overthrown by the meekest in society, when they might well have revolution again!

Yet, despite the moment, despite everything, all he could think was: fucking Clarence.

He did *not* believe him. He did *not* believe his interfering parents. Even though they were confirming his own suspicions, he simply would not.

This was the time to believe the worst of Clarence Hopper. He had glanced so often at his parents throughout the interview, and the couple were so quick to supply him with answers, they must be covering for him. It was obvious what they were doing or trying to do.

Yet, there was nothing in the couple's behaviour inconsistent with what he had long known about them. He had always understood them to be overbearing, quick to defend and mollycoddle their son. Even if they were not the kind, no wish to defend him could imbue them supernaturally with knowledge. No matter how he looked at it, though his heart remained convinced of Luke's innocence, he could not entirely acquit him of blame.

At the very least, he was responsible for stealing the letters – this was how he had learned that Clarence was not his nephew. Luke was also to blame for his complicity. If Daniel had not actually seen him place the note on the mantle, he might well believe it was Clarence who had written it in a fit of rage. But anything was possible when you had a misguided allegiance to a parent.

What was very nearly as bad was that there *were* undeniable, albeit small, changes in Clarence. The regret in his eyes. This new uneasiness, this hating his past behaviour and wishing, by reclaiming his former relationship, to set all to right. Daniel must feel compassion for anyone first experiencing that. Knowing you had been the author of your own misery was not a pleasant place to be. Some part of him did wish to help him through this. Clarence, of course, would only confuse the extended hand as a wish to resume their relationship.

Then there was Luke. Daniel turned the dahlia in his hands, accusing himself again for its being far too paltry an offering considering his great wish to begin afresh. Yet anything more from him would feel obscene and presumptuous. As a receiver, simple gifts had always meant the most. He'd been twenty minutes walking the garden, enjoying his imaginings of Luke when he took the flower – surely his first from a man. Even if he responded with incredulity, it would be a first – and Daniel longed to accompany him through every new thing which lay ahead. God knew he had mishandled one first Luke was unlikely to forget or forgive. But it would be a mistake to let anger at himself prevent him from attempting a new start.

Luke deserved to know not so much that Daniel was sorry, but that happiness between men was possible. Instead, he'd bent him over the desk and had him like a common whore, afterwards tossing a demand in his face rather than twenty quid. When Luke had turned to him afterwards, he had appeared a glass-blown figurine – hot, still pliable as young men so briefly were before the world hardened them. Before societal expectations, as much as experience, taught them to become something meaner than their potential. Daniel had lit the flame, blowing him into the shape best suited to his desire. Then, he had withdrawn, leaving him unfinished, incomplete. And anyone left incomplete by a lover or a parent or anyone who'd had the power to shape them, would seek to fill that void with something, anything, rather than remain as they had been left.

When the coach arrived at the Morley house, he observed that the front door had been left ajar. Inside he could see shapes, or at least one womanly and bustling shape, walking back and forth, to and fro. Given the general upheaval in the town, he had been unsurprised to discover the drapery closed until further notice. As Luke must now be at home, it would be more difficult to speak to him privately. Be that as it may, he *would* find a way to speak to him. He plucked off a couple of offending petals, then slipped the flower into an inner breast pocket.

As he had supposed, it was Mrs Morley crossing back and forth in the vestibule. When she opened the door fully, he observed from her manner she had been expecting someone else. However, her shriek of delight upon seeing him brooked no room for regrets.

"Mr Thornton! My dear man, how *very* kind of you to pay us a visit! We are all in an uproar! But rest assured, dear, sweet Bridget has been left very nearly unscathed! Do you know it was your own Mrs Edwards who saved her from dashing her head against a cartwheel?"

"*My* Mrs Edwards?" said Daniel, somewhat bewildered as Margaret seized him with one hand, held up the tresses of her gown with the other, then swept them down the corridor toward the back of the house.

"From the Park, yes, your own. Of course, everyone is saying that Philip Forsyth was the true hero of the event. He beat that manservant to a pulp, just as he was about to attack Eliza Ringwald. Then he swept her into his arms and leapt with over the melee to safety. Just like in a romance! And now here you are, come to see how we all are. I was at the door expecting my son Stephen, you know. He's gone to fetch our Luke back from jail, but—"

"Excuse me – *jail*?"

"Yes, it was due to some confusion in all the chaos; you know none of my children has ever come within a mile of the jail. Luke was a hero in his own right, tackling that same manservant I told you about. The man was trying to steal an apronful of buns from Mrs Michaels."

"An apronful of buns?"

"Yes, indeed. But as I say, it was Philip who actually pummelled that blackguard. Only I suppose he appeared so dazzling with Eliza in his arms that the constable didn't like to interrupt them, and so took Luke to jail instead. Quite a scene, by all accounts – they say it will be in the London papers. It is our *turn*, they say. Only imagine! But, of course, that is nothing to you, Mr Metropolitan Man! But, as I say, Stephen was only just off to fetch Luke back, so I knew it was too early to expect them back. But still, a mother will hover about the door regardless. And I was well rewarded for my agitations, for I saw you immediately you came striding up my stoop!"

They were by then in the back parlour. Bridget was sitting on a settee speaking with Sophia. Evy was on a large sofa with Cecilia and Maria. Upon the entrance of Daniel, Maria became flustered as one does understanding every eye is upon her. After a significant look from her mother, Maria rose and, curtsying to the newcomer, urged Evy and Cecilia to join her in another room. With some agitation, she told them she must speak to them privately about a certain *beau*, who had begun harassing her again after a slight misunderstanding at the ball had made it appear he was neglecting her.

Daniel understood something in this had been meant for him and was happy to be rid of her. Yet his first questions could not be about Luke once he observed the state of Bridget. He had understood her part in the scuffle to be quite minor, so he was dismayed to find a prominent gash on her arm which Sophia's intervention had not prevented. Stepping forward, he asked how she was feeling. She immediately released the hand of her friend. Then, sitting up, she smiled brighter upon seeing him than he might have supposed, dismissing the gash on her arm as nothing.

Daniel blushed under her gaze. He felt Mrs Morley's eyes boring into his back. Even Sophia was looking at him with an undisguised expectation for her friend. His recent interview with John was, of course, common knowledge in the house. Yet, he had given it scarcely a thought before stepping inside. Now, the expectation for Bridget was so palpable and his belief that Luke would do nothing to stop the marriage plan so certain, that, without thinking, he withdrew the dahlia from his inner pocket and offered it to her.

For a time, he could only just attend to the things that passed – the thanks, the sighs for the beautiful flower and for a man who had been so thoughtful. The combined power of their expectation had completely overwhelmed him. He was shocked. He hadn't felt such fierce pressure to conform since university. Yet, playing the gallant was so ingrained in him, he should have anticipated this. God knew even Miss Williams had been too much for him. Bridget wished the union; this was obvious from her manner. She was justified in wishing this, insofar as she wished a good marriage. She possessed everything a sensible man would wish for in a wife. Her friend, her mother, were justified in wishing it for her.

Setting the flower across her lap, she smiled shyly at him. There was something decidedly arch in the look, but there was an equal part of shyness – in this Daniel saw her brother so clearly it nearly made him ill.

She said, "Sophia has been telling me all about you, Mr Thornton."

Clearing his throat, he looked at the lady. "Has she?"

"About you and your uncle," she continued. "The great amount of time you spend caring for him each day."

Sophia took her hand and squeezed it.

Daniel said rather stiffly, "I had supposed all that was common knowledge by now."

"Not the particulars," was all Bridget would say to this. Then, Daniel said something bland he could not later recall. He was angry. Yet whom was he angry with? He had been completely taken in; he *felt* he had been. The gash on Bridget's arm, her happiness upon seeing him. Mrs Morley, nearly throwing her daughter at him. Sophia, selling what she saw as his qualifying characteristics. Yet *his* task, as the victim of blackmail, for God's sake, was to resist and be indignant. To scheme to find a way out of this forced marriage. Christ, it was like he was a fellow conspirator.

When Stephen at last arrived with his brother, they were all seated and having tea. Daniel hardly knew how much time had elapsed, hardly could recall anything he had said to Mrs Morley or her daughter as he had been speaking entirely by rote. At the arrival of the two young men, he stirred from his numbness. He glanced at the flower, which was of course now proudly displayed next to the tea set in a glass vase. His anger at himself began to rise.

Upon seeing Luke's expression, however, all such anger at himself ceased. In that moment, he understood that the flower had indeed gone to the right person. The look of horror, the look of faintness upon seeing himself, was enough to make Daniel wish he had never come into this house. His eyes quickly on the ground, Luke told his mother he was unwell then excused himself to lie down.

Daniel rose to his feet to follow him, feeling more anger in that moment than perhaps he ever had. Anger at John Morley. At himself. At everyone in this room.

He remained standing. Of course, he could not pursue Luke. He had only stood to take his leave – departing was the only option left to him.

He made a hasty excuse, then departed the house. By the time he had reached the yard, he had his handkerchief to his mouth. He told the coachman in a husky tone to set off immediately. Once he was in the carriage, he let out the one, great sob he had only just been able to contain. To be followed by all the rest.

He wept not just for what he had done to Luke. Not just because he saw himself through Luke's eyes – that coward, that bastard Luke had every reason to believe that he was. He wept for what he had done to himself. For societal pressure, for indebtedness to a favourite relation, for blackmail – for despite all of it, one still had choices in life.

There *had been* a choice. He might have refused to be blackmailed. Thrown Luke out of his study, refused to see his father. Told Erasmus of his sexual persuasion. Told him this was simply how it was for him, how it had been for as long as he could remember. How it had been when he was a teenager when they'd taken their trips, and if Erasmus turned his back on Daniel now, so be it – he was also turning his back on the boy he had saved and claimed to love. His uncle was weak, he was dependant, he was in no position to reprimand his caregiver. He would have been forced to stifle his shock and accept it. Then Daniel would have approached John Morley telling him what he had done, and if he still considered exposure to the town of Grantham, he would see him in court for libel.

Yet, he had done none of those things. He was the author of his own fate, just as Clarence had been the author of his.

Now, he must find his own way out of the hell which had become his life.

CHAPTER SEVENTEEN

B y the time Daniel reached the Park, he had recovered himself sufficiently to appear composed. He located Albert, thanked him for seeing to Erasmus while he and Sophia were out, explaining their delay and the situation in town after the riots. Then, determined to ignore the resistance he still, after twelve years, felt at approaching him with affairs of the heart, he asked if he might have the man's ear for an hour. While they spoke, he heard Sophia return, accompanied by Evy and Philip. They sat with Erasmus while Daniel sat with Collins, and afterward, though he had no clear direction forward, Daniel felt relieved to have shared his burden.

When he joined the group, he found Philip awaiting him, eager to regale them all again with his account of the incident at Ringwald's.

"I carried my sweetheart nearly to Church Street, and I intended to carry her all the way home. Her father had gone to the magistrate's office, but her mother and sister were with us, crying and exclaiming, overjoyed at my heroism! And I *would* have carried her home, but we were stopped by the Eliots in their carriage. They insisted on taking us the rest of the way. I stayed some time at the house, but everyone was exhausted. So, I told them they must all get their rest, and I would see what I could do for them at the magistrate's. It turns out nothing will be done until the militia arrive. Anyhow, I was told by no less than three people that they had seen me carrying my dear up the High Street and that it was likely I would receive a visit from the *Grantham Gazette*! Can you imagine?"

Evy said, "I was to depart tomorrow to see my own John in Yaxley. Now it seems likely he will volunteer to come here, and departing means I might actually *miss* him! So, I suppose I must wait here like a princess in a tower and see if he will come find me."

Erasmus was clapping his hands, extending them first for Evy, who came forward for a kiss, then for Philip who came up to shake his hand. Daniel was not surprised to see tears in his eyes.

"Gracious me! To see you both *so* well off. Evy, your militia man *will* come find you, have no doubt. And Philip – Eliza is one of the worthiest young ladies in town. Saucy as anything, you'll never have a dull moment with her, I assure you! And you, so lovestruck from the moment you saw her! Now you have swept her off her feet *just* as a man should do! Oh, lovely woman! To see everything coming together just as it ought. I can wish nothing more from life – this is very much *the thing*, as you young people say!"

By the end of this, Daniel found he was smiling like everyone else. He could always smile at absurdity and what seemed almost providentially poor timing. Any lingering thoughts of confronting Erasmus tonight and confessing his nature to him had been quite done away with. Yet once the party had departed and he was preparing his uncle for supper, the man said he wished to have a talk now the others had departed. He was giving his nephew one of those old, worried looks he used to give him when he had just arrived for a visit after some trouble with his parents.

"Sit down. I wish to speak to you." Daniel sat, feeling more the fifteen-year-old than ever. "I am not yet so senile I cannot recognise distress when I see it. I see more than you think I see. And, well, people talk. You can always count on people to talk."

Frowning, Daniel nodded, supposing it best to say nothing until he had understood what this was about.

"Much as we might wish to, we cannot always please the people we love – or rather, we do not *think* that we can. You believe that despite all you've done for me since the stroke, you still owe me for the time you spent with me as a young person. And, yes, I did intervene when your father wished you to go into the military, something you have always made far too much of. Those little gifts I gave you when you were a young man newly in London, struggling to live within your budget, were no more than many others would have done had you confessed to them you were struggling. As many times as I have told you that I do *not* wish to be thanked, you continue to do so. I am *fortunate*, Daniel. I am in a position in life which has allowed me to be generous when I can be, and still you wish to repay me. Who knows – I might feel the same in your shoes, though I think not."

Daniel smiled.

"But people do talk, as I say. And this includes yourself – I see this surprises you. I know we had visitors in the house yesterday. John Morley, a gentleman tradesman, visited on behalf of his daughter, a young lady by the name of Bridget. '*Bridget, did you say?*' I asked the moment I was informed, though I will not say by whom. Then, I said to myself, '*This must be the same Bridget Daniel danced two reels with at the ball. Daniel told me of this just before I began chiding him for dancing the same number of reels with Miss Williams.*' So, I manoeuvred and learned by way of a few questions that Miss Morley is a beautiful young lady of seventeen. Lovely, flowing dark hair, a great reader, with a good heart and many other lovely attributes. And so, I said to myself, '*Ah, Erasmus, you old* fool. *Daniel has feared telling you of this because of your preoccupation with Miss Williams.*' And so, I wish to apologise to you. I wish to apologise for being a little... no, I fear far too zealous."

"Please, don't apologise—"

"Well, I did already, and I won't take it back. I won't *again*, I see no need for that – not for having good intentions and wishing the best for you."

Despite the man's rather tragic misunderstanding, Daniel could not help but chuckle and take his hand. He turned it and kissed the palm, then held the man's cold extremity to his cheek.

"I had, Daniel, rather presumptuously assumed you were needing my assistance. It seemed to me that since arriving, you weren't going out nearly enough. How on earth could you meet anyone when you never went out, and I still don't entirely know. That is because you are a gentleman. Every bit the gentleman I always knew you would grow up to be. And a gentleman never tells. You are so handsome and debonair, I never doubted you always enjoyed your fair share of company in London. *Perhaps*," he added, patting his nephew's cheek before withdrawing his hand, "sowing a few wild oats and not wishing your uncle to think poorly of you. But now you are a bit older. You are seeking a life mate, just when a man should do. No need to advertise what you are doing. I *understand* you. I assure you I could not be happier for you."

Daniel thanked him. He could feel nothing but pleasure from this, nothing but gratitude when the man continued, "I will resolve the matter with Miss Williams. I've made a damn mess of things, but I will make it right. She *is* a lovely young woman, as you know, and I am sorry I must now beg her forgiveness. And, I'm afraid, the forgiveness of her parents. I said far too much. But I will handle it, don't give it another thought."

This shouldn't have been much, indeed any, comfort. Yet it was. Daniel still believed he should speak to the man about himself, somehow, at some time. Tonight was clearly not the night, but he took some courage from the man's apology. It was not unwarranted – in small ways, Miss Williams had begun to come between them. Daniel had occasionally been more abrupt than he should have been. The instances were too trivial to have rated comment from either of them, yet he had begun to wonder when these seeds of irritation would sprout into resentment. It was a relief, a small relief, during a state of agitation in which any relief was welcome.

Once he had put Erasmus to bed, he searched out Collins again. Albert was in his dressing gown and gestured him to an armchair. Once he was seated, however, Daniel found he hadn't an idea what he wished to say.

"Oh, dear. You *are* in a bad way."

"Yes, I am." When Collins smiled, he continued, "Please don't laugh at me."

"I would never laugh at you, sir. You are laughing at yourself."

"I am?"

"You have surprised yourself."

It was a moment before Daniel understood what he meant. Surprised that he was ready to move on from Clarence, God help him it had only taken six months. Shaking his head somewhat helplessly, he said, "But *must* it be under these circumstances?"

"That is a question for the Fates, not your valet. It would seem so. In all our years together, I've never known you to be like this about a man. You will say you were with Clarence, but that should be the last of your involvements I should compare this to. You fell for his arts, in my opinion. You wished to see him as good, and the relationship fell apart when he could no longer conceal his true nature. With Luke, he has come out and declared his guilt, his bad nature, yet you believe him to be concealing goodness. You see it, sense it, I don't pretend to understand, but I believe you see what you see."

"Thank you, Albert."

"I remind you again that before we came to Grantham, you declared you wished to find the goodness in the world. Did you expect it to be easy?"

Daniel narrowed his eyes. "You know, I'm tired of you having all the realisations that I should be having. Why didn't you remind me of this before? No, don't say it. You'll say something sage about when the student is ready, and I'll look even more the fool."

CHAPTER EIGHTEEN

"**L** uke!"

"Let him go!" shouted Bridget.

"Luke!" repeated his father from the top of the stairwell. "Come back upstairs and speak to your sister!"

Stephen reached his brother in the vestibule and caught his arm.

"I'm going to the shop tonight."

"Speak to Papa before you go, Luke. Be a man and speak to him, then go if you must."

Their father was soon thudding down the stairs with Bridget in tow. "*G— Almighty and S— in his Inferno*! Go in there, Bridge, and face your brother!"

"I faced him in his room already, and this has been the outcome."

"You both tell me now what has happened between you," said John. "Out with it!"

"I'll tell you," said his daughter, "since my brother hasn't two words to say for himself unless they are to attack me. Luke said he was ill after Stephen brought him home and was all afternoon laying down in his room. When I went up to ask how he was, he began demanding to know if I was going to marry Mr Thornton. Accusing me of... of I don't know what, actually. The trouble seemed to be that I wished to be happy."

John turned to his younger son. "Do you wish your sister to be happy?"

"*Are* you going to marry Thornton?" said Luke.

When Bridget merely swept her hair around one shoulder and looked at him, Stephen lowered his voice to a whisper, still audible to all, "You are *embarrassing* her, Luke. With affairs of the heart, *delicate* affairs, Lord Stanhope as always advised—"

"*Will* you marry him," said Luke, his eyes continuing to hold hers.

Bridget shook her head. "I thought I knew you."

"Everett thought he knew you."

John looked between them. "Everett? George? What has he to do with this?"

"Nothing," said Luke savagely. "We were in a cell together today and with nowhere to go, I got him to speak at last. He was two hours crying his eyes out because he loves you. He fears he isn't rich enough for you, and you'd never fight to have someone of his standing in society."

Bridget looked appalled. "Luke, he never said that. He *wouldn't*—"

"So, I defended you. I said anyone could see you are mad for him, and you are just the kind of girl who would stand up to her parents and demand to have what she wants. But you aren't, Bridget. Are you?"

"*Everett?*" said John, turning to his daughter. "George Everett, your little friend? Has he proposed to you?"

At this, Bridget went uncharacteristically red and shook her head.

John returned to his son. "Everett is no proper match for your sister. You wish her to marry Thornton; you told your mother and me you wished it."

"It doesn't matter what I wish," said Luke. As there was no immediate response, he saw his opening and exited the house.

He was at the front gate when Stephen caught up with him. "Please don't go. Please. Something must have happened to upset you. Tell me what it is. Is it to do with Jenny Paltrow?"

Luke groaned – he really should be annoyed with Stephen, always so dependably clueless. Yet what could he expect? Stephen had no idea who his brother really was. "I don't wish to marry Miss Paltrow. I don't wish to marry anyone."

Stephen appeared not to comprehend the words at first. Then, he smiled. "But that's perfectly natural. You *are* far too young to marry. An engagement would—"

"I don't wish to be engaged."

At this, Stephen appeared genuinely confused and indeed a bit grave. "What *do* you wish?"

Luke might have laughed. Such a simple question. Simple questions deserved simple answers and there were no simple answers for Luke Morley. He didn't know what he wanted, apart from wanting Daniel, whom of course he should not want. Whom he should be urging his sister to marry with all his heart through the bile rising in his throat. Beyond him, he hadn't an idea what he wished. Anyhow, nothing that was achievable. "I want to stay on in the shop, like I said before. I don't want Papa to sell. You won't remember, but he used to speak of buying a controlling interest in that drapery in Pall Mall – Harding, Howell and Co."

Requiring a moment to bring this from memory, Stephen at last said, "I remember. That was years ago, but I do recall—"

"He said to stock a London shop, we'd need to bring in all sorts of exotic textiles. We'd go on buying trips perhaps as far off as the Near East."

"I never understood you to be particularly interested in that scheme."

"I was. I was thirteen and couldn't see myself out of Grantham, but I *was* interested. I have knowledge of the business and would have liked to travel. Nothing ever came of that."

This, at least, was something Stephen could understand. And seeing that he heard him, seeing him consider his words, felt incredible. To express a wish fully and openly and know that his brother understood him felt almost impossibly good. "It *was* a good idea," said Stephen. "It made sense to consider it. But the business began doing so well about that time we hadn't the desire to risk any of the capital. Our goal has been independence, and we already had a clear path to it. By the first of next year, Papa and Uncle Pete will sell not only the business, but our contracts with the association of sheep farmers. Those are almost as valuable, and selling them is what the plan has been since we secured them. We've had many schemes over the years, of which the London interest was one. But our ultimate aim has always been to sell."

Luke nodded. "I know. I should go to the shop tonight, then, while I still can."

Appearing a bit mystified, Stephen nodded and said yes, he supposed he should.

"Will Bridget marry Thornton if he asks her? Has she spoken to anyone about it?"

Stephen looked somewhat conflicted at this question. After considering, he said in a lowered tone, "She asked that it not be spoken of to too many people, but, yes, she said she will. You believe she prefers that Everett fellow because she goes about with him. Seeing as how you became so upset on his behalf, I supposed something must have gone awry with Jenny. A man suffering a rejection empathises with another. As for Bridget, she may well like Everett more than she claims. Mamma has always said she doesn't see any of *that* interest in her eyes, but I'm willing to believe you might be right.

"The fact is, Luke, it doesn't matter. Bridget is practical. She wishes a secure future with a good and caring man, which she believes Thornton to be. She did tell Mamma she couldn't accept him until she knows him better. She wishes to see him often, spend time at the Park, so she can understand his ways and his life there. She said her friendship with Mrs Edwards will give her the perfect excuse to, well, to use her words, *to spy on him and see if he does anything revolting.* So, it isn't all about the money. She does wish a happy existence with her husband. But she also said she would be a fool to decline an offer which might not come again. If I were a betting man, I would say yes, I believe she will accept him."

***

When the bell tinkled in the shop the next morning, Luke was in the back room. The night before, understanding he had outgrown his place under the counter and all it had come to represent, he had been a couple of hours clearing an area in the back, moving around what seemed endless old bolts of fabric to make a space of about ten square feet. The dust had been horrendous, but airing and cleaning out a makeshift bedchamber had been happy occupation for a tormented mind. It also prompted occupation for the morning, as in the process of moving their stock about he determined to begin their semi-annual calculation of the inventory a bit early.

So, at the clink of the bell, Luke looked up from his notebook, considering if he should leave Jenkins, whom he'd sent up a ladder to inventory the stock in the front, to take the customer. He was only a moment, however. Jenkins was quite happy with his dusty bolts and calculations and seemed to consider the customers a necessary evil of the business. He set his notebook aside and went out.

"Hello, Luke."

Daniel stood at the entrance, the book of fabric samples he had taken to him under one arm. He took a step forward, and observing Luke had frozen in place, took a steadying breath and advanced another step.

At the questioning glance from up the ladder, Daniel said, "We spoke of replacing the drapes in a few rooms." To Luke,

"Is there a quiet place we can speak about the details?" Into the silence which answered him, he added, "Please."

Luke caught the hint of sandalwood Daniel often had about him, a smell now redolent of deep, straining arousal as he came in close from behind. Of sweat produced then burned away, diffusing its scent into the air. Of opening himself fully, trusting him not to become too violent. Then, for the briefest moments afterward, pride in what they had done – the sandalwood burned into his nose, into his skin, before Daniel began making his demands.

"How about that table over there?"

Luke agreed, then led Daniel into the far corner. As they proceeded, they passed the doorway to the haberdashery, which stood open during business hours. Uncle Pete was speaking in the loud, stagey cadences he employed when welcoming people into his shop. From what Luke could hear, Daniel's coachman was asking about a suit he'd recently brought in for an alteration. The coachman, of course, was a member of The House, whose true mission in coming inside might be to wander into the draper's side to hear what they were speaking of.

As they sat on either side of a small table, Luke reminded himself he had not been forbidden to speak to Daniel. They might speak, and indeed should so he could encourage his attentions elsewhere. He directed his gaze to the book of samples, hoping Daniel would begin there. But rather than opening it, or speaking of drapes, he merely rapped the cover absently.

At last, Daniel said, "I do wish you would look up at me. What I must appear to you I cannot—" When Luke began shifting in his seat, he said, "I understand you have full management of the shop most days. When did you begin working here?"

Maintaining his eyes on the closed book, Luke said he'd been about eight. He could feel Daniel's eyes on him, waiting for him to look up. When he did not, Daniel took this as a cue to continue this style of exchange. He asked if he enjoyed the work. Luke nodded and said he did very much.

After an extended moment, Daniel said in a lower tone, "I want to apologise for keeping your book so long." Luke looked up, why particularly at this moment he could not have said, and his companion caught his gaze. "I fear I've trampled on your generosity."

"I said you could keep it as long—"

"But a man should know, *I* should know, how long one *should* keep a thing. And when to bring something in return."

Frowning, Luke said, "I shall fetch Mr Jenkins to assist you with ordering the drapes. I must—"

"One minute more. I believe there have been some misunderstandings between us. I was told... or rather, I was led to believe some things which have made me act in what must have appeared to be a very peculiar manner." When Luke rose from the table, Daniel took his wrist. "A cruel manner. Abominably cruel. I'm sorry."

"It's alright. I shall fetch—"

"It was wrong to demand assistance from you. Both how and when I demanded it. I had reached a point of desperation, but I wish you to know that I know it was wrong. And I wish you to know you are not alone." Despite himself, Luke ceased pulling away. "You are *not* alone – in feelings which might be leaving you conflicted. I have them too. I have had most of my life. I understand what it is to feel allegiances which are against your better judgment. Allegiances to a lover. To a father. A wish to please him, whatever it takes. Even if you suspect... even if you know he is doing something wrong."

Luke frowned. What was he implying? Was he accusing his father of speaking to Erasmus? Was he still trying to have him intervene in the marriage scheme?

"You are confused. I see that and you will remain so until we can speak more at length. Out here, I know you do not wish to. Can we go somewhere?"

Luke shook his head and looked toward the shop assistant.

"I will speak to Mr Jenkins about the drapes," said Daniel. "We would like to replace the drapes, that was not a pretence for coming. But is there anything... anything else you might wish to tell me? Anything you might like me to know? Anything at all?"

Keeping his eyes averted, "I wish for things to progress as they ought. I wish you to marry and be happy. I wish *not* to interfere."

Swallowing, Daniel attempted to recapture his gaze. When he did, Luke saw he was dismayed. But this was soon replaced by a look of determination to accept the response.

"Very well. Thank you for telling me. I would have preferred to hear something about yourself. I scarcely know you and am seeking ways to remedy this. What you like, don't like. What you might wish for."

This was not exactly a question. But coming on the heels of Stephen's asking him this, Luke felt the bitterness at his inability to speak all the more. He said, "What I wish is to get as far away from this town as possible."

Daniel sighed. Then, he nodded and rose from his seat. Before he proceeded to Jenkins, he stepped before Luke and forced him to meet his gaze.

"A person can always run. But you will not get far if you cannot accept, if you cannot recognise, help when it is offered. You've prevented us from speaking as I would have liked to speak. It is certainly your prerogative whether you wish to hear everything that I have to say. But Luke, you should never silence yourself."

CHAPTER NINETEEN

"I *am so very sorry, Clarence. Here we are in Brighton, on our holiday, and we, I, have allowed a slight difference of opinion to come between us. We should be together enjoying ourselves in this lovely place, not in different hotel rooms sending notes. You said some harsh words that hurt me greatly. But I know, deep down, you do not mean them. You've always had a passionate nature. I've always loved and will always love that about you. You are all I have ever wanted; all anyone could ever want – not just for who you are, but for your tremendous potential. My love for you is boundless. Take my hand – let us realise* our *potential, together."*

Clarence looked up from the note to his audience of two.

"Very pretty," said his mother. After nudging her husband, the man made an appreciative noise.

"Among all Daniel's writings to me, and he did write some very long, adoring letters, I treasure this note the most. It was written after an argument, the only one of its kind that I still possess. Undying love is expressed in each line. And I recall distinctly when we reunited, he presented me with a single, long-stemmed rose. Just one, perfect specimen. That is what he likes – taste and simplicity. We needn't send something so obscene."

"Do return to your sickbed, Clarey," said his mother. "Your father is fully on board with our plans now. He wrote an excellent note to rid you of your rival, and I support him completely in our next move."

"You might at least have let me read the damned thing before you sent it."

"Oh, poo."

He turned to his father. "I do hope you were not too harsh on the little bugger. I would prefer Daniel return to me for his great and undying love, not because he has been rejected. What did you write?"

"I addressed him," said Charles, "the way one must address his class when seeking to achieve an aim. You have your parents now, son – heaven-sent and the answer to your prayers as you declared the moment we arrived. You must allow us to do things our way. Our way has the great advantage of objectivity. Your way saw you ejected from the Park, shipwrecked with drink and crapulous for days. Incidentally, I agree with your mother that you do look tired and really should lie down."

"I'm sick to death of my sickbed! I'm sick to death of..." he looked at the two but left the remainder unsaid. "I'm going out."

"Out?" said His Lordship. "I would strongly advise against it. You might be attacked; the common folk have run amok!"

"If I leave my necklace of honey cakes on my vanity, I expect I'll survive."

"Understand: it always *starts* with food demands. It is always food with them; you saw that across the Channel. Then they develop a taste for heads on pikes!"

"Oh, Charles, *do* spare us the image!"

"An image speaks a thousand words, Edwina. And a present, an appropriate present after a quarrel, does the same. Thirteen bouquets to represent each month Clarey and Thornton were... together. Thirteen boxes of pastries and goods from the bakery ordered privately at an obscene price. It's taken all day to organise those after these robberies, requiring our carriage to fetch in grain for milling from a local storehouse – we shall put all that in the note to Thornton. I predict Bainbridge Park will be deprived of many such things after these riots. The word we wish Thornton to associate with the Hoppers is *bounty*. Endless bounty. That is what he shall enjoy so long as he remains loyal to his class."

Clarence summoned his father's valet and exited to his bedchamber. A cussed mistake to have read out that note to them. A mistake to begin rereading all the letters again after hearing such a difference in Daniel's most recent. But his mother had made such a damned fuss about it, she should have adored a note from when they had been together. Her face, when he'd read it, had simply confirmed it *was* a note from when they had been together. Had been.

He began dressing, closing the door when his parents welcomed the florist. The valet was tying his cravat when Clarence noticed what appeared to be Daniel's coach down the street, just outside Morley's Drapery and Haberdashery. When he came to the window to make absolutely certain, he observed Daniel just then ascending. As quickly as he could, he tugged on his heeled slippers and exited their rooms. He ran down the flights to the street only to see the coach pulling away.

"Of course. How fittingly ungenteel of him," he said, out of breath, wishing to do something to show his contempt but having nothing to throw or spittle enough to spit.

But wait – Luke had received that note from his father. Clarence had only glimpsed the back of Daniel as he was getting into the coach, but was it possible his visit had not gone as he'd hoped? Had there been a scowl on his face? Disgust? Tears? He had a quick look at himself in a window, touching his hair in place in the breeze of a brisk day tautening with thoughts of autumn. Then, he proceeded to Morley's.

"May I help you?" asked a sour-faced man descending a ladder who introduced himself as Mr Jenkins.

"I wish to speak with Luke. Is he here?"

Appearing to take this as a personal slight, Jenkins went grudgingly into the back room. After a moment he reappeared and said, looking rather pleased, that he was displeased to inform him that he had been mistaken and that Mr Morley had just departed. Clarence then demanded to know where he was going, what were his usual hours in the shop, had Jenkins himself assisted the gentleman who had just departed in the coach? Before anything in the interrogation could be addressed, the door to the back opened once more, and Luke emerged.

"Ah, I see you must have forgotten something and so just returned," said Jenkins, his expression souring just that bit more.

Looking tired, Luke said, "I asked Mr Jenkins to lie and tell anyone calling that I wasn't in." Then, nodding to the front door. "I was about to step out."

"Let us step out together, then."

Exiting onto the High Street, they continued south. They remained silent for a time. Each observed unhappiness in the other, each observed fatigue. When they took a table in the corner of a noisy coffee shop, bustling with talk of the riots, Clarence understood Luke was doing what he was rather late to do, which might bode well – he was assessing him like he wished to discover what Daniel had seen in him. Clarence took up his coffee, enjoying that first sip, enjoying as well the boy's jealous assessment, both of which helped to warm his chill bones. At last, he said, "I observe your lover continues to make you miserable."

Nodding, Luke said, "I never supposed being with Dan— sorry, being with General George Ev—"

"Oh, enough of that," cried Clarence. "I *know* whom you are speaking of! Use his real name, for the love of God!" Realising he had perhaps overreacted, Clarence expelled a huffy breath, then took a moment to touch a speck from his eye. This boy was *such* a manipulator. How the hell was he supposed to attack someone who looked like a child who had just dropped his syllabub into the mud?

You've always had a passionate nature, Clarence. I've always loved and will always love that about you. He must take heart from these words. There *was* a lot to love. He *was* fiery, *was* passionate which made him a fabulous lover. Luke was a confused little fledging scarcely out of his shell. Now he had been shouted at, he had retreated again to silently assess his rival.

At last, deciding he must toss the boy some bone, Clarence said, "*Arrêtez, s'il vous plaît!* I positively shrink under your merciless assessment of me. Rest assured, we are both good looking men, else Daniel would never entertain us. But you *are* younger, so I suppose you win in that regard."

When Luke simply nodded, Clarence said, "You needn't agree so quickly. My bone structure is far better than yours – that is what matters when one ages."

"Alright."

"You needn't agree with that so condescendingly, either. Daniel had many fawning little cherubs before he met me. There's no novelty in it for him, I assure you. It is only ephemera."

Luke frowned, then after a dry swallow, sipped his coffee.

Clarence narrowed his eyes. "And so, you are miserable but are still dead set upon pursuing him."

"I can't pursue him."

Clarence waited for him to look up again before he responded. "Can't you? Why not?"

"I was threatened by someone from The House. I was told Daniel should pursue other interests and that things should proceed as they ought."

"Is that what you told him just now?"

Luke nodded. "I am not..." He paused for a word. "I am not welcome at the Park. People there want Daniel to marry. My presence makes them angry."

"Because you are a tradesman. Ah, well, what can one do?"

Luke appeared confused. "A tradesman?"

"Well, yes. Sorry, isn't that what you meant? If you hadn't considered this, I'm sorry to say you probably should." Lowering his voice, he continued, "Oh, dear. You've been attributing it all to your sex. That, of course, *is* a problem. But your *class,* my dear..." Clarence tut-tutted. Luke looked off toward the ceiling, as though the idea had momentarily dazed him. When his eyes returned to his companion, when he simply nodded, Clarence understood that might have been the nastiest thing he had ever done. *You have so much potential, Clarence. Such tremendous potential.* He cleared his throat. "I *did* just tell you how handsome you are. Very pretty indeed."

Appearing not to hear him, Luke remained lost in thought.

"That note you received," continued Clarence. "It was about your romantic interests, then? It told you not to distract him from his other romantic interests?"

"It said Daniel and I were unclean Pathics, that my father would be told, and that I was interfering in people's plans."

Laughing, Clarence was a moment shaking his head. Then, he was another moment deciding how he must have misunderstood him. "You dramatic boy! It did not say 'unclean', surely. You were just upset to receive the thing."

However, Luke was on an inner train of thought and said only, "I wonder at myself sometimes. If Daniel cannot say no to my father, or to his uncle, or to whoever is pressuring him to marry, why do I still want him? He attempted to make amends and offer me advice just now. He did apologise for asking me to intervene with my father. He told me I shouldn't run away from my problems, shouldn't silence myself, and he's right. But hasn't he done the same? He is being pushed into a marriage because he refuses to say he doesn't want it. That's cowardly."

A moment was required to respond; Clarence shouldn't have been surprised at his father's words, at his mother's complicity. Yet, it had stung.

Then, he resumed his attack: "You are learning that Daniel is weak. That is why I was good for him. You see, although you might not guess it having observed the delicate, sinewy lines of me, I *am* strong in many ways – ways that he is not." His attempt to lighten the mood appeared entirely lost, so he said, "Is it likely your sister will accept him?"

For the first time, Luke appeared agitated. "Yes. She loves someone else, or I thought she did. But she is practical. Daniel is a good man, and wealthy. I'm not a monster; I do want her to be happy. She only wishes to help herself."

"Perhaps she'll marry him to help herself *and* her lover."

"What do you mean?"

"Have you never heard of such things? They do happen, I assure you. A marriage for financial gain. All the time the devious member of the pair is using the money to put up their lover, who is *always* impoverished, in a little love nest. Rarely good for any involved, of course. It usually ends with one, sometimes two, of the three dead in a ditch somewhere. That is why it kills me that Daniel cannot see to let me back into his life just yet. I just know I could put a stop to all this marriage nonsense. Be honest: you'd hate to see him with your sister – what is her name?"

"Bridget."

"You'd hate to see him with Bridget, wouldn't you?"

Clarence leant back at seeing a look of anger the boy had just a moment before seemed scarcely capable of. "*Yes.* She already *has* a lover. If she chose to, she *could* approach my parents about marrying him. It is her *choice* to pursue someone else. I have *no* choice! Daniel and I are—"

Clarence raised a brow. "*Daniel and I,* is it? You speak as though you two are an established thing—"

"Bloody hell! How *do* I say it, then?"

"—and you are *not* an established thing. I've had a belch last longer."

"If she marries him, I could scarcely look at her. I *would* hate to see her with him. I'd almost rather see you..." He shook his head.

Clarence was duly comprehending and, for a time, encouraged this line of thought. He spoke of Daniel's weaknesses and the powerful sway the public expectation to marry could have on such a person, viciously adding the likelihood of a child within the first year. By the time they departed the coffee shop, Luke had fallen silent.

He intended to return to the shop through the alleyway entrance. Clarence offered to walk him, feeling their interview was drawing to a premature close. Progress had been made, though he could have wished for a more categorical dismissal of Daniel. By all accounts, Luke had done what the note had instructed. Yet, somehow, it didn't seem nearly enough. It would not do to let the enemy too far from his sights, so he said, "I'll come round tomorrow, shall I? Will you be here?"

"Why?"

Clarence smiled. "Because *I* am not a monster, either. I have been where you are, and I understand that in a place like Grantham, there are likely few with whom to speak about such things."

"There's nobody."

"There you are. My parents are driving me mad, and I must get away when I can. And, despite our differences, and our unfortunately similar interests, you and I *are* in a kind of brotherhood. One must have someone to speak to. And I like speaking to you."

Luke looked at his shoes. "I do, too. I mean, I must still be against you. And I would rather you were unhappy than have what you wish. But, aside from that, you know…"

Still smiling, Clarence tilted Luke's face upwards with a finger as though telling him to buck up. Just beyond him, Clarence observed through the open alleyway door what appeared to be a makeshift bedchamber. The lost little lamb appeared to have made a bed in there, running from home to avoid his sister in all likelihood. He leant forward. As he did, he observed Luke's eyes expand. And though the boy drew back slightly, Clarence had him cornered – his aim surely would have been accomplished had he not, at the last moment, doubled up to take his shin in his hand.

"Leg cramp, sorry," he said, stumbling a bit for effect.

"I have a chair if you want to come in and sit down for a moment."

"No. Quite alright. I've been in bed so much the last few days I'm beginning to atrophy. Don't mind me."

***

It was a devilish business. What had Daniel ever done to prepare for this? Sitting at the Morley dinner table, directly across from a host who was blackmailing him. The man who was raising a glass of raisin wine in a toast to new moons and new connections. Surrounded by his family, one member of which Daniel was now officially courting. Another he dearly wished to. Two siblings who were sitting as far from one another as possible, making it something of an effort to divide his attention between them.

Luke was eating little, appearing as though he wished to jump from the table and run up to his bedchamber – in short, looking absolutely miserable. Daniel would have liked to tell him of the obscene bouquets and boxes of baked goods he had received shortly before departing for the dinner. He could have told him Clarence's gross offering had been promptly sent to the militia for redistribution. Then, he could have told him the gifts had been accompanied by an invitation to sup at The George, dinner to be ordered in where they might enjoy what was termed *complete security*.

Then, he would tell him of his note declining the invitation in favour of another to be hosted by a local tradesman.

It was the kind of thing Luke would have enjoyed; Daniel knew him sufficiently to know this. Had they spoken at the shop as they should have done, they might have shared this. But they had not spoken. His heart broke for Luke, no doubt forced to attend this dinner to support his sister, regretting whatever part he had played to organise it. He didn't know if he had ever seen anyone as alone – despite the warmth of his family, he appeared almost completely isolated from them. But Daniel had said all he could think to say at the shop. He would make one more move to reach him before the night was over. Until then, Luke must work things through for himself.

Daniel turned his eyes to Bridget. She had such an easy, assured way about her. From the moment he'd given her the dahlia, he was certain she could have no idea what had been done to oblige the connection. And Margaret, whose occasional slips into vulgarity were too braced with a hearty, good-natured energy – she could never be less than winning. Her other children behaved without a hint of self-consciousness. He could not believe any of them knew of the blackmail.

And, God help him, he was beginning to have his doubts about John. As they drank their wine and chatted, Daniel very nearly forgot himself and the situation he had been put in – the situation he believed he had been put in. John *was* gruff, no doubt he could be a bit devious. He had a kind of earthy charm which made him appear unsophisticated until one sat down to talk business with him. This, no doubt, had served him well. He might be capable of blackmail if he thought it would promote one of his children.

Yet where had been the need? A marriage by blackmail was nothing short of degrading to the young woman he saw before him. Her family were nearing independence. She was exceptionally well-spoken and engaging, more so the longer you knew her. She spoke with a great deal of candour, had decided views on Fanny Burney, quoted Dr Johnson. As for the food riots, she had little to say concerning her own experience – she spoke instead of the national trend and a solution currently under consideration which sought to tie a minimum worker's wage to the cost of essentials like grain.

He sensed something else in her, always present but particularly strong tonight. Her heart seemed so clearly to be elsewhere. This had struck him at the ball – a curious unconcernedness which had instantly put him at ease and made it easy to approach her. It was not a question of coldness or confidence. Where were the nerves she should have sitting down with the suitor her parents intended for her to marry? If there was a way through this mess, if he was able to back out of this marriage arrangement, he felt certain her heart would not be broken from any pining or lingering thoughts of himself.

A hint came when they were finishing the main course. A knock sounded at the front door. Bridget leapt up as though she had been expecting it. Once she had departed, there was a strangely silent reception in the vestibule. This was followed by a slightly shrill call for her mother – a call which was answered by both her parents. Once they had reached her, sobbing was heard, not from the family but from what sounded to be a young man. After a passionate exchange and

Mrs Morley's raised voice assuring him he must *hush all that, of course he was welcome here*, John Morley led the visitor upstairs. Before they were entirely out of earshot, Daniel was alarmed to hear John order a servant to fetch a couple of towels.

After some time speaking to each other in the vestibule, Mrs Morley led Bridget, who appeared quite shaken, back to the table. Once she was seated, Margaret Morley took her guest's hand. "I must apologise, Daniel. A friend of Bridget's has had a fight with his father. You may have heard of the Everetts. Parents are drunkards, violent. He asked to stay the night here," she looked at her daughter, "and of course he may. He will stay as long as he needs to. Had we understood just how bad it had become for him at home, we certainly would have extended our hand earlier. I am indeed sorry we did not." This was accompanied by a pat on her daughter's forearm.

For the first time during the meal, Luke was looking up. His eyes were on Bridget, who steadfastly did not return his gaze. Then, he turned to Daniel with a look which was both expressive and unreadable. Daniel understood this to be the opening to speak of what he'd wished to. The family would be grateful to him for taking the reins at this potentially awkward moment. John's being out of the room was a benefit as he hadn't intended to speak of this in quite so personal a manner. Now, he understood no other way.

He spoke of once being at a crossroads in his life, just as Bridget's friend George appeared to be at. He spoke of a rather unhappy childhood, though by no means fraught with the kind of violence George was subjected to. His parents simply hated one another and were not of a station to pursue a divorce. Their outlet had been to use their children as pawns against each other. So, at the age of nine he had run away, thinking he would spend his nights in a neighbour's barn, living off eggs and milk and whatever he could gather from the garden.

Though this was primarily for Luke, whose attention he was pleased to see was undivided, he spoke as well to Bridget and her mother.

"I am grateful to my parents for one thing, at least," he continued. "Whether it was from wisdom, which they never showed in any other facet of our lives, or merely from frustration, they sent me for a summer with my uncle. Erasmus never had children of his own; his wife, whom he had lost and had adored more than life, I understand was unable. He welcomed me with open arms. He said he had heard I liked to travel – would I perhaps like to see something farther away than the neighbour's barn? I told him I *was* seeing something beyond the barn, I had come to Grantham, hadn't I? He said that was quite true, and he had also heard I was a very smart young man, and so I was proving to be.

"But what about travelling someplace a bit farther off? Had I heard of Italy? Yes, I had. What about Naples? I believed I had. What about Greece, the birthplace of civilisation? Yes, I had certainly heard of Greece, but that was on the other side of the world. This he poo-poohed and said the other side of the world wasn't so very far. Then he popped a drachma into my hand and said all I would need was a bit of the local currency, which is what a drachma was, and most importantly, someone to guide me through it."

Luke's eyes never strayed from him. Daniel continued to feel them when he returned to Margaret. "Your taking in your daughter's friend is something he will remember all his life. Over the course of eight years, my uncle took me all over this island as well as around the Continent. I saw everything, indeed more, by the age of sixteen than many a young man sees on his Grand Tour. Yet it is not the sights I recall so much as first being accepted into Bainbridge Park – into his home when I needed it so much. It really doesn't matter where George goes from here. What matters is that he has a place to start from."

Smiling, Bridget thanked him and wiped away a tear. Mrs Morley had a handkerchief to her face. Then, Daniel felt a hand on his shoulder. John Morley said in his ear, "Doesn't surprise me at all. Erasmus Thornton is a fine man. Just like his nephew."

John then suggested that his guest join him in his study to speak privately. Daniel took a moment before he said, "Yes, John. I believe it is time we do."

Now was the time to understand. He would, God help him, ask what he needed to ask. A confirmation of what he feared would likely produce a question as to the soundness of his mind – perhaps not so bad as a move to escape a forced marriage. A discovery of innocence, however, uncovered with a few tactfully worded questions, would save them both from considerable embarrassment. If need be, he would just come right out and ask. But one way or another, he would understand for certain.

Luke was moving toward the staircase when Daniel asked John if he could have a quick word with his son. To his dismay, the man, patting him heartily on the back, assured he most certainly could and called for Luke to join them.

Trying to ignore the man he had better damn be able to acquit after the torment he was putting him through, Daniel extended a hand to his son, quickly rewording what he needed to say.

Luke took his hand hesitantly, aware, as Daniel was, that this was their first physical contact since their dreadful separation in the library. Daniel gripped him a bit tighter and, as he did, he watched Luke's expression change from unease to confusion. Daniel covered their hands with his and held his eye.

"Each day I have left with my uncle, every word he says, every gift he ever gave me – those are the things most precious to me. It was a pleasure to speak tonight of my past with him. I wished particularly to speak of my travels to you as I understand you have a passion to travel one day. My door is open, day or night, rain or shine, should you ever wish my advice."

As he released him, he turned Luke's hand upward to be certain he retained the drachma he had placed there. Luke immediately closed his hand and put it to his side. He looked into Daniel's eyes. And Daniel smiled, certain he saw a bit of light touch those inner places again – places which were so often shut to the world. He held his gaze for just a moment more, for as long as he dared.

Then, he turned to his father and told him he was ready to speak with him in private.

CHAPTER TWENTY

"Fucking Clarence."

That the next day would be one of the longest of Daniel's life he might have expected. Spells of acute dizziness from his sleepless night had left him without any clear direction by morning. The only thing capable of grounding him, albeit temporarily, were two words which, when put together, conveyed the happiness, the outrage, the incomprehension, the sheer insanity that had been, and indeed continued to be, his life.

"*Fucking Clarence.*"

Daniel had burst from John Morley's study, unable to contain his wild joy. Just a few carefully worded questions had been all that was needed to understand the man knew nothing about any old love letters, nothing about any blackmail note – scarcely anything at all, it seemed! John Morley was perfection in his ignorant bliss!

Ignorant though he was, however, he had explained one lingering point of confusion. In taking the private moment to thank Daniel for the interest in his son, he made clear that the note requesting the interview had been entirely Luke's doing. Daniel was heartened, and indeed a bit sick, upon learning that Luke had written numerous drafts of the request over the course of a couple of hours. The note Daniel had only skimmed to confirm there were no additional demands was, of course, the note Luke had insisted he had written.

Learning that he had departed to sleep in the shop, which his mother insisted was not unusual behaviour, had confirmed what Daniel knew he should do, which was to leave him with his own thoughts this evening. Regardless of what he had learned, he had done everything he could do to offer himself to Luke Morley.

Now, in the light of a new day, he paced about any room he found himself in, drawn to the nearest window, hoping to discover a sign of him. About the drachma, he alternated between full confidence in Luke's sensitivity and understanding, and certainty that it had not been nearly enough, that it must seem a mere pittance without the intended impact.

At about two that afternoon, he thought he saw movement in the forest. Not precisely where Luke had been when Elsworthy had confronted him, but further back by the pond. He'd been playing cribbage with Erasmus and so was easily able to excuse himself. Five minutes of observation from a window had shown him no other movement, if indeed there had been any. Of course, if Luke was out there, he should leave him to approach when he was ready. Still, it was a trial when Sophia strode by on one of her walks, not to ask if she could see anyone out there.

A short time later she entered the house, declaring that it looked like rain. When the rain began an hour later and no Luke driven to the door to escape it, his hopes of seeing him today sank to nil. By four, a steady rain had settled over them, curtaining off the woods and the outside world. It was something of a relief for his anxiety, yet it was agony to think of Luke staring out some window, perhaps wishing he had come sooner. And of course, he might simply be too revolted by what must have appeared in the library to be Daniel's rank cowardice. If he could only explain it to him. If Luke would, despite everything in their brief, chaotic history, come to him of his own accord, it would mean everything. Absolutely everything.

Oh, for the relief of a fiery note dashed off to Clarence. But he refused to be led by his emotions. He must gauge just how much damage had been done to the relationship with Luke before he expressed himself. Though not nearly enough, it was some satisfaction to have sent the Hoppers' footmen from the house three times today with the verbal message that he was unavailable. If he knew Clarence at all, a verbal dismissal would be almost unendurable.

About a quarter to five, he heard Philip's heavy footfalls descending the stairs. The coach was readying to take him across town to dine with the Ringwalds, which seemed to require much fluttering about the house before he departed. Fifteen minutes before he was to depart, a knocking sounded at the door. Philip called to the butler from the first floor, asking him to tell the coachman he would be out in ten minutes. The butler passed to the vestibule, and Daniel had only begun to question why the coachman would choose to remain outside in the rain when a frantic conversation commenced at the front door – a conversation which pulled Daniel so rapidly to his feet he nearly lost their support as he rushed toward the sound.

The joy of hearing Luke was quickly alloyed by the near-frantic quality of his voice. Daniel arrived to find the butler had closed the door behind him and was attempting to contain the guest on a floormat. Luke was wet clean through, his hair a mat of seaweed, his frockcoat pitifully unequal to withstanding a storm. As for the book of fabric samples, which was apparently indispensable to each anytime one wished to see the other, it was soaked through entirely and coming apart in great chunks.

"I have business with Mr Thornton!" cried Luke. "I have every right to be here! Every right to come. *Every* right!"

"Luke!" called Daniel, sprinting forward, shocked at his condition, which seemed approaching mania. He exchanged a look with the butler, who appeared ready to set the young man back out in the rain. He quickly assured him he would handle the matter.

"Sir, I would advise—"

"Here is how you can help me, Samuel. Locate Mrs Edwards and ask her to see to Erasmus until I find them. Will you do that for me?"

"Yes, sir. But—"

"Then fetch a housemaid and have her bring out as many rags and towels as she can find to sop up the water. A large bowl, perhaps two, will be needed to place beneath this coat once I've hung it up."

"But, sir—"

"Thank you, Samuel."

The butler sighed, understanding a dismissal when he heard one. After another glance at the wild-eyed, trembling young man whose sodden state had already surmounted the limits of the floormat, he proceeded down the corridor.

"Luke, what on earth has happened to you? Are you unwell?"

"No, Mr Thornton! I am quite well! I am making a house call to follow up on our plans to redo the drapes in eight rooms!"

As Luke was nearly shouting, Daniel quickly decided that, though they might well need to call a physician, his first order of business would be to get him into a dressing gown, get some tea, perhaps something stronger, into him and get him to calm down. He asked for Luke's assistance to remove the worst offender, his cascading frockcoat, which felt to weigh about as much as its owner. As he was setting it on a hook near the front door, the head housekeeper and one of the chambermaids came hurrying down the corridor. After depositing rags and a large bowl, the chambermaid was quickly off to fetch more rags. Slipping the bowl beneath the coat, Daniel assured the horrified housekeeper if she would be so good as to follow them to his bedchamber to mop up the trail, he would see to Luke from there.

Looking slightly faint, Mrs Michelson stooped to retrieve a good number of rags. After setting the book, now in ten volumes, upon the drenched floormat, Daniel led his visitor towards the staircase.

"It's never too late to consider brightening a room!" shouted Luke. "And one of the best places to start are your window coverings! From a delicate lace which can create the dappled effects of a cherished summer walk, to a heavy damask to cut the light entirely, now in our new Spring Green dye to lighten the effect..."

Daniel closed them inside his bedchamber just as a pronounced trembling overtook Luke's limbs. He'd done no more than fetch the blanket he intended to wrap him in after he got him out of his clothing, when Luke took the blanket in one hand, Daniel's shoulder in the other, and brought them to their knees as he collapsed. Daniel let out a grunt as his knee hit the floor, quickly extending a leg to prevent them from toppling over entirely. Then Luke grabbed him around the waist, and with his other hand brought his face to his own. Seizing Luke tightly, Daniel leant in to return his gasping kisses. Then, he tossed the blanket under them and lay them down, only just sparing Luke the impact of his fifteen-stone descent before all thoughts but of kissing him left his head entirely.

"*Our first kiss!*" Daniel managed, laughing, before an arm hooked around his neck and returned him to that sweet, scalding, beautifully sucking little orifice. At last, tearing himself away, he said, "Oh, *Christ*, Luke!"

It soon became clear that his guest was intent upon receiving more than just kisses. Daniel worked to slow him, kissing him, telling him how inexpressibly precious it was to kiss him at last, as Luke struggled from his wet breeches and began to rut against him. When Luke retook a fistful of his hair and forced his mouth firmly over his own, Daniel quickly set to devouring him, rutting in turn, cherishing that sweet press of this trembling little fish beneath me – trapped, eager. All his.

"You mad little fool!" he gasped, coming up for air. "What the devil possessed you to traipse over here in the rain?"

"You convinced me!"

Daniel stooped to warm his ear with kisses. "Ah, the Devil himself, then." He came up to look him in the eye. "Thank you for coming. *Thank you.*"

For the first time since arriving, Luke actually appeared to have heard him. Yet, he looked so wretched it seemed something beyond mere sexual desire. He was a sailor on the last night of his leave unsure if he would ever see land, ever have the chance again.

Luke rolled to his side, then pulled his companion in closely from behind. Daniel closed over him, placing a hand on his naked flank which was all damp chill and expectation. Coming in to kiss his neck, Daniel slid a hand along that smooth, pale flesh and asked, "Is this an invitation?"

"A command."

Surprising to hear from Luke, yes – but it did unquestionably have the desired effect. With some reservations Daniel began undoing his breeches, when the sound of footsteps scurrying past the door gave him fresh pause. They must slow down. He glanced over his shoulder at the door, primarily to confirm that he had locked it, then he returned to Luke. "Let's take a breath and calm down. All in due time."

"No – right now! *Please!*" But Luke already sounded defeated. He reached back and began pulling at the cursed, constraining garments, but Daniel leant away out of reach. Returning Luke to his back, he climbed atop and eased his weight gently upon him. Then, he took both wrists and held them to the floor.

"In due time. I promise."

"But—"

"I promise. This is not the last moment on earth. Let me make a promise. And let me keep it. Will you do that for me?"

Though looking almost tragically frustrated, Luke at last said, "I'm sorry. I'm afraid. I don't—"

Daniel kissed his lips to still him. "Sshh... sssshhhh... how about this?" he whispered and began gently to lap at his lips until Luke parted them. Daniel dipped down, opening him still further, caressing Luke's tongue with his own, licking first the course topside which flattened and curled, slipping then to the silky underside, down to that tender valley, the rise from which brought him over a rigid row of teeth. Smiling, Daniel withdrew.

When he descended again, he brought their mouths together at an angle. Opening his companion wide, he found a place to take hold. Now quite docile, Luke allowed himself to be lifted. He smiled as his head was brought to one side, then the other, one side, then the other: Daniel, a lion with his cub. The urge had risen like a long-dormant instinct. It was the most exquisite, intimate play Daniel had ever experienced, his heart filling to near bursting as Luke's smile became a grin, and then a laugh.

"Now, let us take another direction."

Still laughing, Luke said, "What direction?"

"Let us go back in time. Let *me* go back in time." He waited for him to agree, needing him to agree before he understood what he meant. Luke agreed. Easing off him, Daniel allowed one leg to rest languidly between Luke's naked thighs. He reached down and cradled his tight, wet bollocks, nearly dizzy with love as he observed the vulnerability of his exposed sex. Absolutely adoring the instant stiffening his hand inspired, that helplessness to do anything but respond.

Daniel leant down and took him in his mouth.

Exhaling tremulously, Luke said, "Is that what you call this – going back in time?", giving the distinct impression he didn't care what it was called.

After a moment, Daniel leant back and said, "It is when I am determined to do things differently this time. No doubt I should have done many things differently before we reached the study. But that is where I'd like to begin." He flicked his tongue just to watch Luke jump, then shudder, before adding, "You remember the study, don't you?" before returning more diligently to his work.

Luke's response seemed to be an affirmative, caught as it was in trembling and a sudden arching of his back which clipped his breathing.

Daniel sucked the chilled exterior of his swelling erection until it warmed, nearly forgetting his technique as he felt a grin tug the corners of his mouth – so easy, so true was a young man's pleasure. And when the young man was Luke Morley, who had so much more to show him of himself, who had so much more to teach Daniel about himself, Daniel offered his mouth to the bottle, sipping as it began to rise, a thick, heady smell filling his nostrils as that strong liquid crested the brim.

"Don't hold back," he said. Luke gripped his hair in tremulous, urgent longing, guiding Daniel's movements until he suddenly released him, his hands slapping the floor. His back arched and he began spilling convulsively, prolifically, failing almost entirely to stifle his cries. Daniel quickly slipped an arm under him, catching him as though he had fallen, keeping his body suspended to prolong Luke's pleasure, extend his relief, make sublime his delight. Then, he lowered him gently, maintaining the arm around him as he came up to lay beside him.

"I love you," said Luke.

Feeling his own words, whatever they would have been, dissolve in his mouth, Daniel said, "What did you say?"

"I said I love you. Back to the study, back in time – I went just as you did. The study was when I longed more than anything to take your hair in my hands but was too shy. Then, after, I nearly told you I loved you. But it seemed you did not wish to hear it." He met Daniel's eyes. "Then I wished to do this."

Before Daniel could think what to do or say, Luke had slipped from his grasp and gone down on his knees, unbuttoning his half-undone breeches and taking him without hesitation into his mouth.

"Luke..." but more words were lost as he felt that curious tongue grow bolder and more intent.

Coming up for a moment, Luke said, "I was outside for hours, unable to come to the door. Even after it began to rain, I still couldn't make myself come in. What a fool I am!"

When Luke resumed his work Daniel found it impossible to voice his questions, impossible to string two coherent words together. Luke was intent upon changing what had happened in the study. His eagerness occasionally made him too forceful but, having no other aim than to give pleasure, he obeyed Daniel's gentle guidance without embarrassment or hesitation. God, he was just like Daniel at his age – that blind determination, his self-esteem, his very self-image depending on his ability to bring a man off this way.

"Just like that," he said, once Luke had, no doubt unknowingly, begun precisely what he would need to complete. "*Just* like that... yes..." Daniel bit his lip to supress a moan. Another minute at the very most.

Oh, that was good.

A knock sounded at the door. "Sir? Is everything alright?"

Daniel had already gone too rigid with thoughts of his destination to start up – eyeballs-deep in that state of pre-death *rigor mortis* and Collins *must* come now to check on them. And Luke, the devil, was paying no attention at all to this interruption and simply carried on.

So, working mightily to produce that natural, easy sound, Daniel announced, "*Yes, Collins. Quite alright. Never better... just a moment.*"

A short silence. Then, a thud which sounded suspiciously close to where the valet's head might connect were he to send it resolutely into the door.

"Never mind, sir. Take your time."

This order, however, Daniel could scarcely obey. Luke had now brought him to the precipice. Daniel was raising a knee from a sudden urge to stamp his foot upon the ground when

Luke abruptly held back, ceasing that controlled, steady movement to tease him with a feather-like delicacy.

Completely bewildered, he cried, *"Please*, Luke!" coming up on an elbow, shocked that he must suddenly chase his pleasure.

Luke quickly resumed his focused, steady rhythm, but he had already missed a few beats. As he worked harder, Daniel felt his body seize forward. Then, rising onto both elbows, he locked his jaw to stifle the explosion which began to rock him. He was spending, his arms shaking from the effort. His chest heaving, he stared in amazement as Luke led him, meticulously careful of his rhythm. Each wave depended entirely on Luke's whim. Each grew exponentially more pleasurable as it was mixed with a kind of profane gratitude. Daniel was brought steadily, unflaggingly to completion. His rigidity began to slacken. His upper body shook free from its grip, and he collapsed back onto the floor. Finally, he was left peering through the stars.

Good God. Was it possible Luke had done that knowingly? Surely not. Yet he had taken on that attitude he had in dance – self-possessed, decided, and playful. Daniel would not; he dared not ask him.

Once he had the wherewithal to look at him again, he found Luke wiping his grinning mouth with a hand, laughing with sheer pride in himself as he purveyed his felled prey – the exposed, still pulsing, prostrate form of his ravished lover.

Then, falling back on his hands, he began to shake.

Coming up on an elbow again, Daniel took his shoulder. Though he was initially uncertain, Luke was indeed laughing.

Yet, he found nothing to laugh at and felt only dismay when, after asking what was the matter, he was brightly informed:

"I have destroyed my life!"

Observing once more the manic behaviour he had displayed when he'd arrived, Daniel came to his feet. He pulled up his breeches, then extended a hand to assist Luke up. "For God's sake, what is going on? Why were you outside this house for hours before coming in? What do you mean you have destroyed your life?"

"Because coming to see you here means I have angered someone in The House. That is why I was so long deciding to come inside. But I *would* do it. I will *not* creep. I will *not* cower. If I must run to France now, I will, I don't care!" Then, looking suddenly as though he might care, and care very much, he added, "Will... you come with me?"

Horrified, confused, Daniel was yet unable to do anything but bring him forward, wrap his arms around him, and kiss him. The sweet, pungent taste of himself was momentarily too primal a sensation to see beyond – Luke was *his*. Holding his face as he kissed him again, and again, then just once more, he at last drew away. "But who can you have angered? Nobody in this house, surely."

"But I have. I've angered whoever sent me the note telling me I must encourage you to marry and let everything take its course. Or else Erasmus, and my father, would be told about us. I was ordered never to see you as a lover. Never to come to this house at all. It was in a blackmail note."

Daniel might have lost consciousness for a moment, he wasn't sure. "*Blackmail*. You mean someone from this house, *my* house, actually threatened you if you came to see me here?"

Luke nodded. Daniel was still dumb with shock when a knock sounded at the door, and a voice asked if everyone was alright.

"Yes, thank you, Sophia," he said, not taking his eyes from Luke. "Please wait for me downstairs, I shall be down shortly." He was disheartened to hear her speaking to both Evy and Philip, who had apparently postponed his departure. Shushing the siblings and ordering them downstairs, Sophia led them away.

"*All* this," said Daniel, "whatever *this* is, has gone quite far enough. We *must* sort this out; we will sort it out. God knows I still have things I need you to explain."

When Luke frowned, Daniel let out an irritated breath, more than a little angry at himself. But there was no way around the subject now; too much had been left unsaid and for too long.

"I received a blackmail note as well."

"What?"

"From Clarence. Only I didn't know it was from him, not until last night. This is why I have acted as I have... I... I'm sorry, Luke, I thought it was from your father."

"From *Papa*?"

"Yes." Christ, he didn't want to say it this way. "Initially, I did think it was from you. I'm so sorry. I saw, or I thought I saw, you put that damned note on the mantle in the sitting parlour. Please God, tell me you forgive me."

Luke, bless him, began to laugh. "*That* note? The one Clarence asked me to retrieve for him when I came to see you?

I met him in the alleyway beyond The George the morning after we met. That is how I learned about you two. That's quite funny, really!"

Daniel had a choice then. It took a moment. But then he laughed as well. With Luke. With gratitude. "For God's sake, didn't your parents tell you never to speak to men in dark alleyways?" He ran a hand through Luke's matted hair. "Let's speak no more of it just now. I can tell you, almost for a certainty and soon it shall *be* for a certainty: *nobody* from this house is threatening you. Nobody would do that to you. Or to me. It must have been Clarence."

Luke shook his head. "He has been quite kind to me, all things considered. He's been giving me advice."

"I'll bet he has. He can be very charming when he wishes to be, I know that better than most. But I doubt he has had your best interests at heart. How did you receive the note?"

"In jail. Your gardener, Mr Elsworthy, brought it to me."

CHAPTER TWENTY-ONE

A fter speaking to Jacob Elsworthy, Daniel returned to the room in which his guest was resting. At his approach, Luke opened his eyes. He smiled as Daniel sat on the bedside and began to stroke his hair.

"You are safe here, darling," said Daniel, placing a kiss on his forehead. Though he dearly wished to dismiss all talk of blackmail, he felt obliged to tell him immediately who wrote the letter and why. Luke took it in, frowning as he considered. Daniel leant down and kissed him again, allowing his lips to linger on his forehead. It felt extravagant to have this – a prince to cherish and protect. The feelings Luke inspired encompassed the best parts of him: his paternal instinct, his empathy, his lust. And his love, so long suspended.

Luke said, "If nobody in this house wrote that note, then I just made a complete ass of myself."

Smiling, Daniel crawled onto the bed and lay an arm across him. "Given your understanding of the matter, your lifelong fears, what you did was one of the bravest things I've ever seen. Do you see that?" Grinning crookedly, Luke glanced at him and, shrugging, said he supposed he did. "It's certainly the most flattering thing anyone has ever done for me. You came to this house brandishing your musket and broke down the barriers. For me."

"With a musket that wasn't loaded, aiming at enemies who were not there."

"*Someone* wrote you that note."

Luke said, "Everyone wrote it."

"Do you really feel that?"

"It doesn't matter who actually wrote the note. There is no place for me, or you, in a town like this. Perhaps in a city, where we could be anonymous. But that isn't truly being accepted, is it? It is only going unnoticed, getting lost in the crowd."

"I accept you. Do you accept yourself?" Luke was perhaps three times longer affirming this than Daniel would have liked, but he did at last affirm it. "Let us begin there. And if there are no more, then let us expend no effort chasing them."

"Is it *us*?"

"It is if you can forgive my terrible treatment of you. I showed you a side of myself I should have been ashamed to show a... show anyone. No matter the provocation, I had no right to attempt to bend you to my will, just as you were seeking to discover yourself."

Luke was trying, or trying not to grin – Daniel couldn't quite tell. He said, "As first times go, do you think it was so bad?"

Daniel nearly said *the worst*, but on second thought refrained. "Well, and this is not to excuse my behaviour by any means, but no, perhaps not so much worse than most."

"What was your first experience like?"

Daniel laughed. "Quite absurd and appalling, really. Not as absurd and appalling as yours, but bad enough that I've never told a living soul."

"Tell me."

Taking his hand, Daniel said, "Very well. I was two or three years older than you, which was not good for someone like me. Had I had some of the mystery taken away a bit sooner, I shouldn't have gone so long afterwards with no other goal for myself. At Cambridge, with scarcely any other aim than to be near other young men, I found I was still more confined by fears of making a mistake with them. One or two opportunities may have presented, I'll never know. So, I moved to the city on my independence, approaching my twenty-second year and in a state of desperation to begin that part of my life. Wretched at the thought of never experiencing what other men, somewhere, whoever they were, whatever they looked like, were able to accomplish. Desperation, of course, is never a good place to start.

"Not knowing where to go, I took to haunting the alleyways behind taverns where men are always happy to expose themselves taking aim at exterior walls. My great, cunning calculation was supposing that, while in drink, they would be more open to a proposal. It wasn't unusual to see one or two in states of mild arousal. So, at last, I approached one whom I'd seen once before who hadn't minded my observation. I made my proposal, ready to run if he became enraged. Instead, he merely chuckled as though I'd given him an amusing compliment. With hardly a look at me, he said, 'I don't mind,' upon which he directed us into a corner of absolute pitch. Then, he encouraged me over the first thing we encountered, which felt to be an old wooden crate."

Luke was all eyes. "What did he do?"

"He took me, roughly and quite painfully. As he was buttoning up afterwards, he said, 'Lend us tuppence for another drink, would you, love?' So, I handed over the money, supposing it the friendly thing to do. I remember wishing to say something, anything, to him, to keep him from returning inside so soon. I began to, and he hesitated. But when I said nothing, he simply went in. I proceeded home terribly pleased with myself.

"Then the regrets came: why hadn't I asked his name? What if I couldn't find anyone else? What if he had been the only one? So, the following three nights I returned, increasingly desperate to find him again as no one else I was observing seemed at all promising. Then, I decided he hadn't returned for fear of encountering me again. It hurt me terribly. I supposed I had done something wrong."

"But you hadn't."

Daniel gave a smile just short of a laugh. "The only thing I did wrong was driving myself mad with regrets about a quick, dirty fuck in an alleyway."

"But then you got over it?"

At this, Daniel did laugh. "Oh, yes. I got over it, and many subsequent men in the process. For years I thought of little besides *getting over*. A young person should have a vocation or else sex, or some other pleasure, becomes that vocation.

Ignorant as I was and now fancying I had been rejected, once I understood where to go, I went after conquests with a red-eyed, single-minded determination.

"But I do wonder, had that man in the alleyway been of a different sort – had he invited me to join him in the tavern, to share a drink and a bit more about ourselves – if I might have turned out a bit differently. I'm not saying I regret the subsequent ten years of my life. Part of me supposes it must be like that for most. But part of me wonders if young men were handled with care, the same care as we wish for our young women, if the assumptions we make about them would not so quickly become the assumptions they make about themselves. If it might not be better for all." Daniel shrugged. Then, he glanced somewhat shyly at Luke to see what he made of that, and, indeed, of Daniel Thornton.

When Luke appeared struggling for a response, Daniel patted his hand. "On some level, I was living that period of my life again when I thought you were blackmailing me. I was seeking to inflict the same kind of pain and confusion that I had felt."

"Only to defend yourself. I'd have done the same, had I... well, thought of it." When Daniel smiled, Luke continued, "And I don't want a lot of men. I know you think that I will, but I promise one has been enough."

Daniel laughed, bringing Luke to him. "The best compliments are those so without art they couldn't be made out by the most discerning of us. But I do know what you mean. And I do love you for it."

"Do you?"

Holding his companion's gaze, he said, "I love you desperately, Luke. So much that I won't seek promises just yet about what you may or may not want in the future. If you promise to be open and honest with me, always, I shall work to be everything to you."

Chapter Twenty-Two

When a second round of knocking at the front door began, accompanied by a violent tugging at the bell, Daniel was writing to the Morleys, informing them of their son's whereabouts and intention to remain at the Park for a time. At the noise, just three hours after Luke had arrived, he experienced the strangest sensation. Convinced it could be none other than Luke, he hurried from his desk and down the corridor to the spare room. The opening door and sweep of candlelight stirred the sleeper, and after telling him to go back to sleep, Daniel hurried downstairs. Sophia was at the front door, speaking over the sound of cascading rain to a visitor just then entering the vestibule.

Coming forward, Daniel took in the sight of the normally pristine Clarence spattered to the waist in mud. His heeled slippers were so tortured they had the appearance of wet paper set to peel clean away. Half draped across Sophia, whose task of supporting nearly everyone she came into contact with seemed doomed to continue indefinitely, Clarence reached dramatically for Daniel.

Here was an act of maturity Daniel would later have no qualms giving himself full credit for – he did not scream at Clarence, he did not kick him in the arse or between the legs, neither did he slap him or push him backwards to tumble down the stairs onto the drive. Instead, he came forward and said in his steeliest tone, "Give me one reason not to turn you around and throw you the hell out of here."

"Because you are a good man, Danny. You cannot have that on your conscience. I ask just a few words after which you are free to throw me out again – it's all the same to me."

Struggling with the guest to rid him of his frockcoat, Sophia raised her brows but said nothing. Clarence worked what was left of his heeled slippers from his feet, stripping away his stockings as well, both of which were unrecognisable for the mud. "Christ Almighty," said Daniel, "couldn't you take the coach?"

"No," said Clarence simply, as gooseflesh spattered his cold, clammy legs, and he began to tremble. They were at the top of the stairs when Mrs Michelson and Samuel arrived at another travesty downstairs. Daniel quickly closed out the cries of horror as he sealed them into a spare room.

Then, like Luke, Clarence grabbed for him and began dragging him to the floor. Only he did not attempt to hold on when Daniel pushed him away. Instead, he knelt, head bowed. After a moment of silence, Daniel understood that Clarence was crying.

"What has happened? Come up off the floor. Sit on the bed, or in that armchair..."

Clarence shook his head. When he was recovered enough to speak, he said, "*You* happened, Daniel. You and your wretched notes. One after another, you merciless, heartless bastard."

"My... notes?"

"The damn love letters. I read and reread them. But I only just *begin* to read them, you see? Only begin to understand them. You win, Daniel. I can take no more of your praise, your good wishes. So here it is." And with this, he rose to his feet to face him.

"*I* wrote that note the night we quarrelled. Somehow you came to believe Luke had written it. I don't know how that came to be. All that matters is that I wrote it, and when I had the chance to set matters right, I took the coward's way out. I continued to let Luke take the blame, which is the *damned if you do* part of this, and now I am confessing, which is the *damned if you don't* part, because it makes no damned difference to you what I do. You don't want me either way. All I accomplished was a better knowledge of Luke, who is a sweet boy with a good heart who didn't deserve that or what came next to him."

"The second blackmail note."

"*Mais oui*! Upon receiving it the courageous little man no doubt overcame his fears and ran to you for help, falling into your arms with even more of that irresistible, succulent appeal with which he initially attracted you. Very well, and so here appears the true villain to confess: *I* am to blame for that as well."

That his father had written the note, which, according to Elsworthy, Clarence had not even seen before he'd taken it, made no difference just then. Daniel let loose.

"How *could* you?! He's eighteen fucking years old! Never been with a man before, utterly terrified of discovery!"

Clarence motioned for him to continue, pulling apart the buttons of his sodden shirt, happy to take his blows like any good martyr. Though Daniel was nearly too livid to speak, he held out his hand for the shirt, then retrieved a dressing gown from the wardrobe and threw it at him. "Put that on before you catch your death."

Clarence appeared disappointed with the offering. After a moment he snatched it up from the floor. "Why not let me catch my death? What does it matter? I have nothing. Not even any more confessions." After slipping the gown on, he said, "Actually, I *do* have another confession. This should do the trick. My next plan of action was this: meet with Luke once more, for we have been meeting for little enlightening chats and so that he can cry on my shoulder. Only this time I take him to the tavern in The George. Once he is drunk, I seduce him, driving a wedge between you two by ravishing him until the sun comes up – or letting him ravish me, whichever he prefers. Then let the guilt eat at him until he no longer feels worthy of you."

Daniel could only shake his head. "I have no response to that."

"Of course you do: you hate me even more."

"No. I'm simply confused. All this for me?" Clarence looked away. "This is too much; you know it is. Let me ask you: you planned to seduce him, then chose not to. Why did you choose not to?"

Clarence took a seat on the bed, glaring at Daniel for where he was taking the discussion. Then, he shook his head. "Because the way my luck is going, I would have fallen in love with him as well, only to have him dump me for you anyhow."

"Clarence..."

"Because he doesn't deserve that. I couldn't have lived with myself." He glanced briefly at Daniel, then down at the floor. "I did not *personally* write the note to him. I didn't know what my father intended to say. I never saw it before it was sent."

"You are both to blame. But at least I can rid myself of that image of you actually sitting down with pen and paper."

Clarence was quite a long time considering before he muttered, "I've reached an age, and don't you dare tell anyone I said this, but I've reached an age when I feel I have gained... I suppose you'd call it *wisdom*. That was your cue to laugh, Danny."

"I'm not laughing. I think you mean *a conscience*, but I'll let you give it a name."

"How about I be generous and say it is a bit of both? One recognises things dealing with an innocent. You *will* laugh at this – but looking at Luke, I felt I should like to guide him. Properly guide him. Though my life to this point has been an exercise in selfishness, I have learned about human nature, in myself and in others. If nothing else, a narcissist can speak eloquently of the downfalls of leading a vapid, pointless existence. Once you realise there is less self to be seen, the more you stare at him. That one blurs into something not quite human until one steps away and observes as others observe. Speaking with Luke, I did begin to wonder if being the 'Daniel' in a relationship might not force me to apply some of what I have learned. Not now, of course – I'm too much of a jealous, insecure bastard. But perhaps eventually."

Daniel was so surprised words were momentarily failing him. But this was not the time to be tongue-tied. "It really is extraordinary to hear you speak like this – opening yourself to new roles, new ideas about yourself. Being open to this in yourself must eventually open you to new and better things." Then, though perhaps fibbing a bit, he said, "If your intentions remain good, if you let your conscience continue to speak to you, I think you would make a good 'Daniel' one day. Once you leave off pursuing the original."

Clarence made a face. "Pithily put, as usual." He sighed. "It's true, isn't it? That bit of tripe I picked up from a romance novel I used to win a point in an argument – that if I hadn't a heart, which I have long taken pride in not having, you could not have loved me."

"Yes, I'm afraid that is true. I'm sorry it can't be otherwise."

"Figures."

***

Unable to return to sleep, Luke was immediately aware of a disturbance in the house. Rising from bed, he soon understood Clarence to be the instigator. Though the words were unclear, there seemed no love lost between him and Daniel, who sounded to be giving him a verbal drubbing.

Once it grew quiet, he moved to an armchair. His had only been a restless sleep, and though so much had now been resolved, it felt scarcely less still had to be. Particularly where Bridget was concerned. Daniel would break things off with her, of course. However, he had not mentioned it yet, and Luke could not quite ask, knowing he did not wish to disappoint his uncle. That was not reason enough to marry, yet still he did not wish to be the one to bring it up. Wasn't it obvious he would break things off now there was no obligation? It *was* obvious and there would be time to speak of that tomorrow.

After a time, a knock sounded, after which Collins entered the room. When Clarence came in behind him, Luke rose from his chair.

"Excuse me, Master Luke. I was asked to retrieve a nightshirt and a few other things for our latest guest. As you see, Master Clarence is paying us a visit. He must stay the night but hasn't any of his belongings. I offered to fetch a nightshirt on my own…" he paused meaningfully, "but as you can see, he wished to join me. He would like to speak with you."

Luke came forward as Collins passed by to the wardrobe. Clarence had the look of a castaway about him, weather-beaten, his hair a flattened tangle not unlike Luke's own, swimming in one of Daniel's dressing gowns.

"You'll hear it from someone, so it might as well be from me," he said. "My father wrote that note you received in the jailhouse. I wish to apologise."

Luke nodded. "Once I told Daniel and we had worked out what had been happening, it seemed likely. I didn't think it was from you; I hoped it wasn't."

"You won't care either way," continued Clarence, in cadences of military precision, "but I promise I did not know what the note said and would never have allowed it to be sent had I known. That said, I of course knew whatever he would write would not be particularly nice, so I am still a rotten scoundrel who does not deserve to live, who should burn in hell."

"Your change of clothes, sir," said Collins, passing them on his way out the door, superbly indifferent.

"Stay, Albert. I might have fetched these clothes myself."

The valet stooped his head. Then, with a sigh, he turned on his heel and faced them.

"I've caused Daniel nothing but grief since arriving in Grantham. I caused him scarcely less when we were together. I regret my behaviour very much. You all will be rid of me just as soon as I can make arrangements to return to town."

Extending a hand, Luke said, "I forgive you." Clarence immediately took his hand and as quickly released it. Though he would not look at him, Luke saw that he wished some response from Collins. As nothing seemed forthcoming, Luke continued, "Won't your parents bring you home?"

"No, they will not. I arrived on my own, I shall depart on my own. I refused to take their carriage here tonight. I wish to God they had never come. If I might—" he swallowed and looked intently at the floor. "Daniel said to ask you if I might remain at the Park until I can make arrangements to leave. I will have my portmanteau brought here, though God knows

I'd remain in dressing gowns all the way back to London in order to avoid those two. I simply haven't the strength to face them just now. But if you are uncomfortable with my presence here, given my history with Daniel and my appalling behaviour since arriving, I will make other arrangements."

CHAPTER TWENTY-THREE

With Clarence staying at the Park, Daniel suggested they get away the following evening. Having agreed it best to spend the night in separate bedchambers and nearly climbing the walls needing to have Daniel close, Luke had assented immediately. He knew instantly he wished them to spend a night in Morley's. He set it down so strongly as their rendezvous, he felt obliged to revisit the plan about noon in case Daniel had any misgivings about spending a decidedly rugged night on the floor of a draper's shop. Daniel, however, insisted he would be thrilled to experience the place as he had so many nights of his childhood. So, Luke set out from the Park three hours before him to prepare for his overnight guest.

By eight that evening, however, when the coach deposited Daniel at the shop door, Luke had begun to have misgivings. He met him on the front stoop.

"Let's go to The Angel instead. I've never been, and everyone says it's nicer than The George." He was halfway through this plea when he understood from Daniel's expression this was futile. The man had packed his bag for a night in the shop and he would be staying in the shop.

"Open that door, Luke. I've been looking forward to this all day."

Luke remained where he was, hoping the violent blush that was now beginning to sting his eyes might change Daniel's mind. It appeared not, but only from a fear of actually angering Daniel did he at last open the door. Upon entering, his guest looked about, understanding something unusual had been done in anticipation of the visit. They might have remained in the front for longer, but he was now on the hunt for whatever it was and soon arrived in the back. Once he saw it, he was silent so long that Luke was obliged to ask what he thought.

"Good *God*!" he said at last, setting down makings for a cold collation to step forward. After looking in, around and up, he returned to his host. "Luke, this is extraordinary. All I've contributed is claret and a hunk of cheese. But you've... this isn't how you used to spend the night here as a child, surely?"

"Not exactly. I was always out front under the counter. This is only for tonight. Just some things I used to think of doing. But it's too much."

During his cleaning and subsequent inventory, Luke had discovered yards of eye-catching old scraps: glimmering damask, some exceptionally fine lawn cloth, even silks. With the lawn he had built a tent of about ten square feet, crosshatched with emerald and cobalt damask, pinning black silk where it would catch the light of lit candles. The tent came to a focus at the back around a collection of silk cushions stuffed with scraps, expanding onto a floor cushion more than half the length of the tent.

Coming forward, Daniel wrapped his arms around his companion's waist and bent to his ear. "You little devil. Was your aim to create something straight out of a Persian harem?"

Smiling, "I wanted to excite you. Mostly you. But once it was done, I knew I had gone too far. And—" Daniel slapped his bottom smartly. Then, leaning into his neck, he told him he had done his job only too well. "But... sorry," he continued. "Could we just kiss?"

Rising up, Daniel said, "Luke, of course we can. If truth be told, I wish us to take things slower as well. I wouldn't have gone in for the kill at your neck had you not knocked me over the head with this harem of yours."

"I mean, I do want the other, too. It'll kill me if we don't do it tonight." Daniel was laughing. "I just don't want you to think I'm... you know, cheap."

Daniel silenced this by placing his mouth gently over Luke's. "If it takes all night doing this to convince you you are not cheap, that is what we will do."

Standing in the entrance of the tent, they drew arms around one another and kissed chastely. Luke did have another motive in creating this harem-like atmosphere. He wished to distract him from talk of Bridget. Daniel's silence on that subject had initially seemed consistent with a foregone conclusion. Today there had been other things to speak of – Clarence to settle in, then outfit after the request for his portmanteau had been denied. His parents insisted he return and tell them what was happening with Daniel, and together with daily trivialities, it had never come up.

Yet neither had one sentence been uttered referring to *after* – after he had told his uncle, after they had told the Morleys they would not be marrying. This was not missed by Luke, and it was becoming less obvious that they would break it off and rather more how many people breaking it off would hurt. And given the adoring way he had spoken of his uncle at dinner... how long before Daniel stepped back from him, set out the wine and cheese and said it was time they sit down and have a talk? A talk he had been putting off.

Growing more aggressive, Luke pulled him into the tent. Seeing he must take off his shoes, Daniel kicked them away, then turned and lay on his back on the mattress. Luke climbed on top of him.

"Sorry," said Daniel, slipping a hand behind his head. "We did agree to just kiss. This will make it more difficult to keep our agreement." When Luke tried to distract him, he continued, "I must tell you I am a bit concerned about this hot and cold toying with me. I don't want you to think I'm cheap."

"Never."

"No, now... I *am* the one who paid a public intoxicant tuppence to tup me in a dark alley. I've never quite thought that through until now, but that makes me somewhat worse than cheap, doesn't it? What is the word for that? Ah, yes, desperate."

"I'd tup you free of charge."

Luke found himself on his back, Daniel hot in his ear. "Would you, would you really? Is that what you are planning for tonight? I thought I knew you."

"No, not tonight... perhaps... after some additional research."

Daniel suddenly had Luke's knees so far apart they were threatening the seams of his breeches. Luke's foot collided with the overnight bag, setting the wine bottle on its side. Daniel had straddled him, his fingers at Luke's shirt, when his companion began squirming away. "Wait. Is wine and cheese all you brought?"

Letting out a breath, Daniel ceased with the buttons and set his hands on his thighs. "And a few grapes. Sorry, are we speaking of food now?"

"You said you would bring something else. From the binder's desk."

Groaning, Daniel slumped forward. "*Must* you refer us back to the scene of my very worst behaviour? *The oil*; that's all you need to say."

"I like you on your worst behaviour."

Daniel made a fist and set it lightly on Luke's forehead. Then, pinching the bridge of his own nose, he took a deep breath before returning to him. "Let me look at you, darling. Laid back on silk pillows, skin softly illuminated in the candlelight. Red lips, bright eyes. You are so beautiful."

"I've thought you were beautiful from the moment I first saw you."

Daniel settled over him. Once their breathing had fallen into sync, he whispered, "Tell me how you want me." To

Luke's grin, he tilted his head. "Do you like the sound of that?"

Nodding, "Like I own you."

"Let us say... ownership is on offer."

His grin subsiding, Luke said, "It's up to me not to ruin the offer."

Daniel hesitated quite a long time before affirming. "Yes. I find that incredibly difficult to say, considering the way I have behaved. It goes without saying that I must do the same."

For a moment this seemed another detour on the rocky path to that lovemaking which reappeared at each attempt to delay it. Yet when Daniel looked down at him and repeated the words, "I must do the same...", it came out as both a sigh and a growl. Luke registered the words deep in his gut, in his loins. He extended his arms; Daniel took the sleeves and rid him of the shirt. Then, he leant down to kiss the shallow muscles of Luke's chest, took his diaphragm in both hands and kissed the meeting place. "I forgot to mention: I most certainly did not forget the oil. So may I assume—"

"Yes."

Daniel reached for the bag. Luke found he was holding his breath at the production of the bottle. The thumb easing up the cork, the palm of the same hand catching it. Daniel's rising up on his knees to straddle him. The loosening of his clothing. The readying himself with oil. Luke emerged from his trance only when his leg was patted. "Oh," he said, squirming away so he could unbutton and kick off the breeches. When he turned, intending to flip himself onto his stomach, Daniel took his hip and returned him to his back.

"My one request is that I see you." Somewhat uncertainly, Luke agreed. "You will have me as you want me, I promise. But you are my prince laying on a bed of silks on his wedding night. I wish to see you." When there was no reply, Daniel looked slightly concerned.

"It's nothing. It's just," Luke sat up and whispered in his ear.

Daniel looked like he didn't know whether to laugh or cry. The former at last won out and he said, "Dear Lord. Is *that* your concern?" Luke nodded.

Taking a pillow and placing it beneath Luke's lower back, he continued, "I can assure you, my lusty lad... but no, better to show you..."

Finding he was once again holding his breath, Luke was brought down into the warming bath – head just above the surface, heart thudding as Daniel brought his legs into the air. After prodding him with a generously oiled finger, as he moved to enter him, Daniel ran a pacifying hand down the back of his thigh.

"I won't hurt you. I do suspect you may like it even better this way. But you must relax, or you will hurt yourself. That's right... let me. *Let* me... there you go..."

As one they turned their heads, a sock and buskin of relief from Luke and something just short of perfect bliss from Daniel, who said, "God in His Heaven; you cannot imagine how glorious you feel."

"More..."

"Are you sure?"

"*More.*"

When Daniel pushed in a bit farther, Luke dispensed with additional preamble. "*Fuck me*. As hard as you want. Do it now."

Daniel brought one leg around his back, slipped an arm beneath Luke to grip his opposing shoulder, and thrust in.

When Luke gasped, Daniel came in close. "Any more orders for me?" then thrust again, and again, never letting him quite catch a full breath. Luke threw his head back and forth, slightly panicked, before he understood he could breathe if he allowed Daniel to set the pace. After a time, after acclimating to the rhythm and the reach inside him, his eyes rolled into his head.

"It *does* feel better like this..."

"Does it? I was right?" said Daniel, setting his hips higher onto the pillow, then straightening a knee to angle himself. Opening Luke's legs wider, he drove upwards.

Luke cried out, spasming under an upsurge of pleasure. "OH! Don't move! Right there, right *there*!"

"You were fearing I couldn't locate a certain place in this position. Have I found it?"

"*Don't* move, Daniel. Don't!"

"Luke."

"*Fuckin' hell*! I *love* you!"

"I love you too, darling. But trust me now, it *will* feel even better if you allow me to move."

"Don't move..." repeated Luke, finally without much conviction, bringing his hands to Daniel's buttocks to show his willingness. A tingling began in his nose, down his throat, surging into his stomach as his eyes teared. Daniel reached down and took Luke's erection, not so much stroking as testing to assess how close he was. When he asked, Luke told him to go as hard and fast as he wanted, it was almost too late already.

Daniel came down more fully over him, slackening the agitation on that inner place just enough to slow Luke as he, Daniel, quickened. He set his hands wide on the floor, keeping Luke splayed with his shoulders as he pummelled him, grunting, sweating, pounding him until he swelled, the pain excruciating as he bruised his lover to the spine. Luke was spending without knowing that he could or when it had started. When he began crying, Daniel clamped a hand over his mouth. Then, he buried his face in the hand as he pulsed, and pulsed, and pulsed.

"Don't move," Luke said as Daniel took him in his arms, kissing the beads of sweat from his forehead, the damp at his temple. "Don't move," he said again. Somewhat puzzled, Daniel smiled at their joke and placed his lips over Luke's.

When Luke turned his head from the kiss, Daniel observed tears – in his eyes and running down his cheeks. And, he realised. "Don't move," he may have said initially. What he was saying now was, "Don't marry."

"Luke?"

"*Don't marry. Please don't marry her.*"

When Luke saw Daniel's comprehension, he descended into sobs. Daniel took him close as he began to shake, pleading that he needed something, he needed *this*, only for himself. He wished things to be as they had been with Bridget – if Daniel married her, they never could be again.

"Even if you swear you don't love her. Even if you swear you never will, I cannot bear it! It isn't *fair*!"

"I—"

"Swear you won't do it!"

"Luke, I won't marry her if you don't wish it. I *won't* marry her."

He drove his head onto Daniel's chest. "Not her. Not anyone."

"Nobody at all. Not if it upsets you like this."

"But wouldn't it upset you? Wouldn't you hate to?" When Daniel hesitated, Luke sat up, looking fearfully at him. "Wouldn't you?"

Daniel needed a moment to organise his thoughts. "Yes, of course. Only I had... in some fashion I had begun to make peace with the idea. Your sister is a lovely young woman..."

"I *know* that! I'm not saying she isn't; I'm saying—"

"I know. I know what you are saying. I'm merely saying I shouldn't wish to disappoint her. I shouldn't wish to disappoint Erasmus. Or your parents now that I finally understand them. Rights or wrongs of the matter aside, they are good people who have every right to wish for this. It will be regrettable to disappoint them. I *will* disappoint them. Your happiness, your peace of mind, *you* mean everything to me. I understand why you wish an end to the plans, and I wish an end as well. Your sister will not lack for suitors. And if, as you suppose, she might be using a marriage with me to help fund some plan with Everett... they do certainly have my sympathy, but I should have no qualms about terminating the engagement."

"And your uncle?"

The long silence which followed Luke must have anticipated. This was, of course, where the real problem lay. Where that tinge of reluctance he could never quite banish from his voice originated.

"As regards my uncle, it won't be so simple. We will have to have a talk. A talk I've never considered having with him until recently. I should have long ago – certainly, once Miss Williams became his great passion for me." He looked to his companion, who was watching him earnestly, simply wishing for a future of his own. Daniel took Luke's hand, kissed it, then closed it into his own. He kept his eyes averted from those of his companion to suppress the emotion he felt rising in his throat.

"I find the prospect of facing my uncle exceptionally difficult. Difficult and quite extraordinary. I've fashioned my life to answer every question he might ever have on the subject. I've always been a very respectful nephew – because it is his due, but also because understanding the type of man he is, I have known he will maintain that respectful distance I've taught him that I require. He is credulous, but only in the best of ways. I've given him to understand the women of London, a city he has never liked, have evolved since his day into something altogether more aggressive, money-hungry and difficult to please than even he had supposed. God help him, he has believed his open-hearted, all too easily wounded nephew has had his heart run through the mill over the years.

"All lies. And of course, the last thing on my mind when I came to take care of him." Daniel at last ventured a look at Luke. "Do you understand?"

"Of course. I couldn't imagine telling my father; I couldn't imagine telling anyone in my family. I never used to be such a cold and reserved person."

"Cold and reserved? Are you?"

"Not around you, but around everyone I grew up with. Bridget I knew was the most perceptive, so once I understood how things are with me, I feared she could not help but discover it. I wished to let her know by my behaviour that she should think twice before approaching me, before asking questions as freely as she used to do. All because I couldn't bear speaking of it. I don't want you to do something I couldn't do. You can tell your uncle you don't wish to marry, just now, and leave it at that."

"I know I can. I know that it might not be the thing to make him at last look at me as he should have done years ago. Then, I ask myself, will I be content pulling the wool over his eyes yet again? When that becomes too uncomfortable to consider, I've even sought to acquit myself by believing my confession would be too much for his heart – I might have his death on my hands for not having the judgment to simply hold out until he passes."

"It really could be too much for his heart."

"Maybe in a novel – maybe if Mrs Radcliffe needs a fresh source of terror for one of her heroes, such a revelation would do the deed. Otherwise, I doubt it." Daniel patted Luke's hand. "I won't bring you into it. Don't think anything like that. But I will do it; I think I must. For myself."

CHAPTER TWENTY-FOUR

It was noon when they arrived at the Park. The house was unusually quiet owing to an unseasonably warm day – after looking about, they discovered everyone out on the terrace. Stepping to the back parlour window, Luke observed a party which included not just Erasmus, Sophia, Evy, and Philip but also Bridget, looking very much a member of the household. This day was for Daniel, he knew it must be, yet observing his sister among a family she believed she would soon be a part of, Luke did feel rather ill.

Daniel was some time staring out at the group as well. His uncle should have been alone with Sophia after his morning routine. A request to speak to him privately should have passed as nothing. But with the weather having inspired a garden party, and Daniel's intended bride visiting, a request to see the man alone must cause concern. It might even cause alarm – Erasmus would of course be in no mood to re-join them after speaking to his nephew.

Luke looked at Daniel, half expecting him to give this up as lost. He now appeared a bit irritated but seemed undeterred; he was simply considering how this should be done. Yet now Luke felt entirely conflicted – perhaps they should delay. This was cruel. Taking Erasmus away from the party would be cruel. Destroying Bridget's introduction at Bainbridge Park would be cruel. Yet, wasn't her being here today really a good thing? They had not foreseen the opportunity of speaking to her so soon. This *would* be best for her; she should know as soon as possible. Surely, it would be just as cruel to delay as to break up a garden party.

When they observed Mrs Edwards breaking from the group to return to the house, Daniel seemed to take heart. He would see if she couldn't get the rest of the party away for a time. Settling into a corner, Luke took up a newspaper, hoping to appear at ease though his heart was in his throat.

Understanding Daniel was to be out most of the day, when Sophia came into the back parlour, she appeared taken aback.

"Oh dear, you startled me. How nice to see you. You too, Luke," she said, raising a hand. "You both must come out and sit with us. Bridget is here and it's so lovely. What a surprise this warm day – I just came in to grab my sunhat, I had been too precipitate packing it away already."

Luke continued to study his newspaper until a low exchange produced this from Mrs Edwards: "Is something the matter?"

Daniel assured her nothing was wrong, but he did need to speak to Erasmus about something important. Observing them over his paper, he saw Daniel look from Mrs Edwards toward the terrace. Then, in a lowered voice, he added something Luke couldn't hear. Nevertheless, he saw its immediate effect upon the lady, who looked both concerned and quite grave.

Sophia said, "I don't believe Bridget intends to go home anytime soon."

"All the better. I would like a moment with her afterwards, so if you would, please try to keep her close by."

The look which came into Sophia's face said she could guess Daniel's intention clearly enough. She looked down at the floor. Then, without a word, she nodded and exited to the terrace. Daniel returned to his pacing of the room as they waited for the others to be ushered inside. Bridget's being here was decisive. It would be best to get this done today. Luke must feel a pang, but he steeled himself. Daniel was doing this for him as much as for himself, and that was what mattered. Bridget, at best, was making a practical match, and there had only been a few days of serious talk on the subject.

When footsteps approached, Luke looked once more to Daniel, who strode towards the back parlour door. He did look dreadfully uneasy, that stiff posture, that fidgeting. He bowed as Bridget entered, nodding at Mrs Edwards who followed behind her. He looked past them as the others followed on their heels.

Only no others were following on their heels.

Bridget crossed the room and stood before the mantle. Mrs Edwards closed the door.

Daniel turned to Luke, a look of alarm on his face. Luke instantly came to his feet, looking first to Bridget, who had gone red and was steadfastly staring at the floor, refusing to look at anyone. Then, he looked to Mrs Edwards, who was staring defiantly at Daniel, betraying her unease only by a faint swallow. Daniel looked angrier than Luke had ever seen him.

"What is the meaning of this? I asked a favour of you, Sophia. I asked that you please bring everyone inside so I could speak with my uncle on a matter of great importance to me."

"You wished to speak to Bridget, too. You said so."

After a moment to check whatever he actually wished to say, Daniel said, "You know damn well I wished to speak with Bridget *after* I spoke with Erasmus. I was quite clear about that; are you going to tell me I was not?"

Though blinking a couple of times at the language, Mrs Edwards continued to hold her ground. She said, "Bridget is my dear friend, Daniel. I know what you intend to tell our uncle, and I merely ask you to reconsider. Please. She needs this marriage more than you can know."

"Does she?" said Daniel, turning to Bridget, who continued steadfastly to look at the floor.

"Yes. Even though... someone in this room might not wish it for you."

"Please, Sophia," said Bridget, at last looking up. Then, a tear running down her cheek, she added, "Don't," before pressing a hand to her mouth to contain a sob.

Luke shot a look at Daniel, who turned to him with a look of astonishment which told him he was not wrong in what this seemed to imply. Daniel took a step back. Then, he came to stand beside him.

Luke turned to his sister, refusing to let himself think too long about what was all but being said. He asked as calmly as he could, "What do you know?"

"Please, Luke," said Mrs Edwards, stepping forward. "We do understand. You have every right to wish your friend to remain single. He is very special to you. I wish you to know that I, that we, do not blame you for it. But there *is* something else to consider." She looked at both. "There is Bridget to consider."

"*Why?*" said Luke. "*Why* do I have the right to wish my friend to remain single, in your opinion?"

Mrs Edwards held his gaze. She looked away, taking another moment to consider. She walked across the room and took her friend's hand. Bridget kept her gaze averted as Sophia spoke to her in a low voice. At last, she nodded and swiped at her eyes. Together, they turned to the men.

Sophia said, "The reason, Luke, why you have what I term *the right* to wish Daniel to remain single, is the same reason I might wish, with all my heart and soul, that Bridget remain so as well."

Luke looked from her to Bridget, who had collected herself enough to bring her eyes to his. She said, "Do you understand?"

Luke did not understand. Not at all. "What?" He turned to Daniel, who appeared much longer taking this in as he seemed to comprehend more about what was being said.

"Dear God," he said, finally. "I apologise. Bridget, for my tone. Sophia, I apologise sincerely. I should never have spoken to you like that."

"It's alright, Daniel."

"It is *not* alright. You are the kindest, most giving soul."

Luke felt as though he were staring at the surface of a pond. He could not see past the surface beyond the glimmer and his own reflection. Daniel had seen to the bottom. He had seen to something that made sense to him. Luke could see only that Bridget was like him. Just like himself.

Feeling he was reaching across months, perhaps more, he took her hand. She gave it easily. "Bridge. I have to say it. You and Sophia are..."

"Yes."

"Lovers?"

"Yes."

"But..." he lowered his voice. "And you two are... happy together?"

She smiled and turned to her companion. "Yes, when we are not clumsily confronting my brother about a secret I begged she would keep."

Blushing violently, not quite able to attend to the apology offered by Sophia, Luke said, "How long have you known?"

Bridget said, as kindly as she could, "For a while. I'm sorry."

"What's to be sorry about?"

"Because I am so damned nosey. And I know that you know I am. I know you saw me watching you last year when you were staring at Michael Kensington."

"Kensington? Staring at him? You are mad – I never liked Kensington."

"Well, you liked the tight white breeches he wore one Sunday because his family are too cheap to take his brother's hand-me-downs to Uncle Pete, and his mother thinks she can sew."

This was so absurd, both the unwanted, forgotten memory and Bridget's run-on sentence, that Luke nearly laughed. Seeing this, Bridget smiled as well. Daniel took his hand and kissed it, at which Luke reddened even more, glancing back to his sister to judge her reaction. But Bridget was looking at Sophia who was appearing so distressed it bordered on fear. She did appear as though she were about to faint. "Will you not reconsider?"

Daniel expelled a breath, looking about the room as he attempted to collect his thoughts. He did appear to be considering something. However, Luke had no idea what he meant when, after returning to the lady, he said, "The girl by the punchbowl?"

When Sophia nodded, anything more seemed beyond him.

Bridget took her lover's hand and sat her down. Coming in closer, she set a hand on her knee and said, "We'll find another way. It's alright."

"There *is* no other way. You know that." Returning to Daniel, "Won't you reconsider?"

Luke felt forced to interject here. "What do you want him to reconsider? You *wish* Bridget to marry him?"

"Yes, of course. We've been planning this for nearly a year." The only compensation for the confusion he felt at this was the look of fresh bewilderment on Daniel's face. The lady continued, "That makes no sense to either of you. Oh, dear. Do allow me to explain."

"If you would," said Daniel. "I'm afraid I'm not feeling very quick at the moment."

As the men drew up chairs Sophia thought back for a place to begin.

"During a visit to see Erasmus last year, at a church function, Bridget saw me sitting alone and came over to introduce herself. Initially, without her mother, Daniel. I suppose she felt sorry for me – a stranger in widow's weeds sitting off to one side. I wasn't as tragic as I know I must have appeared. Everyone in Grantham, whenever I have visited, has always been very kind and welcoming. But I had gone to that function only to please Erasmus; he didn't wish me to stay at home alone. I simply wasn't in the mood to be chatty, so I told anyone who asked I was a bit heated and wished to sit." She glanced at her companion, who smiled at the memory. "When Bridget ventured over, she was by no means the first. Yet she *was* the only young person to do so. A beautiful young girl, not lacking for companions by any means, found it in her heart to notice and pity me."

"Upon my word," said Bridget, "it was *not* pity; I was curious. Nosey. I'd never seen a woman your age in weeds."

"Very well," said Sophia, "but do allow that some of it was that you did not like to see a stranger sitting alone at a church function."

Sighing, "Well, of course, that was part of it. I'm not a brute."

Smiling, Sophia patted her hand. Then, she turned to Luke. "It all happened terribly fast, I'm afraid. At least for me. Bridget was kind and interested. Absolutely radiant. But she was one other thing, which was perhaps even more important: she was frank. Candid. Because she was candid, I found myself being so as well. By the end of that conversation, I had told her more of substance than I had told almost anyone in my life, no matter the years I had known them. There was a childlike directness which cut through the nonsense people so often speak, myself included. Within the first minute, she had learned that I had lost my husband three years before, and after offering her condolences and my saying I had made peace with his death, she asked why on earth I was still in weeds."

"A bold pullet," said Bridget. "I don't know how you could stand me."

"I understood later she was simply wondering I didn't wish to wear something else. I, however, assumed she meant I would never catch another husband, which I had heard many times before, along with all the assurances that I was still young and pretty enough. And... I don't know, I suppose the boldness of my companion emboldened me, and I asked if she thought weeds might not be worn for more than just mourning a husband. That perhaps if one was not interested in another match or in being approached, weeds might not be ideal for keeping attentions from the male sex at bay."

Raising his eyebrows, Daniel turned to Bridget. "That was quite a response for a girl of sixteen. What did you think of that?"

With blood in her cheeks, Bridget said, "I thought I had made the right decision approaching her. I thought she was clever to think of her strategy. I didn't think to wonder why she didn't wish another match." She turned to Sophia, "You told me that first day about your husband, didn't you? That he was a dear friend, only, whom you had wished to care for until the end of his illness?"

"Oh, yes, I told you of Henry that first day. It was so very easy."

Bridget hummed. "I *was* listening. But I was also wondering how you would look in something light and airy. In my head, it was a sprigged muslin, pink and yellow flowers." Turning to Luke, "I didn't know why I wished to see her like that. Not then. But I did believe it a tragedy that I would resolve because she was too attractive to have retired from life so early. So, I fetched Mamma, determined she should befriend her too so we could have her around as often as possible."

Sophia brought Bridget's fingertips to her lips. "That initial exchange set a very clear tone, with many, very clear openings for understanding, during our subsequent conversations. And our many letters."

Bridget returned to her brother. "But even though we met more than a year ago, and we spoke with exceptional honesty, I only understood what sort of relationship I wished a few months ago. I did understand the idea of finding one's own sex more interesting than the other. But can you understand this, Luke? – I didn't have a label for women being together; it is such a non-idea it isn't even against the law. When Sophia spoke of herself, I took it to be just that – feelings she alone had. But I *did* have a very clear idea about men. It was where my interests lay because I had a name, many names, for it. That made it real for me. It was nothing you did, Luke, or didn't do, exactly – rather that I was *looking* for it. Does that make sense?"

"Yes," he said, though he believed it would take time thinking it over before it did entirely.

She continued, "And, now... do you feel better? I know how terrible it has been for you trying to keep your secret. I don't wish to make it worse, make you feel that you somehow failed."

Luke frowned. "Nobody else knows?" When Bridget hesitated, he added, "Besides Sophia, I mean."

When Bridget continued to hesitate, Luke, after a quick look at Daniel, said, "Who else knows?"

His sister blushed. Only after Sophia had taken her hand and told her her intentions had been good and she had nothing to be ashamed of did she say, still not looking up, "George."

Luke had to work to compose himself, to quell the stinging in his nose the sharp intake of breath had produced. "*George Everett*? You told George Everett!?"

"Only because," she said, wiping a tear from her cheek before daring to look up. "Because I had *found* George. After I understood about you, I searched him out." Then, she added, scarcely above a whisper, "For you."

CHAPTER TWENTY-FIVE

T wo hours had passed since the conversation in the back parlour. As surprising as it had been, as uncertain as it had left them as to how to proceed, the conversation had been going well until the moment Bridget said she had sought out a young man as a companion for Luke. The discussion had continued, but with her brother noticeably subdued until he was merely staring at the floor. Daniel had motioned to the women that they would speak later, today certainly, but that now was not the time. Observing Luke's behaviour, both had agreed, though it left them in an uneasy state, Sophia nearly wretched, which he regretted sincerely.

When they were up in Daniel's bedchamber, Luke had come immediately into his arms but had remained unresponsive. When they lay down, he set his head on Daniel's chest, but to Daniel's asking for his thoughts about what had just passed, he said only that it was a lot to take in. So, they had lain together listening to the sounds of the house

– Luke with his head on his chest, Daniel with a hand in his hair.

The return of that withdrawn, unhappy young man was unsettling, but Daniel took heart from knowing him on a deeper level. Theirs was an acquaintance of only a week, but they had been days of strong and unusual intimacies. He knew Luke Morley. He understood that he needed time on his own to reflect. However, he also knew that without intervention he would likely fall back into old habits. And his habit, Daniel suspected, was to conclude private reflections with silence.

He said into the silence, "The conversation has upset you. Will you tell me why?" Shrugging, Luke said again that it was a lot to take in. "One of the best things about being in a relationship is that you have an intimate with whom you can share your thoughts and fears. Let me be that for you."

There was a momentary pause. Then, he said, "Now you won't speak to Erasmus as you had planned? About yourself?"

"Do you wish me to?"

"That's your choice. But if you don't..." He lowered his voice. "How can they ask this of you?"

Daniel stroked his hair. He certainly understood the concern. What Sophia was asking was extraordinary – a way that she and Bridget might be together without either raising questions difficult to answer or living in Northampton in near poverty.

Five months ago, after word had reached her of Erasmus's stroke, Sophia had seen a way forward. She would dispose of her house and accept Erasmus's long-standing offer to move into Bainbridge Park. Knowing Daniel Thornton, a lifelong bachelor whom her uncle very much wished to marry, was already with him in the house, she would arrive and offer to assist caring for their uncle. Upon hearing Bridget's description of him and his continually resisting Miss Williams, though in favour of nobody else, it seemed possible his single state might be due to sexual persuasion and so even more favourable to their schemes. After befriending him, she would, in a private moment, very tactfully ask if he might not consider a match with Miss Morley. The marriage would bring her into the house with Sophia, fulfil his uncle's wishes, and she would take the care of Erasmus onto herself. After Erasmus's death, she would stay on as a kind of lady's companion to her friend, and Daniel would be free to pursue his own interests – whatever they were.

"It's absurd," said Luke. "How could that ever have worked? What were they thinking?"

"I think a better question is, what other option had they? Desperate people try desperate things. Sophia said she would have been willing to share Bridget, *actually* share her, sad as that is to consider. So, Bridget's description of me must have been strong encouragement. I appeared to have no interest in women, and perhaps my inheritance depended on my marrying. I don't find that so outlandish."

But Luke was clearly battling with himself. He'd felt the same kind of desperation yet could see no way to be happy about this. "Now you think I'm a horrible person," he said. "I'm the worst brother in the world, without any compassion."

"It *is* a lot to take in, I agree with you. I've had much more experience of the world and hadn't any idea such a thing going on. But I do think you aren't saying something. Why did learning about that Everett boy upset you so much?"

"It didn't."

"Luke."

"Because," he said. After quite a long delay, he continued, "Because it is *humiliating*. How must I have looked to them? Bridget said a hundred ways George wished to speak to me and was only too shy. All the time, I thought she was making excuses for his standoffish behaviour. I thought she thought I'd be easier to get to like him, then she could make the rest of my family believe how great he is... as a match for *her*. I've run every conversation a thousand times in my head. Every time it was me who cut her off, me who said I didn't wish to speak, me who told her how much she had changed and that I didn't like who she had become. Yet she would not admit the truth even to win an argument because it would have meant betraying what she knew about me. Out of compassion for my feelings, she said nothing and took the abuse. I didn't *deserve* any compassion."

He turned from Daniel and lay on his side facing away. "I didn't know what I wished to do or where I wished to go in the world, but I had figured out for certain Grantham was *not* the place. Grantham was a stupid place where everyone was different from me, everybody was against me. Of course, now that I have you in my life, I wish to stay. But even without you, my judgment is so bad I shouldn't dare leave because I could never trust myself out in the world. This all seems like a joke intended to degrade me."

"Life often *is* nothing but a grand, cruel joke. The trick is to understand that it *is* a joke and that you *can* laugh about it."

"For Christ's sake, how can there suddenly be so many like us? All around us. It's ridiculous."

It was difficult to contain a smile here, yet it was a sad smile. "It may seem like that now," said Daniel, "this suddenness. But the only true coincidence is your sharing the same proclivities with your sister. And I am not certain at all that this is especially rare. Once we get beyond demonic possession and rank depravity as explanations, I find a biological inclination, whatever reason there may be for that, most suits my own experience. Biology, familial traits are what you share with your siblings. Aside from her, what you are understanding as being magically surrounded by people like yourself is the result of attraction and conscious effort. Bridget sought out someone for you from the hundreds of boys living in Grantham. She was attracted by, *and* she sought out Sophia, who might simply have been a visitor she never saw again. After they spoke, they felt bound together. When you and I met, our attraction bound us – it obliged us to continue."

"But I was deluding myself about this town. I've lived here all my life, and I don't know it at all."

"You weren't deluding yourself entirely. I fled Aylesbury in the belief that I couldn't possibly find anyone like myself. And though odds make it almost a certainty that there must have been men and women like me, being of a like mind is not the same thing as being able to accept it in yourself or in others. What you are experiencing is, quite frankly, owing to your having quite a remarkable sister. You simply could not see it through your fears of discovery. But *you* too, Luke, are just as remarkable."

"How is that?"

"You overcame your fears, your shyness, and pursued me when you hadn't an idea I would have any interest in you. You also pursued me when you believed it might well be the end of life as you knew it. You refused to be denied access to Bainbridge Park simply because of who you are."

"I *was* terrified of doing that, that's why I was out in the bloody rain for two hours. In the back of my mind, perhaps I thought doing it would make it easier to run away from Grantham. Then, I realised it wasn't such a great plan if you didn't come with me."

"Desperate people do desperate things. I understand why you did what you did that night. And I understand why Sophia and Bridget planned what they planned."

"I *do* understand," said Luke. "Yet I cannot bear the thought of Bridget coming here *instead* of me. I know we can't be married, and I know she can't be married to Sophia. Yet I am still so jealous that she might actually stand at the altar before all the world and become your wife."

With a sigh, Daniel said, "So, what do we do?"

Luke said miserably, "I shall marry Sophia, just to spite them."

Daniel laughed and kissed his forehead.

Luke crawled on top of him. He kissed his mouth. Then, he leant back to look him in the eye. He said, "I'm not the child that I sometimes sound like. I know what we have to do."

When Daniel departed, Luke sent him with his full support, understanding it would take time to accept their decision. Daniel would marry Bridget. He felt somewhere beyond resigned, somewhere short of accepting, but that, for him, was progress. Daniel was in this with him.

As Luke watched from the window, he observed the man crossing the green. The women rose from the terrace to approach him. Daniel's intention was to ask them to take a walk, informing them only where their privacy could be assured. The group had only exchanged a few preliminary words, however, when Bridget leapt forward to embrace him, then fell into the arms of Sophia, who collapsed into tears on her shoulder. Daniel smiled up to the window. His shrug said so clearly that he had never been great at adhering to a plan that Luke laughed. Alone in Daniel's bedchamber, he laughed because he had understood even without the words. And he laughed because he now felt in his heart, looking at his sister and her lover, that this was the right thing to do. He couldn't imagine doing anything else. He and Daniel *were* in this together. But they were in it with two more, bound just as closely in the agreement.

As Daniel put an arm around the pair and led them down the green on their walk, Luke watched the trio moving forward as one. It was the movement of many towards a greater happiness they could not have otherwise attempted. The newness of such a direction for himself initially left him feeling somewhat overwhelmed. Then, his thoughts returned to Wednesday morning when he'd watched Mrs Musgrove lead her group toward a common aim. The women were now working with the militia, within the bounds of the law, redistributing what had been collected and compensating those who had sustained losses. Mrs Musgrove must now live with uncertainty, with the prospect of prosecution by the local magistrate. Should she receive a prison sentence, she must content herself with what had been achieved: the prospect of a Minimum Wage Reform Bill to be introduced the following year. The attention of their Prime Minister who, should the first bill fail, intended to introduce of bill of his own to reform the Poor Laws.

Yet, the uncertainties of potential outcomes must be preferable to the certainties of inaction. Luke had the certainty that there was no other acceptable alternative. And he had the contentment that they need not withdraw the happiness of their loved ones in pursuit of happiness for themselves. The happiness of his parents, of Erasmus, was a happiness widely distributed. A happiness worth whatever continued effort must be made.

It was not perfect. But it was a solution. He had Daniel. Bridget had Sophia. And that was better than he could ever have hoped for.

He was coming downstairs when he heard a knock at the front door. He stepped into the vestibule as the butler received a note from a footman sent from The George. Coming quickly forward, he offered to deliver it and was back upstairs.

Though Luke had assured him he had no problem with his presence in the house, Clarence had been careful to stay out of everyone's way. He had made progress in his plans to return to London. He had taken the coach to arrange for his departure by post in a few days. However, as his parents were steadfastly refusing to allow Daniel's footman to retrieve his portmanteau, threatening severe displeasure if he was wavering in their ambitions, he had had to do so wrapped in a hastily altered three-quarter-length frockcoat from Daniel's wardrobe.

Clarence admitted Luke to his room, groaning at the sight of another message from The George. "Have a seat," he said, gesturing his visitor toward an armchair. "I'm sure this will be good for a laugh."

Once he had read it out, Clarence failed to laugh; Luke thought it best to refrain. Upon closer examination they had discovered the note was addressed to Daniel, threatening legal action if he did not release their son. *Theft of an Heir-Apparent* was to be the charge, which was a capital offence, applied in history most often to members of the royal family but which a good lawyer would have no trouble arguing applied to a family only a couple tiers down. Clarence tossed the note aside, assuring Luke he was fully prepared to purchase a few new suits to travel home in. But all his money was at The George as were the letters from Daniel which were all he had left in the world.

Falling into a stupor, he collapsed onto his bed. Luke was unsuccessful in reviving him until he ordered tea and persuaded him to join him for a cup. After nearly an hour questioning him about his parents, both what they were like and what their experience had been since arriving in town, an idea came.

"It will take some doing, and we must begin right now. But I think it could be organised by this evening."

"Ah, thank you, my good man," said Clarence. "Who says necessity is the mother of invention? Just give the problem to the new lover; he will have the old lover out *tout de suite.*"

"You *do* wish your things back, don't you?" said Luke, his colour rising.

Clarence made a face. "Yes. Thank you. Daniel's a lucky bloody bastard to have you. What do you have in mind?"

Luke, in fact, had two things in mind. As the second was somewhat more involved and dependent on the success of the other, he merely hinted at it as he set out his plan for the first. For this, he consulted Daniel who, after consulting Clarence believed it had potential. They then sought out Jacob Elsworthy, who joined the group breathless at the thought of a new commission. He agreed even before he understood the details as Clarence promised to pay him exceptionally well should he succeed. He promised, too, if he played his cards right, additional compensation from the Hoppers themselves.

CHAPTER TWENTY-SIX

The coach returned at quarter to midnight to a Bainbridge Park breathless with anticipation. Upon arrival, Jacob Elsworthy descended from the cabin, waiting as the coachman brought forth Clarence's portmanteau. Then, he hurried inside where he was met with a reception he was not soon to forget.

Daniel, Luke, Clarence, even Sophia and Bridget Morley, lately informed of the scheme, were present to welcome him. The mission, which he admitted through a toothy grin, had succeeded quite well, he would inform them of presently. He wished only a few moments at the fire to warm his hands. And, if he might, a slight nip of brandy to loosen his vocal cords so he could relate what had happened properly. This, then, is how Jacob Elsworthy not only retrieved Clarence's portmanteau but solved the problem of Lord and Lady Ludlow altogether:

ιτ was by no means easy to gain that interview, I can tell you. The George is locked down as the Hoppers wished nobody admitted inside! Only once they understood I was the same Elsworthy who had informed them the little he knew of the Morleys – very little indeed Luke and Bridget – and had delivered a note to yourself, Luke – which I hope sincerely caused no trouble for you, given what I saw of that deranged family tonight – was I finally granted an audience.

"'Your Lord and Ladyship,' I says, 'who were so generous as to employ me formerly. I am privy to a piece of information I feel obligated to inform you of, though at the risk of life and limb.' They looked immediately alarmed and bestowed a down payment for the communication, promising more if this information was indeed as valuable as I had intimated. Upon reception of said payment, I says, 'Thank you, my Lord and Ladyship, much obliged to you both. And so here it is: in one hour's time, your palace is to be invaded!' And as God is my witness, they began packing even before I could tell them what was at hand.

"'It's the housewives, just as you suppose! As you may know, they have never been jailed as every member of local law enforcement is terrified of prosecuting them. It is widely believed that you recently placed two exceptionally large orders for baked goods: one for pastries from Madison's Patisserie, another for an assortment of breads from Ringwald's. Have I been correctly informed of this?' To which they said, *Yes, Good God! though every bit of it had been transported to Bainbridge Park!* I said I was sorry to tell them, but that piece of information was not known at all. I myself had not heard it, and it most certainly had not reached the renegades. So, now they are readying for an invasion, determined to retrieve every crumb. And they are saying, if they discover nothing remains of that order, they will wreak terrible havoc on The George and her inhabitants!'"

Daniel ruffled Luke's hair and wrapped his arm around him. Clarence clasped his hands together, and all leant forward as Elsworthy continued:

"You'll be pleased to know, Sir Clarence, that your parents wished to retrieve you and were horrified to learn that all roads between gentlemen's abodes were being watched. They said they feared the Park must certainly be next under assault. I said that sounded a certainty once the final destination of those baked goods was discovered! I would be off directly to inform you. I would also be happy to transport your portmanteau which you would certainly need for your midnight flight from Grantham! For a small fee. And so, I have brought it."

Clarence leapt from his seat, placed a kiss on Luke's forehead, then returned to Elsworthy. "Anything more, before I kiss you as well and give you your reward?"

"Only to assure you that your very particular message, sir, I did relay to them. As they were packing everything into trunks and every servant on the top floor was in an uproar, I told them I bid them Godspeed on their journey. They must travel quickly and must be exceptionally careful where they stopped and whom they spoke to before they reached the safety of London. As they no doubt knew, many country towns were now under siege by renegades and anti-royalists, and I would be remiss if I failed to remind them of the terrible lesson learned at Varennes."

***

Two days later, at about ten in the morning, Clarence emerged from the main house and stepped into the coach waiting to take him from Bainbridge Park. Daniel followed him in, taking the seat opposite, pleased to see him off and, at long last, put a dignified end to their former relationship. Daniel observed him as they progressed toward the coaching house, pleased to have spent a few tranquil days with his tempestuous former lover. Pleased by the improvements in his behaviour, pleased especially by his civility to Luke.

Perhaps more than anything, he was pleased to observe the uneasiness on Clarence's face as the coach rocked along. It was an expression he had never seen there before – that of a person who understood he was moving into a new phase of life without the old crutches to rely on. The relationship with his parents Clarence was determined to alter, understanding the roles they had played were incompatible with his future life as an independent adult. Daniel had promised his friendship, begged him to write often, daily if he wished, for advice, encouragement, and support. It would be the encouragement of a friend, he hoped a dear friend, but it would be different from their former relationship. By this morning, Daniel's reassurance of this was met with a wave of the hand and an insistence that he was not daft, he had heard him and would certainly remember that. The reality of his new life, and new responsibility, was truly dawning on him.

They arrived at the coaching house with time to spare. Clarence leapt out, leaving Daniel to watch his portmanteau as he strode across the street to stare in a few shop windows. Only, Daniel was certain, he was seeing nothing. He was scarcely at one long enough before he was on to the next. When he returned with quite a bad imitation of his former jaunty lilt, Daniel took him to one side and set a hand on his shoulder.

"I have full faith in you, Clarence."

"Do you? That's refreshing."

"All you must do is have faith in yourself. It's that simple."

Clarence nodded. Then his face altered as his attention was drawn to a place a short distance away. Daniel turned, smiled, and raised a hand. After Clarence agreed he was ready, Daniel took him by the arm. Bridget was waiting for them in the distance. After greeting them, she took the arm of the man beside her. With a little prompting, Everett looked up. He tucked his hair behind one ear. Then, he looked at Clarence.

"General George Everett, as I live and breathe," muttered Clarence as they proceeded forward.

Frowning slightly, Daniel asked, certain he had misheard, "What was that?"

"He's looking at me..."

Daniel said, "I should think he will do a lot of that in the next two weeks. He will also look *to* you – as a guide. Hopefully, eventually, as a friend. You've spoken to him enough over the last two days to understand his history. You know what he has been through."

"I know he can defend himself, certainly – Bridget, through that dazzling smile of hers, said it ten different ways both times we all sat down together. I shall be alone with him now, won't I?"

"Yes, you will. As for Bridget, she cares for him and wants to make certain you understand where he is coming from. But she also trusts my judgment in recommending you. He is looking for a fresh start. But if you reach the end of two weeks and he decides London is not for him, I have been assured he will always have a place with the Morleys. You are under no obligation to support him if things aren't working out."

Clarence hadn't time for whatever tart dismissal of this he might have wished to bestow. He had extended his hand. Bridget was the first to take it.

"Top of the morning, Clarence. Here he is for you." Spoken with an exceptionally sweet lilt, though Daniel doubted if he had ever heard a greeting with such teeth in it.

George now had his hand extended.

Before taking it, Clarence said, "And here *I* am, for George." Then, turning to Everett, he took his hand. "How are we feeling today?"

Bridget had nothing to say to this; Daniel could not have been more pleased.

"I'm well. Thank you again, sir, for what you are doing."

Clarence inclined his head. The *sir*, Daniel suspected, was Bridget's doing. Clarence was too used to hearing it to notice, though he would have noticed the omission. However, after a second look, Daniel believed he could discern a slight reaction. A slightly warmer expression, perhaps.

Either way, the two would have to take it from here. Daniel had a nearly overpowering urge to grab Clarence and tell him how very proud he was of him. But he would wait; he *should* wait; he *would* wait for the first letter to arrive.

"I believe that one is for us," said Clarence, gesturing at an approaching post-chaise. "Are we ready?"

CHAPTER TWENTY-SEVEN

Marriages in St. Wulfram's are, by their nature, grand affairs. Indeed, so grand it is often left to the wedding party to live up to its enclosure, or else be remembered as a grand disaster. A party of a few hundred guests can do it if well-positioned to fill the aisles with the proper number of attendants waiting in the wings.

"That was the case with Stephen and Clarissa last month," said Margaret Morley, sitting in the front row on the bride's side. "I wish you could have been here to see it. A wedding the first week of November is a fine thing when the weather cooperates, and of course it did for those two. Stephen did so wish to be here today, but he is away on his wedding tour. The date could not be helped, you know – everyone agreed the sooner the better in regard to Daniel's uncle. Ah, look! There he is over on the groom's side; when did he sneak in? I must go speak to him in a moment." Leaning forward, she blew Erasmus Thornton a kiss. The man, already in tears of joyous expectation, caught the kiss and put it to his lips. "Dear me," said Margaret, "I do hope he will be alright over there. He does have Mr Collins, but I don't imagine a substitute can ever be quite the same."

"Don't trouble yourself, Mrs Morley," said Clarence, rising to his feet. "George and I shall take a turn to stretch our legs, then we will sit with him. As intimates of both the bride and groom, we might select seats on either side. I have often heard of the pleasures of going both ways, and I suppose this must be one of them."

Margaret turned and squeezed Everett's hand, which she had retained since he'd sat beside her. "Ah, very well. How *lovely* it is to see you again, George. We would have been happy to have you back in the house, but I am so glad city life has agreed with you. Bridget was overjoyed you could make it today. She did wish to speak to you a bit more but with a wedding, you understand."

"Of course, ma'am," said George, inclining his head. "We meant to arrive yesterday but were delayed."

"Ah, that is because you departed on a Friday which is never propitious for road travel. Do stand up so I can look at you again. My stars! So much changed from the day you left us. What a handsome young man you are!"

"Yes, he is, isn't he?" said Clarence, raising a brow.

"Mr Hopper keeps me, well, hopping," said George, brightly. "Attentive to every detail – well-groomed and, I must say, exceptionally well-exercised. It improves a fellow."

"Listen to you!" cried Margaret. "Just like a little puppy! Are you a little puppy, George? I should think not!"

"Well, I *am* obedient when I know it will get me a treat. Entirely loyal to my Master, Clarence won't argue with that. Rather overfond of licking everything, but you know Clarence has never protested to—"

"*Let us take a turn about the room*," said Clarence, eyes blazing. "Before you give *me* a turn."

"Oh, you two," said the lady. "Such is the London way – such droll comedy I cannot understand a word of it."

The couple took a decidedly circuitous route to Daniel's uncle. Much was discussed in hushed tones, much laughter from George, much scolding from Clarence, who, as they arrived on the groom's side, was heard to say, "*What in God's name have I created*? Ah, Erasmus! Hello, Collins."

"Young Masters."

"Clarence!" cried Erasmus. "I observed you speaking with my friend Mrs Morley. *Cla-rence*! You see? I always recall your name, but I do tend to forget whose child you are."

"So do I, usually. But I *am* Daniel's adoring nephew, which you do *not* forget. That is what counts, of course."

"That *is* what counts, isn't it? He'll be so pleased you made it."

"How are his nerves?"

"Oh-ho-ho – with a beautiful, vivacious young woman like Miss Morley waiting for him you can *imagine* his nerves on his wedding day!" He winked at George. "And you must be Everett."

"Yes, sir. It's an honour to finally meet you. I've heard so much about you from Bridget."

"All good I trust. I'll tell you something: we are *blessed* to have her join our family. She practically lives at the house already. My niece Sophia also lives with us, so Daniel and I are uncommonly fortunate in female companionship. How they have warmed the place, I cannot tell you. And I did used to worry Sophia might grow lonely for companionship surrounded by so many men. But she has Bridget now to chat to, and chat they do. Always together, the most harmonious pair. Clarence, tell me, how did it happen that two women brought together under the same roof, where there is a household to manage and every detail to organise, unite so perfectly it was like they were made to live together?"

"I can't imagine."

"I do expect Sophia allows Bridget the final say when it comes to it. George, I want you to be careful when it comes to opening your heart in London. Daniel was just about your age when he went, and it took a return to the country, more than ten years later, to find his life mate."

At this, George looked at Clarence. The comment passed without so much as a raised eyebrow, or a nasal aside. Luke, of course, was here, somewhere. It had been three months, but the sight of Daniel again, of his old rival—

"Sorry, what was that?" said George, coming out of his reverie.

"I said," said Clarence, taking his gaze, "I concur. It *does* take a trip into the country to find one's life mate. Erasmus is correct."

George regarded him. He smiled, though with some uncertainty. The walls initially between them, of formality, of insecurity, of fear on both sides, had at last fallen after they'd discovered a similar taste for banter. Verbal play had become their outlet, then their common occupation, then their display to one another. One night early in their second week, banter had put George sufficiently at ease that, after a fit of laughter, he had leant in and kissed Clarence. Light-hearted banter had done it and had simply become their way. Clarence Hopper was not one to speak without a punchline.

After another minute speaking to Erasmus, Clarence suggested a visit to the water closet. George nodded, feeling words continuing to elude him, and they remained silent as they proceeded toward the antechamber. Clarence slowed their pace before they reached their destination and waited for George to look at him before he spoke.

"That was perhaps the wrong time to do that. You know I am a rather impulsive creature." George nodded, but before he could decide whether he should try to make light of the comment, Clarence continued, "The impulse was taking an unforeseen opportunity. The impulse was not the wish to tell you. I have been happier, George, these last three months than I ever believed I could be."

George said quietly, "You have?"

"Yes, I have. Seeing this church, seeing the High Street and her shops and hotels again did not make me realise this; I knew it long before we arrived. What returning to Grantham has done is make me understand that I must say it. I have known the error of being late to understand. I will *not* know the error of having understood without speaking."

"I—" said George, then cleared his throat before trying again. "Neither will I. You see, I have already done what Erasmus told me not to do. Isn't that funny? I opened my heart in London, though it was entirely yours for the asking already. I... I don't need to tell you what returning to this town has meant to me. I should have been in tears an hour ago had we not proceeded directly to church – the one place that doesn't remind me of them!"

Clarence embraced him to still him. George set his forehead on his shoulder, grateful to be excused from saying anything more. After a moment, Clarence whispered, "Thank you, my sweet boy. That is everything, and more, that I could ever wish to hear. That is all we need say at present, I think. How about we resume our jester's hats for the rest of the day? Then speak a bit more this evening?"

George nodded. He rested his forehead a moment longer on Clarence's shoulder. Then, he stepped back and smiled at his companion before they continued toward the antechamber.

***

"Papa, you are crying!" said Bridget, withdrawing from the man's embrace. She reached for a handkerchief from her dressing room vanity.

"Bah!" said the man, taking the kerchief and blowing his nose. "Confounded dust. This church doesn't need a new roof, it needs a green and a bit of shrubbery around it. Dust to dust, that is St. Wulfram's, faith." He cleared his throat. "I won't keep you long. Just stopped in to say I'm proud of you, Bridge. By G—, you do look beautiful."

"Thank you," she said, touching the delicate gold chain Daniel had given her when they'd become formally engaged.

311

She wore a simple white gown which just touched the floor garnished with red bows for pulling off and tossing to all the marriageable women in attendance. John Morley tugged one gently.

"Well, you'll be an old married soon, just like the rest of us. Your mother has..." he cleared his throat, "...*spoken* to you about the wedding night. Told you everything you should know?"

"Oh, I expect so. We've had some good talks."

"Three months is a whirlwind romance; I hope you haven't felt rushed. When I gave you and Daniel my advice in the matter it was a sound principle but with the assumption that a date *after* Lent might be fixed on. I hope I didn't err."

"Not at all, Papa. We are indeed grateful for the guidance. Daniel said he'd never considered it but hasn't a doubt that, by marrying in Lent, we *would* live to repent. An earlier date suits us in regard to Erasmus, you understand."

The pair turned as Bridget's bridesmaid stepped into her dressing room. "Well, how do I look?"

Looking up from an errant thread she had discovered on her sleeve, Sophia immediately apologised, having not understood John was visiting his daughter. When she observed Bridget's eyes filling with tears, when she turned to her vanity, hand to her mouth, Sophia stepped forward and took John's hands. Directing him gently to the door, she thanked him for his good wishes. Then, she told him she was afraid the bride had a bit more to do to prepare herself if he'd be so good as to leave them. John quickly acquiesced, though not before he had informed her it was good to see her in a pretty flowered gown – she wouldn't be requiring any of those red bows by any means. She was indeed lovely.

"I thank you kindly, sir. I have been determined for some time to have done with my weeds – today shall establish a new trend in what has been a decidedly dour wardrobe: now, a lighter, brighter Sophia."

When the door closed, she approached Bridget. She stood behind her where she was blotting her eyes before the vanity. Bridget looked up to observe her in the reflected image. She shook her head, chastising herself and calling herself a goose. When Sophia simply smiled, she turned and embraced her.

After a time, Bridget leant back to look up at her.

"I am not so altered, surely," said Sophia. "My hair is pinned as it always is. This is by no means the first time you've seen me in something other than weeds."

"But this shall be in public. I don't know; it just struck me. And the gown: just what I had imagined when I first saw you. Sprigged muslin, pink and yellow – it is hardly a surprise, and the meaning today is still our own. That's why it surprises me to have it feel so public."

"Perhaps," said Sophia, after a moment's consideration, "you are understanding a greater freedom than you had foreseen for yourself. One reforms the world where one can. One has faith that things will be reformed. Yet, I think it would be a mistake to discount tradition. That is important, too, as is the greater happiness of our loved ones. Yet, we are *not* confined; we move within the boundaries we have established for ourselves. We feel free, Bridget, because we are."

Bridget took a moment to consider this. Then, smiling, she said, "We are, aren't we?"

With a nod, Sophia swept a lock of Bridget's hair behind her shoulder. Then, she took that shoulder, brought her forward, and kissed her – fully, deeply. For the rest of their lives.

***

The wedding was a lovely affair, though by St. Wulfram standards fell short of the grandeur the place was capable of. Attendance neared three hundred, nearly all for the bride given the groom's limited acquaintance in Grantham. The organ swelled as John Morley walked his daughter down the aisle. Waiting for them at the altar stood Daniel with their attendants – Luke Morley for the groom, Sophia Edwards for the bride.

"I *should* have liked to be flower girl," whispered Cecilia to Maria, who was taking mental notes on the things she would improve upon when she married Mr Shapely. The date was tentatively scheduled for next year. After Lent. Provided they were still together – which of course they would be.

"They wished *simplicity*," said Maria, rather scraping the word off her tongue.

"But so *very* simple! Those four look quite lonely up there. With hardly any in attendance, they might have had the ceremony a bit closer to us."

This was indeed true. Maria made a mental note to have four in attendance on each side.

"It was sweet of them to ask Rev. Wallace to perform the ceremony. But he *is* a bit frail and sad-looking. I didn't know he was even still marrying people!"

"I had heard he was dead," said Maria. The poor old Reverend was a dear, but he was hardly an ornament to what should be a spectacle in honour of new lives and bright futures. She made another note to recruit someone fresh from his divinities.

When Daniel turned to Luke, and Bridget to Sophia, their attendants offered up the rings, which were tied with a bit of ribbon to silk cushions.

After a time, Cecilia was obliged to mutter, "Oh, dear. Something has happened, hasn't it? Neither one can get the ring loose!"

"Is *that* the problem? I can't see anything – Sophia and Luke have come around to stand far too closely. Don't they understand they have an audience?"

Maria glanced around in some amusement as her fellow attendees began murmuring about the delay. There they were, Daniel and Bridget, in the middle of the biggest day of their lives, obliged to chatter on and on with their attendants to resolve their troubles. And there, smiling above it all, stood Rev. Wallace, quite oblivious to it all.

Sounding dismayed, Cecilia said, "Reckon Rev. Wallace *would* try to assist them but he's half blind. He doesn't seem to know that there *is* a problem. Oh, look! Luke got his ring away. And look, he just put it on Daniel's finger, I think!"

"Cecilia? What are you thinking of? Daniel was given *Bridget's* ring, which he is holding certainly. He will put it on *her*. You need to come down from the clouds now and then."

"I saw it!"

"Bridget's ring would never fit him, so now do be quiet."

Nevertheless, Maria was pleased by the chuckles of a couple in the pew behind them. Then, she collected herself and added to her mental notes: rehearsals. *Rehearsals.*

***

By midnight, Bainbridge Park had gone dark. The guests had been sent home fat and happy, the servants exhausted and ready to sleep the sleep of the dead. They would be well compensated for their efforts. The next day, the bride and groom would depart, leaving them for three months with only Erasmus and his new attendant, a man selected by Erasmus himself as his wedding gift to the happy couple.

Daniel walked Bridget to the door of their bedchamber, took her hand, and kissed her cheek.

"You are happy with how the day proceeded?" he asked.

"Marvellously happy. Happy to have it official. Even happier to have everyone out of the damn house so I may proceed to my bride."

"Go on, then. I believe the coast is clear."

Her hand on the doorknob, Bridget returned to Daniel. "And Luke. He assures me he has made his peace with all this. Has he?"

"He has."

"Promise?"

"I promise. If there were any lingering doubts, your father's gift most certainly did away with them."

"You'll wish a break from us two old biddies by the time we get to Florence anyhow. What better time to go on a six-week buying trip?"

Daniel grinned. "Indeed. Textiles *are* my private passion. How very careless of you to let slip that I've always wished to own a little London drapery. How very fortunate that you have a brother who knows the business and has time in his schedule to accompany us. A contract with an association of sheep farmers is not the most romantic of wedding presents. But it *did* suffice, together with what I contributed, to buy a controlling interest in Harding and that does warm the cockles of my heart."

Fifteen minutes later, when Luke crept in the door, Daniel was waiting by the window. In the darkened room with only moonlight to see by, he waited for Luke to secure the door then make his way toward the silhouette.

Luke seized him and tugged him backwards until they collapsed onto the squeaking bed. They embraced, rolling over and under, back and forth. They were at last left facing each other, laughing softly, catching their breaths.

"It will be so nice to be away, won't it?" said Luke. "No servants creeping about besides Collins and the ladies' maid."

"Yes, it will be."

"You shall worry about Erasmus while we are away."

"He will have letters to look forward to. I have made my peace with whatever the future might have in store. He has his wish fulfilled, and this is part of what it took to achieve that. But do leave off about all that. I need to tell you this: when you slipped this ring on my finger today, you smiled and looked up at me. That moment, Luke, was the happiest of my life. And yet I do wish, so much, that I could have slipped one on yours. It was the most we could do, I understand, but it does feel half-finished. Am I being foolish?"

"Yes."

After a prolonged silence, Daniel said, sounding decidedly hurt, "Upon my honour, that was succinct. Is that all?"

Luke sighed. "No, but it was worth it to get your reaction." Daniel flipped him on his back and pinned him. Struggling for breath, laughing, Luke managed, "It was worth it to get *this* reaction as well. I'm not an amateur at this."

Daniel leant down blindly in the dark. He found the place, then nuzzled his nose. "I love you so much."

"I love you, too. We have too much to regret what we haven't. Anyhow, I might not have a ring, but I have something even better."

"What is that, darling?"

"A string tied around my finger – my index finger, the one used to beckon. The string is tied to your end finger. Reckon you hadn't noticed it, but it is there."

Daniel was laughing. "Oh, I have noticed, believe me. I've felt it from the beginning, albeit for a time obliterated from view by a big, ugly blackmail note. The note was put to the fire, yet I feel no less obligated to satisfy your wishes. Only it is myself, my body, my very essence obliging me to comply. Now it is nothing but pleasure."

"Is it?"

"Oh, yes. Because I know you are being blackmailed, too. What is mutual attraction but the shared delight of blackmailers? You pulling my strings, I pulling yours.

Sometimes, it is lovely to have one's choices taken away. Sometimes, it is a delight."

A Note from the Author

G entle Reader – If you have enjoyed this story, please take a moment and leave your rating on Amazon. This will help the book find its way in the Almighty Amazon Algorithm and will mean the world to me.

Thank you!

David

Further Reading

These books are in the public domain and available on sites like Project Gutenberg.

The Village Labourer 1760-1832 – A Study in the Government of England Before the Reform Bill
by J. L. Hammond and Barbara Hammond pub 1912

Letters to his Son on the Fine Art of becoming a Man of the World and a Gentleman
by the Earl of Chesterfield pub 1774

About the Author

A native of the American Southwest, David Lawrence has spent much of his life living and traveling in Great Britain, France, and Finland. He now lives in the American Northwest – Helena, Montana – with his Finnish partner.

By day he loves hiking under the Big Sky of his beautiful adopted state.

By night, however, he prefers editing lost manuscripts and wandering the byways of 18th century London...

You can learn more about David Lawrence and his penned works by subscribing to his newsletter and visiting his website https://www.davidlawrenceauthor.com/

Also By David Lawrence

Hugh: A Hero without a Novel
Blue Billy's Rogue Lexicon